KT-560-135

WREXHAM | Marlborough Library

5 289743 000

NOTHING VENTURED

NOTHING VENTURED

Anne Douglas

This first world hardcover edition published 2015
in Great Britain and the USA by
SEVERN HOUSE PUBLISHERS LTD of
19 Cedar Road, Sutton, Surrey, England, SM2 5DA.
Trade paperback edition first published 2016
in Great Britain and the USA by
SEVERN HOUSE PUBLISHERS LTD.

Copyright © 2015 by Anne Douglas.

All rights reserved including the right of
reproduction in whole or in part in any form.
The moral right of the author has been asserted.

British Library Cataloguing in Publication Data

Douglas, Anne, 1930- author.
  Nothing ventured.
  1. Nurses–Scotland–Fiction. 2. Brothers and sisters–
  Fiction. 3. Love stories.
  I. Title
  823.9'14-dc23

ISBN-13: 978-0-7278-8537-1 (cased)
ISBN-13: 978-1-84751-640-4 (trade paper)
ISBN-13: 978-1-78010-706-6 (e-book)

This is a work of fiction. Names, characters, places and incidents
are either the product of the author's imagination or are used fictitiously.
Except where actual historical events and characters are being described
for the storyline of this novel, all situations in this publication are
fictitious and any resemblance to actual persons, living or dead,
business establishments, events or locales is purely coincidental.

All Severn House titles are printed on acid-free paper.

Severn House Publishers support the Forest Stewardship Council™ [FSC™],
the leading international forest certification organisation.
All our titles that are printed on FSC certified paper carry the FSC logo.

Typeset by Palimpsest Book Production Ltd.,
Falkirk, Stirlingshire, Scotland.
Printed and bound in Great Britain by
TJ International, Padstow, Cornwall.

One

Isla Scott was going home. Only for a weekend, from Friday at five to Sunday evening, when it would be back to Edinburgh Southern Hospital, ready for Monday. Not a break that came round very often, but nice when it did – seeing her parents in Edgemuir and her brother, Boyd, if he could get time off from the hydro where he worked.

Here she was, then, lucky enough to get a seat in this train so full of people going home from work on that early January evening, and lying back with her eyes shut, glad of the rest after the rush of getting ready.

Rush, rush, rush. That was hospital nursing anyway, which was not to say she didn't enjoy it. She did and, at twenty-three, could see herself doing well in the future, maybe doing different things, gaining different experiences. Meanwhile, she had her weekend to think about.

Help! Time had passed and she sat up with a start. Must have dropped off, and as this train trip took no more than half an hour, she might have missed her station. Sitting up straight, now fully alert, she tried to peer through the windows to see if she could recognize where they were. Of course, it was too dark and she had to settle back into her seat again, returning the smiles of the passengers opposite with an uncertain smile of her own.

'Just coming into Edgemuir now,' a middle-aged man told her, rising, his eyes very attentive as she straightened her hat over her dark red hair, newly bobbed in 1925 fashion, and buttoned up her coat. 'Like me to get your case down for you?'

'Oh, thanks, that'd be kind.'

A pretty girl, with wide-apart grey eyes and a turned-up nose, Isla was used to attentions and always fielded them well, except perhaps in the hospital. Some of the male patients, when they began to feel better – oh, watch out! Thank goodness, she worked in Women's General.

With her small weekend case, handbag, umbrella, and carrier containing chocolates for her mother, tobacco for her father and a car magazine for Boyd, she thanked the man who'd helped her before moving to the corridor packed with standing passengers.

'Edgemuir!' a hoarse voice shouted. 'Edgemuir now!'

Someone was opening the door, letting in a rush of cold air and showing a view of a dimly lit platform where people were queueing to show their tickets.

'Manage all right?' asked the middle-aged man at her side, but she was already on her way, only turning back once to smile, before waving to the familiar face she'd spotted in the small waiting crowd.

'Boyd, you came to meet me!' she cried, hugging him as soon as she was through the ticket barrier, 'Oh, that's grand – I never expected it.'

'I usually close the gym at seven,' he told her, 'but I got Larry to take over early so I could meet your train. You remember – he's the one who helps out for me if he's not busy with the saunas? Didn't take me ten minutes to walk down from the hydro.'

'Never takes more than ten minutes to walk anywhere in Edgemuir,' Isla laughed, pausing on the slippery pavement to gaze up at her brother.

Tall and broad-shouldered in a tweed coat, he looked the ideal man to run a gymnasium, which was his responsibility at Lorne's Hydro, but as he bent to kiss her cheek and take her case, Isla marvelled, as she often did, at his classic good looks. Even in the poor street lighting outside the station, his wonderfully straight nose could not be missed, nor his fine brow, his high cheekbones, and the tendrils of his fair hair escaping from his cap.

She knew where he got his looks from, of course, and that was their still handsome father, Will Scott, a foreman at the woollen mill in the town, while Isla was like their mother, who had the same sort of red hair and turned-up nose. If they didn't have the striking good looks of the menfolk, they were attractive – yes, Isla wouldn't deny it – but that didn't stop her wanting to smooth down her nose from time to time, even though it never did any good.

Moving away a little, she looked up to the end of the street where Lorne's Hydro, the long, elegant building that dominated the town, sparkled 'like Christmas', as the locals put it, with every window lit, though behind, in the winter darkness, not much could be seen of its fine backdrop of hills. This was the place known throughout Scotland – and in England, too – as one of the centres for the famous water treatments that had been fashionable for some years, attracting people – mostly rich, Isla guessed – to Edgemuir, which was, of course, useful to the town.

'Better watch your step,' Boyd told her, as they turned into a road that would take them to the woollen mill, their father's workplace, and his terraced house nearby. 'There's a bit of black ice around and we don't want you breaking a leg or something.'

'And ending up in Women's General?' Isla laughed again. 'That'd teach me a thing or two — being nursed myself!'

'Here, give me that bag and take my arm,' Boyd offered, but Isla said she'd be all right; she knew as much as he did about walking on black ice, having experienced the same winter weather when growing up, and there was plenty of ice in Edinburgh, anyway. All she wanted was to get home, see her parents and find out what Ma had been making for their tea, as she was starving.

As she'd said, it didn't take long to walk anywhere in Edgemuir, and even moving at a cautious pace, they were soon in sight of Meredith's Woollen Mill, a two-storey building now burning only a few security lights, the workforce having gone home.

'There it is,' said Boyd, with a grin. 'Dad's pride and joy, the woollen mill. Remember when he wanted me to work there?'

'That was before—' Isla began, then stopped. She'd been going to say 'the war', but it did not do to speak to Boyd of the 1914–18 war in which he'd served. He never spoke of it himself and would not discuss it, which meant that now she could only say hastily that he was much better where he was now. 'I mean you did that course for it and now you're getting the experience.'

'Too right. I was lucky Doctor Lorne gave me my chance, and I'm very happy where I am. Why would I want to spend my life messing about with sheep's wool?'

Boyd was beginning to walk faster. 'Come on, it's better here; let's get to Meredith Street for the grand welcoming ceremony!'

Passing by the mill, they came to the first of the three terraces built years before for mill workers of all types, and toiled along to its last house, number forty-six, the one reserved for the foreman. No change there in the house they knew, where Boyd spent his nights, if not his days, and Isla returned to from time to time, always feeling glad to see it again.

Being the foreman's house, forty-six had a couple of extras to make it special — the huge bonus of a bathroom and a handsome front door with a brass knocker, always lovingly polished by Ma. There was no doubt that Will Scott's wife, Nan, took her duties as foreman's wife very seriously, so that her curtains were the prettiest, her front step was the cleanest, and, in a pot by the front door, her collection of flowers in spring and summer was something no one else had thought of. It was a shame she had no garden – no one in the terraces had that – but there was a yard at the back of the house and a drying green to share with others. Everything you could want, really.

Not that Isla herself would have wanted it, but then she was young, as Boyd was young. They had their way to make and a big question mark over their future. That was what was exciting, eh? About being young? You never knew what might lie ahead.

All that lay ahead at the moment was being home again, and as Boyd opened the door with his key and motioned her into the narrow hall, Isla was already calling, 'Ma! Dad! Are you there? I'm home!'

Two

Of course they were there, hurrying down the hallway, Nan flushed from her stove, Will in shirtsleeves just back from work, both ready to hug and kiss and draw Isla into the kitchen, while Boyd, grinning at the welcome he'd known there would be, took her case upstairs.

'Oh, my, it's grand to see you, then!' cried Nan, holding Isla at arm's length while Will took her coat and hat. 'But you've lost weight, eh, since we saw you? Mind, that was long enough ago, I'll have to say, though I'm not complaining—'

'It's not that long, Ma,' Isla protested, loosening herself from her mother's hands. 'I do try to come on my days off, but I can't come every time.'

'But you didn't even make Hogmanay, did you? We'd to see the New Year in on our own, seeing as Boyd was on duty.'

'She was here for Christmas, Nan,' Will put in mildly. 'And she's here now, so don't keep going on.'

'Now, who's going on? I'm only saying it seems a long time since Isla was here!'

'Ah, well, "seems" doesn't always match up with what's right.'

'How about a cup of tea, Ma, before you dish up that steak and kidney I can smell?' asked Boyd, coming into the kitchen. 'And Isla, what's in the carrier, then?'

'A magazine for you,' Isla told him, grateful for the change of subject, 'with chocs for you, Ma, and tobacco for you, Dad.'

There were soon smiles all round, as her family exclaimed over Isla's gifts – *oh, you shouldn't have* – then drank their tea until it was time for Isla to run upstairs to have a quick wash while Nan finished off her cooking.

As usual, when the meal was ready, they took their places at the kitchen table, for the kitchen was a welcoming place, warm and comfortable, with a large range, solid chairs, a dresser filled with china, and thick curtains at the windows to block out the January night. Afterwards, though, Nan said they must all go into the parlour where Will had lit a fire, so they could sit and talk and sample the chocolates Isla had brought.

'Doubt if I'll want a chocolate after that grand steak-and-kidney pie,' Boyd remarked, leaning back. 'One of your best, Ma. But what's all this "parlour" stuff? We call it the front room, eh?'

'I always think "parlour" sounds nicer, that's all – I'm not meaning "grander".'

'No, no,' Boyd agreed, rising, but when his eyes met Isla's, grey like his – their only likeness – each quietly smiled. Nan just liked to think that what she had was superior to what others had, a harmless enough fault and she never made too much of it.

'Ma has a kind heart,' Isla always maintained earnestly, and Boyd never disagreed. They both felt they were lucky in their parents.

'Now you laddies go next door and see to the fire,' Nan ordered, beginning to bustle about with dishes, 'and Isla and I will do the washing-up.'

'But Isla's tired, I bet she's been on the go all day,' said Will. 'Maybe Boyd and I could give you a hand, Nan.'

'As though I'd ever expect you to do that!' she cried smartly, but Isla was already at the sink.

'Nae bother, Dad. I'll help Ma and we'll have a nice chat before we come in next door.'

'And then I'd like a chat myself,' said Boyd, lingering for a moment. 'I've got some news that might interest you, Isla.'

'Interest me? I can't wait!'

'See you next door, then – don't worry, we won't eat all Ma's chocolates.'

Three

The room Nan called her parlour always seemed to Isla to look like some sort of small museum. Everything so neat and polished and unlived in, which was not surprising, of course, seeing that it was so little used and Nan cleaned it every week as though it had never been cleaned before. Even though she had a part-time job in a tweed shop, she never missed out on her housework, keeping a sharp eye on how soon other women got their washing out on Mondays, or if their brass was cleaned on Fridays.

Oh dear, thought Isla, coming in from the kitchen, *this room's just as I remember it*. Except that the fire Will had lit did make things look more cheerful, and Nan's chocolate box lay ready and waiting by her chair.

'Only one each,' Will declared. 'They are Nan's, after all.'

'No, no, help yourselves!' she cried, taking her seat. 'I'll only put weight on if I eat too many!'

At which they all laughed, for it was well known that Nan had been skinny all her life and never put on an ounce, however much she ate.

'Burn it up, that's what you do,' said Will, selecting a caramel. 'Rushing about like there's a fire – and you're the same, Isla. I bet you're a whirlwind in that ward of yours.'

'Talking of wards, or, rather, nursing, that's what I want to talk to you about,' Boyd told Isla, having eaten his choice of a strawberry cream. 'I think you'll be interested.'

'In nursing?' Isla was studying the guide to the contents of the chocolate box. 'Well, I'm a nurse, sure enough, but what's your point, Boyd?'

'My point is that there's a vacancy for a qualified nurse at Lorne's. Should be just right for you.'

'At the hydro?' Isla, taking a truffle, had raised her eyebrows. 'Why should it be right for me, Boyd? Like I said, I'm a nurse already. Why'd I want to work at the hydro?'

'Well, because it's here, in Edgemuir!' her father cried. 'It'd be grand to have you home again – eh, Nan?'

'Oh, it would, it would!' Nan's eyes were shining. 'Of course, it'd have to be the right job, Will. We don't want Isla moving just to be near us.'

'No, but folk come to Lorne's Hydro from all over the country – I reckon it'd be grand place to work. You think so, Boyd, is that no' right?

'Certainly is – it's fascinating, really, what they can do with just water. I honestly think you'd find it interesting, Isla. Something new, you see. What do you say?'

She hesitated, dabbing at a smear of chocolate on her finger with her handkerchief.

'I'm not sure,' she said at last. 'Where I work, we help all sorts, but at the hydro – that's for rich folk, eh? I didn't go into nursing to help people who can afford to pay.'

'No, no, it's not like that,' Boyd said eagerly. 'All sorts come to the hydro, too, and some of 'em are just ordinary folk who haven't had luck with conventional treatments. The main thing is this'd be something new for you and I am sure it'd be worth your while to think about it.' He gave a sudden grin. 'And the money's good, and all. Wages are generous because Doctor Lorne wants the best.'

'There you are, then!' Will put in. 'Money's important, Isla – don't we know it! Remember what it was like, Nan, before I got to be foreman? Living in one o' the wee houses in the terrace – scrimping and saving, trying to make ends meet!'

A shadow crossed Nan's face and she pursed her lips.

'No need to bring that up, Will. We're better off now.'

'Aye, I'm just saying, money's important. When you see the way folk have to live without it, you ken why you've to fight for it.'

'I know, I know, but we're talking about Isla, and she's got to be sure she wants to work at the hydro, not just think o' the cash. Mightn't be for her at all.'

'That's right, Ma,' Isla said quickly. 'I'm not even sure I believe these water cures work, anyway. I know you're convinced, Boyd, but—'

'But what do I know?' he asked wryly, raising his hands. 'Yes, well, I'm no doctor, but I can tell you that Doctor Lorne who founded the place is first-rate, and so is his assistant. They've written books and papers; they're very well respected. And so are the nurses – the best to be found. So why not try for an interview? You'll find out a lot more that way than I can tell you.'

'That's a good idea,' said Will. 'Why not try it, Isla?'

'I can give you all the details where to write,' Boyd added. 'The closing date's mid-January.'

'Heavens, you're well prepared!' Isla cried. 'I can see you've done your homework.'

'All right, I have, because I'd like you to come. It'd be grand to have you around, not stuck in Edinburgh. What do you say, then? Will you apply?'

'I don't know, Boyd. It's a big decision.'

'It wouldn't do any harm to apply, though. Like I said, see what you think when you know more.'

Glancing at her parents, Isla saw their eyes fixed on her and looked away. Of course, they'd made it plain what they would like her to do, even though Ma had understood that what mattered was what Isla wanted. And that, of course, she didn't yet know.

Maybe, she should, after all, just apply. See what it might be like, make up her mind if it would be worth it for her career to make the move. She'd just been thinking about the future and what might be coming her way, and had often thought she'd like to try different things. She'd have nothing to lose by applying, and if she decided the hydro was not for her, at least she'd have given it a try and her family would appreciate that.

After a long moment, she gave a little shrug and turned to Boyd.

'All right, I'll make an application,' she said quietly.

'You will? Isla, that's grand!' His smile was broad. 'Just the thing to do – go for it, see what it would be like.'

'So you can be sure,' Nan murmured. 'We just want you to be sure, don't we, Will?'

'Definitely. Oh, yes, got to be sure.'

But they were all three smiling now, even though they still didn't know what she was going to be sure about. And if she eventually said she was sure about staying at Edinburgh Southern, how bad would it make her feel when there were no more smiles? Pretty bad, maybe, but one thing was certain: even to please those who loved her, she was not going to take on something she didn't want. And – it made her smile to remember as she was going to bed – with all her soul-searching about taking the job at the hydro, there was no guarantee that she would even be offered it, which might be the solution to the whole problem.

With so much on her mind, sleep was long in coming. So much for her nice, restful weekend!

Four

A pale, wintry sunshine filled the town on Saturday, not strong enough to melt the ice underfoot but lightening the atmosphere, cheering the spirits of those out and about. Certainly, Isla and her mother were enjoying themselves, first looking round the shops, later having coffee at a café busy with smart customers – who might well be patients from the hydro, Nan whispered.

'Oh, yes, they're allowed out,' she told Isla, who wasn't used to patients going out for coffee from the hospital where she worked. 'Quite a lot don't need to be in bed; they've just got, you know, conditions they want treating. Boyd says some complain that the hydro doesn't have its own golf course, but there are tennis courts and they play in the summer.'

'I guessed they'd be well-to-do,' commented Isla, buttering a scone. 'Golf, tennis and good food and wine, I expect? Nothing like that where I work!'

'Wine at meals, maybe, but there's no alcohol allowed on Sundays, seemingly, and no games, either. A lot of places are like that, of course. We're no great kirk-goers, as you know, but I think it's good to make a difference on Sundays, eh?'

'I'm usually too busy at work to know what day it is,' Isla said with a laugh, beginning to eat her scone and keeping an interested eye on the customers who might be from the hydro, thinking she could be seeing people like that in a different setting if she got an interview.

She'd been disappointed that Boyd had had to work that Saturday, but he'd promised to bring her all the information she needed when he came home that night, and her father, at least, would have the afternoon free.

Frost being still about, Isla and her parents had given up plans for a long walk in the hills, deciding instead to take the bus to Galashiels, to look around and have high tea somewhere. First, though, before they went home that morning, Isla told her mother she'd like to walk up to the hydro, just to take a better look at it. Although it was very familiar to her as a place dominating the town, she had never really studied it and was now interested enough to know it better.

'Grand-looking place, eh?' asked Nan, as they stood together, looking through wrought-iron entrance gates at the stone-built, three-storeyed building, with its elegantly framed windows and double doors sheltered by a portico. Several cars were parked on the wide sweep of gravel driveway, and as they watched, a man in a lounge suit came out to open the door of one of them and take out a briefcase. Nan and Isla drew back, taking cover behind the bushes and trees lining the railings.

'Don't want to be caught peering in,' Isla murmured, but Nan said it was all right: he hadn't seen them and had now returned inside. 'But it's worth looking at the place, eh? Used to be a hotel, you know, before the doctor bought it – that'd be about 1910.'

'A hotel? Well, it's big enough.'

'Aye, my mother's sister, my Aunt Julia, used to work there. As a waitress, I think. You'll not remember her – she got married and emigrated to Australia – but your gran told me she loved working at the Marquess – that's what the hotel was called.' Nan gave a little sigh. 'Shame your gran passed on, eh? My dad, too. They could have told you such a lot.'

'I know,' Isla said softly. 'Thing is, we've no grandparents at all, Boyd and me, seeing as dad's folks are gone, too. Why do some folk have to die so young? Life too much of a struggle, do you think?'

'They always worked very hard, but then so do we all.' Nan turned away. 'Think we'd better be getting home.'

'Wonder whereabouts Boyd is in there?' Isla asked, looking back. 'Wish we could've popped in to see him.'

'Never allows that. But if you get an interview, you'll see his gymnasium.' As Nan wrapped her scarf more firmly round her neck and pulled on her hat against the wind, she gave Isla a cautious look. 'Think you're more interested, now you've seen it close to?'

'Maybe. I'd certainly like an interview, anyway, so as to check out just what goes on. First, though, I'd like to see what information Boyd brings me tonight – if he remembers.'

'Oh, he'll remember all right. He's keen as mustard for you to get that job. Thinks it'd be just right for you, seeing as he thinks the hydro's just right for him, eh? Now let's go home and see if your dad's back and get out of this wind for a wee while.'

Five

Boyd was true to his word, and when he arrived after work that evening, he gave Isla not only details of how to apply for the job at the hydro but also a copy of its brochure.

'Now you can read something specially written to tell people what the water cure really is,' he explained when they were sitting in the kitchen with their parents, drinking tea. 'Seemingly, Doctor Lorne's secretary is sending one to all applicants, and she gave me one for you, plus the form everyone's getting. That gives you Doctor Lorne's name – he's taking the interview – the time, date and where it is, which you know anyway. Seems you'll need the names of two referees – one from someone who supervises you now and the other from school or where you trained.'

'All very formal, eh?' asked Will. 'Suppose it has to be.'

'Oh, sure, they need to know all about the people applying. But you'll like Doctor Lorne, Isla; he's a really nice chap – a widower, with a daughter, but she's away at school. Patty MacIvor, the nurse who's leaving, told me she's really sorry to be going, just because he's been such a good employer.'

'So why is she leaving?' Isla asked.

'She's getting married and her husband-to-be has got a job in England, so she's away south. Very pleasant girl, easy to get on with. But I think you'd get on with everyone, Isla – even Matron's not too tough, they tell me.'

'I'll believe that when I meet her!' Isla laughed. 'Matrons aren't known to be easy. And this Doctor Lorne sounds a saint – and rich, too, eh? Well, he must be, if he can own a whole hydro!'

'Oh, he doesn't own it now, Isla. It's been a limited company for some time – most of the hydros are. They cost too much to run for one owner, and, of course, there's not the risk there would be for one person. Just got to keep the shareholders happy.'

'I see,' Isla said thoughtfully. She didn't actually know much about limited companies, but if they made things less risky, they seemed a good idea.

'But listen, Boyd, thanks very much for all this information. It'll be a great help to have some knowledge of Lorne's, especially about the water cure.'

'Hydropathy is its formal name,' Boyd told her. 'Or, as some say, hydrotherapy. If you read up on it in the brochure, you'll have an idea of what to say at the interview.'

'And now I can see what my bedtime reading's going to be tonight, eh?'

'But don't you go worrying about the interview,' Will said seriously. 'You'll walk it, I'm telling you. They'll be lucky to get you.'

'I say the same,' declared Nan. 'If they want quality staff at the hydro, you're it, Isla.'

Oh, if only they wouldn't talk like that! Isla groaned inwardly. They were going to be so disappointed if – for whatever reason – she didn't end up at Lorne's. She didn't yet know herself what she really wanted, and they'd said themselves she needed to be sure.

Jumping to her feet, she said she'd take the cups away and then, as a change from talking about the hydro, why didn't they get the cards out and play rummy or something?

'Rummy would be grand,' said Boyd, grinning. 'I like it because I always win.'

'Not this time!' called Will, already at the sideboard, taking out the cards. 'I feel lucky tonight.'

'I don't care who wins,' Isla declared. 'I just want to think of something else before I start on my homework.'

'Never know,' said Boyd, fixing her with a steady look, 'you might get really interested.'

'No more job talk,' ordered Nan. 'We're ready to start.'

After the card games, which Boyd, true to his prediction, won again, they had more tea and said goodnight, Isla with some relief. She was anxious to study the brochure Boyd had given her, to see if it might help her make up her mind what she wanted.

Settling into bed in her room, the smallest of the three bedrooms the foreman's house provided, she was glad to be on her own, sparing a thought for the way some folk had to sleep in the tenements, packed in like sardines. Imagine only having a bed when someone else had left it, and then having to share it with others! Better not dwell on the troubles of those poor folk now, though. She'd enough to occupy her, with the hydro's brochure.

Six

It was certainly a fine production, with paper of the best quality and clear photographs, but what mattered to Isla was how much it showed of the real work of the place, for of that she hadn't much idea.

First, she studied the frontispiece which showed a picture of Dr George Lorne, the founder and director of the hydro, now looking to be in his fifties, dark-haired with a little grey at the temples, large, thoughtful eyes and a generous mouth. Formally dressed for the photograph, he looked as if he would prefer to be formal anyway, but though you could never rely on photographs, he also looked as nice as Boyd had said and – better still – a man to be trusted.

Would she like to work for him? Too soon to say, but at least he knew how to put things simply for patients, not to mention possible applicants for jobs. For instance, his definition of hydropathy, the water cure on which his business was founded, was just described as the treatment of illness by water itself, a form of therapy that was nothing new, having been traced back to Ancient Egypt. After developments abroad in the nineteenth century, it had become popular and successful in modern times, in hydros such as Lorne's.

In Scotland, England and throughout the world, there were doctors and nurses all treating and satisfying patients, as Dr Lorne and his assistant, Dr Woodville, were glad to do. In fact, any patient who came to Lorne's would be offered such a wide range of treatments – saunas, steam and sitz baths, wraps, cold water rubbings, among others – that their symptoms would almost certainly be improved.

In addition, they would find their stay most comfortable, in a building offering single rooms, two well-furnished lounges, an excellent dining room, as well as a fine terrace, a gymnasium, tennis courts – and beautiful countryside on the doorstep, for those who just liked to walk and breathe pure Scottish air. Finally, Dr Lorne strongly recommended a study of the brochure, which would show photographs of what treatment was available, and for all further information, application could be made to the secretary for Lorne's Hydro at the address given at the end of the brochure.

Certainly knows how to 'sell' his hydro, doesn't he? thought Isla, finishing the doctor's introduction. But who could blame him? At least, he hadn't attempted to guarantee success for his treatments, doing no more than suggest that patients who tried them would see some improvement. And although she was still unsure how they worked, Isla had to admit that having read what Dr Lorne had to say, she did feel a little more confident about them. So many hydros, so many satisfied clients – there must be something in them that brought a certain success.

Sighing, she went on to study the photographs, skipping those of the accommodation and facilities (except for Boyd's gymnasium which seemed well equipped, though lacking a picture of Boyd himself) and moving on to the treatment rooms. These were her real interest, but in spite of showing a number of patients wrapped in linen and blankets, or tactfully swathed in towels beside baths and pools – all accompanied by smiling nurses, of course – they didn't really tell her very much.

A Selection of our Treatments, read the caption for the section, and obviously not all could be shown to public gaze, but it was already clear enough to Isla that to get the real feel of Lorne's Hydro, she was going to have to see the establishment itself. That would only happen if she got as far as an interview, which, of course, was as yet not certain, but as she put aside the brochure and switched off her light, she really hoped she would be successful.

On Sunday, before she went back to Edinburgh, she'd have to get down to filling in the form Boyd had brought her, and think about the names of the two referees she'd have to provide. Her old head-mistress would do for one, and the other – well, that would have to be Sister Nisbet, in charge of Women's General. Here, alas, her spirits went rapidly downhill. She wasn't exactly going to be the blue-eyed girl, was she, perhaps wanting to leave where she'd been trained?

Don't think about speaking to Sister Nisbet, she told herself. *Not just now. Put it right out of your mind and try to get some sleep.* Which, surprisingly, was what she did.

Seven

The next day, though milder air had melted any ice, steady rain prevented a last walk. Instead, Isla concentrated on filling in her application form, finally letting Boyd read it through.

'There you are. That should do it, eh?' she asked.

'Reads well – now all you need are your references.'

'Don't remind me. I'll have to speak to Sister Nisbet when I get back.'

'Now, why shouldn't that Sister give you a good testimonial?' Nan cried. 'I'm sure you've always worked hard on the ward!'

'She'll think I'm being ungrateful – maybe wanting to go somewhere else when I trained at the Southern.'

'A piece of nonsense,' put in Will. 'You don't have to stay there for ever just because you trained there!'

But after they'd had their Sunday roast dinner and it was time for Isla to go for the train, she took no comfort in her parents' support. They didn't know Sister Nisbet . . .

'Don't worry,' Boyd told her at the station. 'I'll take a small bet that you'll get an interview, anyway, whatever happens with the Sister.'

'Maybe.' She smiled and gave him a hug as her train came steaming in, and said she'd be in touch.

'This is all your doing, you know. I never in this world thought I'd be applying for a new job when I only came home for the weekend!'

'Make it what you want,' he told her seriously. 'In the meantime, best of luck with Sister Nisbet!'

Luck, she thought, was what she'd need.

Back at the hospital, changing into uniform, she felt she'd been away for weeks. Greeting her colleagues, though, she judged it wasn't the time to speak of her plans. Best catch Sister Nisbet first, and then – well, wait to see what happened.

See what happened? Just as Isla had expected, when she heard Isla's request and her reason for it, the ward sister's expression grew glacial.

'You want to use my name as referee for your application to Lorne's Hydro, Nurse Scott?' she asked through tight lips. 'Why ever would you be applying there?'

'I'm . . . I'm sort of interested in the water cure, Sister. I mean, the hydro's in my home town, so I've always known about it. Always wondered how it works.'

'I'm sure you're not alone in that. Some people believe in it, others don't, and I can't imagine why you'd want to leave the Southern to work there. After all we've done for you!'

'I know, Sister, I'm very grateful – indeed I am – but I'd . . . well, I'd just like to maybe get an interview – see if Lorne's is for me.'

For a long moment, Sister Nisbet fixed Isla with a cold, pale blue stare.

'You've always worked well here, and I won't refuse your request,' she said at last, 'but I'd like to advise you to take great care in making any decision you might in the future regret.'

'Thank you, Sister. I do intend to make sure I do the right thing.'

'Very well, then. If I am approached for a reference, I shall reply.'

'I very much appreciate that, Sister. Thank you.'

After a brief nod, Sister Nisbet turned away and Isla, returning to her work, felt sweat on her palms and a thudding ache beginning in her head.

Oh, Lord, even the interview couldn't be worse than that, she thought, but at least it was over and there was the promise of the reference, if Lorne's wanted to follow her application up. As she moved quickly down the ward to see what the patient waving in the end bed wanted, Isla was, though, beginning to wish she'd never got involved in applying for a new post. Should have stayed where she was and not caused herself trouble.

'All right, hen?' asked Mrs Barnes as Isla brought her the glass of water she'd requested. 'You're looking a wee bit pale.'

'Just tired,' Isla told her, finding a smile. 'I'm fine, thanks.'

And so she was, some days later, when she was asked to report for interview at Lorne's Hydro at one thirty p.m. on a date at the end of January. At least she hadn't fallen at the first hurdle and was going to get her chance to see the hydro. When she'd sent Boyd and her parents postcards with the news, she felt quite relieved, and only laughed when her colleagues told her she was crazy even to think of working with the water cure. That piece of nonsense!

'All I'm doing is seeing what it's all about,' she told them, at which they only shrugged.

'And getting on the wrong side of Sister Nesbit!' someone commented, to which Isla had no answer.

All the same, they wished her luck the day before the interview, except, of course, for Sister Nesbit herself, who had grudgingly given her permission to take the day off and had said nothing of being approached for a reference. *Ah, well, nothing ventured, nothing gained,* Isla told herself, and when the day came for her to dress for the interview in her dark jacket and skirt, with matching hat and polished black shoes, she managed to put Sister Nesbit from her mind and concentrate on what lay ahead.

At the appointed time on the following day, as heavy rain poured down beyond the portico, she was at the hydro's handsome door, ringing the bell, and within moments was being admitted by a young, smartly dressed woman.

'Do come in, Miss Scott,' she said cheerfully, when Isla had introduced herself. 'I'm Joan Elrick, Doctor Lorne's secretary. If you'd like to let me take your raincoat, I'll take you to the waiting room.'

Eight

Oh, no, we're all wearing the same! Isla groaned inwardly when she entered the small room at the rear of the hydro, where two young women were already waiting, unread magazines to hand. But as they exchanged smiles, she realized it was only what she should have expected. They were nurses applying for a nurse's post and wouldn't be trying to look colourful and smart, just sensible and practical; the dark suits, the small hats and lace up shoes were bound to be what they'd all choose. Yes, even as a fourth young woman was shown in, her fairish brown hair slipping from a knot under her hat, her face flushed from hurrying, it was plain enough that her outfit matched all the others. *Hope the doctor can tell us apart,* thought Isla, taking a chair.

'Doctor Woodville will be showing you round before the interviews; he won't be a moment,' the secretary told them.

'Are there just the four of us?' asked a tall, bony young woman, who, with her height and her manner, looked as if she was on course for a Sister's job at least.

'Yes, just the four.' As Joan Elrick smiled and withdrew, the young women looked at one another.

'I thought I was going to be late,' the latest arrival gasped, taking off her hat to pin up her hair. 'Hello, everyone, I'm Margie MacCallum, from Dundee.'

'Jess Dixon, from Glasgow,' the bony young woman announced, while the third candidate said she was Penny Anderson from Musselburgh. All eyes then went to Isla, who gave her name and hesitated a moment.

'I'm from right here in Edgemuir, oddly enough, but I work in Edinburgh at the Southern.'

'So you'll know all about the hydro?' Penny asked, with some unease.

'I wouldn't say that.'

Glances were exchanged and a silence fell, to be broken by Jess Dixon, who asked abruptly what the Southern was like, as a place to work.

'Not bad,' Isla replied. 'I've been happy there.'

'Why d'you want to work here, then?'

'I think it might be interesting. Why do you?'

'Well, the money's better, for one thing. I love ma work but I don't see why I shouldn't be paid more.'

Nor did Penny or Margie, when you considered the way they were run off their feet. And all were nodding sagely when the door opened and a tall, sandy-haired young man in a white coat strode in.

'Good morning, ladies! Welcome to Lorne's Hydro. My name is Doctor Woodville. I'm Doctor Lorne's assistant and will be showing you round for a short while before the interviews begin. Like to follow me?'

Exactly as they'd been shown in the brochure, the public rooms of the hydro were comfortable and cared for, well-polished and swept: the lounges with flower displays, the library with magazines and a writing desk as well as the expected books, the dining room furnished with small tables, now cleared after lunch.

'Nice,' whispered Penny, as they exchanged polite smiles with three middle-aged, well-dressed women in the library.

'Like a good hotel,' commented Jess when they withdrew, and Dr Woodville grinned.

'True, it's often said that hydros are like hotels, only with treatments. But we must move on – next stop, the gymnasium.'

A slight flush rose to Isla's cheeks, which she hoped no one would notice. She hadn't mentioned to the others that her brother worked at Lorne's in case they'd thought it might give her some advantage, which, of course, it wouldn't. But now that they were to meet him, she thanked heaven that Boyd was sensible: he wouldn't speak to her as his sister in front of them.

And, of course, he didn't. Excusing himself from the patient he was helping, Boyd moved to greet Dr Woodville and the candidates, his eyes meeting Isla's only briefly, his smiles being for everyone, as the doctor introduced him.

'Sorry to interrupt, Boyd and Mr Winterton – we won't keep you a moment – just want our visiting nurses here to see the gymnasium. Ladies, meet Mr Scott, our instructor in PE, which we take very seriously here, as I think you can tell by the equipment we've provided.'

'I'll say!' Jess exclaimed. 'I've never seen anything like it in a hospital.'

'Amazing,' Margie and Penny agreed, but it didn't escape Isla that their eyes were not so much on the gym equipment as the handsome gym instructor, and she would have smiled to herself, except that the doctor, with a thank you to Boyd, was hurrying them on. As she left the gym, she did glance back at Boyd, but was glad he didn't risk a grin or wave that the others might have seen. Anyway, she was hoping now to visit the treatment rooms.

It turned out that these were situated in a large extension to the original hotel; a long, light-filled modern building of polished corridors and doors that opened, the candidates were told, to bathing pools, bathrooms, sauna and steam and massage rooms, though only those empty of patients were shown to them.

Everywhere, there were nurses, quick to smile at the visitors, and patients, some in dressing gowns, who looked at them with interest. And everywhere there was a calmness, almost a tranquillity, that would not have been found in the busy wards of a general hospital. In fact, when they were introduced to the sister in charge – a Sister Francis – and Isla mentioned how quiet everything was, she agreed that it was so.

'Oh, yes, we like to keep everything peaceful here, don't we, Doctor Woodville?' she asked, her smile a wide beam. 'Rest and peace – they're part of our treatments. Now, if you'll excuse me, I must move on, but may I welcome you all to Lorne's Hydro and say how lovely it is to meet you?'

'What a nice boss she must be,' Margie whispered as the sister left them. 'No' much like the ones I know.'

'Snap,' said Isla. 'But she'd be the type they'd want here.'

Jess, meanwhile, was addressing Dr Woodville. 'Doctor, are we allowed to see anyone actually having treatment here? Or is that no' possible?'

'I'm sorry to say it's not, Miss Dixon.' The doctor's smile was rueful. 'You see how it is? We can't really invade the privacy of patients – it just wouldn't do – but at least we've been able to show you the workplace, so that you can get some idea of what's involved.'

'That's all right, Doctor,' Margie told him. 'We quite understand. We've all seen the brochures, anyway, and the pictures were very helpful.'

'That's excellent, excellent.' He glanced at his wristwatch. 'If there are any questions, Doctor Lorne himself will be glad to answer them, but now, I'm afraid, we must return to the waiting room. It's almost time for the first interview.'

'And I suppose that'll be me?' asked Penny, sighing. 'If we're being seen in alphabetical order.'

'Spot on, Miss Anderson. You are first. Would you like a few moments to, er, freshen up?'

'Oh, no, thanks, Doctor.' Penny swallowed hard. 'I'd just as soon get it over with.'

'And there'll be tea afterwards – that should cheer everyone up.'

'As though it would, if we haven't got the job,' Jess muttered as they made their way back to the waiting room, but Isla was silent, disappointed that so far she'd not seen enough to know whether she wanted the job or not.

After Dr Woodville had left them and Miss Elrick had called Penny in for interview, a silence fell on the three young women waiting their turn.

'Maybe we won't be told today who's got the job,' Margie at last suggested. 'Maybe it'll come by a horrible letter.'

'Maybe.' Jess turned her eyes on Isla. 'That handsome guy in the gym had the same name as you, eh? He any relation?'

Isla cleared her throat. 'As a matter of fact, he's my brother.'

'Your brother?' cried Margie. 'Why, you never said!'

'Why didn't you?' asked Jess coldly.

'I . . . didn't think it was important. He doesn't have anything to do with the running of the hydro.'

'Seems funny, all the same, that you didn't say.'

*　　*　　*

Time passed. No one spoke, until Penny came back, all excited, Dr Lorne had been so nice, she hadn't felt nervous at all – oh, it was a lovely interview!

Margie and Jess said the same, Jess perhaps not being quite so bubbly. Then, at last, it was Isla's turn to be shown into Dr Lorne's office, and she was taking her seat opposite the man of the picture in the brochure and thinking that in person he looked exactly the same. So kind, so understanding. A family man, of course, as was evident by the two framed photographs on his desk, one of a good-looking, dark-haired woman, the other of a pretty little dark-haired girl – surely his wife and daughter? But hadn't Boyd said the doctor was a widower? Oh, what a shame – such a lovely-looking woman, and quite young.

With a start, she realized that he was speaking her name and smiling, and she hurriedly composed herself for the interview. Would she enjoy it as the others had done? She thought she would.

Nine

And enjoy it she did, even though aware that Dr Lorne's easy informality concealed his skill in finding out just what he needed from a candidate such as herself. Certainly, he'd soon discovered what sort of person she was, what sort of nurse, and why she'd chosen to go into the profession.

To care for others, she'd told him, to make lives better, even, because she knew what sort of lives many of the hospital patients endured in the poorer tenements of the city.

'And the hydro?' Dr Lorne asked casually. 'What made you decide to apply for the post here? Something to do with your brother?'

'My brother? Oh, no. Except that he told me about the vacancy and I knew he'd like me to apply. He's been so happy, working here.'

'But you didn't apply because of Boyd, or your parents, who live in Edgemuir?'

'No. I made it clear it had to be something I wanted to do myself.'

Dr Lorne smiled and rolled his pen between his fingers.

'Which brings us to the main question: what was it that drew you to working with hydropathy? If, indeed, you did feel drawn? Maybe there was some other reason that brought you here?'

Isla was silent for a moment.

'I applied,' she began at last, 'because I'd got interested in the water cure and I wanted to know how it worked. I mean, folk talk of a cure, so there must be something that *causes* the cure, and I thought, if I got an interview, I'd maybe see the treatments and sort of understand.'

'And then, of course, you didn't actually see any patients being treated. I'm sure Doctor Woodville explained why that wasn't possible.'

'Oh, yes, and I should have known it, anyhow. We did hear about the treatments, though, and read about them in the brochure, so I knew what was available.'

'But not *why* they work.' Dr Lorne shook his head. 'And you have heard, I expect, that the whole thing is quackery and doesn't consist of any real medical value at all?'

'I suppose some do say that,' she answered reluctantly.

'Yet it's not true, Miss Scott.'

Dr Lorne laid down his pen, his gaze on her long and serious.

'There's much evidence of the remedial use of water from way back in history, and many people will tell you how much better they've felt after the therapy. But we needn't talk just about feelings. In terms of hard fact, it's known that water therapy, for instance, has a stimulating effect on the blood – on blood flow, the circulation, the regulation of blood pressure. If it did no good in any other way, hydropathy would be valuable for that.'

'I see.' Isla considered what he had said, thinking that this was something she hadn't heard about before and was glad to hear now. Hard fact, instead of feelings. Yes, it was good to have heard it. 'Thank you for telling me that, Doctor Lorne.'

'Makes you feel better? Well, we could talk on this subject all day, but for now, Miss Scott, I'll thank you for your time and ask you to rejoin the other candidates. I believe there will be a cup of tea.'

They shook hands, smiling, and Isla was turning away when Dr Lorne asked if she would be seeing her brother before she left. When she told him she would, he made no further comment, which struck her as strange, but she was so preoccupied with the interview and what she had learned that she only hurried on to the waiting room, giving no further thought to it.

Tea was already being served by Miss Elrick, together with crumbly

scones, and as they finally relaxed, the candidates enjoyed in retro-
spect their time at the hydro.

'Och, yes, it's been grand,' commented Jess, 'but wait till three of
us get the wrong sort of letter.'

'Will we be getting letters, Miss Elrick?' Penny asked. 'I suppose
they won't tell us today who's been selected?'

'It's not really for me to say,' the secretary answered, adding hot
water to the teapot. 'But I think you will probably hear by letter.
They don't usually make a decision on the day.' She gave a bright
smile. 'Now, who's for more tea?'

The long afternoon had drawn to its close, with Penny, Margie and
Jess already having left for their trains. They had been told by Dr
Woodville that they would indeed hear the results of the interview
by letter. There'd been friendly goodbyes and good luck wishes
made, before Isla had waved them off and made her way to the
gymnasium, where Boyd left a patient for a moment to come
hurrying over.

'Isla, how'd you get on? I've been thinking of you – same as Dad
and Ma, I expect.'

She shrugged a little. 'Who knows? We all enjoyed our interviews
with Doctor Lorne – he's as nice as you said – but it could be any
one of us he chooses.'

'You'll take it if he offers?'

She hesitated, then smiled. 'It's a funny thing, but I wasn't sure
until the interview that I would. As soon as he told me how the
water cure can really work, even for one thing, it decided me. I
want the job.'

'That's grand, really grand! Don't forget, it was my idea!'

'Boyd, who says I'm going to get it?'

Grinning, he turned to return to his client, then halted and
whistled.

'Hey, look who's here, Isla! I think he's looking for you.'

It was Dr Lorne who'd appeared at the door of the gym, and it
was true: his eyes were seeking out Isla.

'Miss Scott? Might we have a word?'

'Why, yes, Doctor, of course,' she answered calmly, but her heart
was hammering.

'May we use your room at the back, Boyd?' asked Dr Lorne.

'Certainly, sir, if you can find space.'

'It'll be fine.'

As Boyd returned to his patient, the doctor and Isla squeezed into Boyd's cramped little office, which also acted as store room, moving aside boxes of equipment, rubber balls and dumb-bells until they were facing each other.

'Miss Scott, this is all rather unorthodox, and I will be sending you a formal letter, as to the other nurses, but you are a little different – being a local girl and with a brother here – so I thought I'd break the rule and tell you now.'

'Tell me?'

'That I'm offering you the job.'

There was a silence as Isla's grey eyes widened and her lips parted.

'Me?' Taken aback, for a moment she had no words. When she hadn't been sure she wanted the job, she might have been confident of getting it, but after she'd changed her mind, no, her confidence had faded. 'Doctor Lorne, I . . . don't know what to say. I mean, why me?'

'Why? Well, I could say because you were the best candidate, but all four of you were excellent, so there had to be something extra.' He began to ease himself from the little office, again pushing aside equipment and brushing at his suit. 'Something you offered and the others did not.'

'But what was that?' she asked, mystified, following him from the office. 'What was different about me?'

'The fact that you were the only one who thought to ask me how hydropathy might work. The others would have made wonderful nurses here, but you were interested to know just what our water cure could do. It's always what I look for, Miss Scott – that interest I haven't had to put there myself.'

As she was silent, considering the strange way things worked out, he asked with a smile,

'So, what's the answer, then? Yes or no?'

Coming fast from her reverie, she returned his smile.

'It's yes, Doctor Lorne. And thank you. Thank you very much.'

'That's fine, then. You won't be seeing the others, will you? I'd rather you didn't say anything until we've sent out our letters.'

'I won't be seeing them, but I wouldn't say anything, anyway.' Of course not. As though she would, when they were getting the dreaded letters! If only they could all have been given the job . . . But that wasn't the way of the world.

'That's fine, then, Miss Scott. All that remains is for me to say welcome to Lorne's and to wish you all the best here.' He put out his hand which she shook, then turned to leave. 'Now you'd better go and tell Boyd; he's been looking across at us for some time. And watch out for your own letter – it will have all the details you'll need.'

As he left her, at last it sank in – the change in her future, the new choice she had made, the heady excitement of what was happening.

'Oh, Boyd!' she cried. 'I've got the job. I never thought I'd be so thrilled! Never thought I'd care so much.'

'Can't give you a hug here,' he told her, beaming, 'but I couldn't be more pleased. You're making a good move, Isla, and you won't regret it, that's for sure.'

'Wait till I tell them at home!'

'And at the hospital.'

But she didn't want to think of that. She'd been happy there and they'd done so much. It would hurt to say goodbye – maybe, even, to Sister Nisbet. Have to be done, of course, but for now she wanted to enjoy her little moment of triumph, especially at home.

'See you back at the house,' she told Boyd. 'Don't be late.'

Ten

If Isla had ever had doubts about her change of direction, they vanished as soon as she began work at Lorne's. From that first wild rainy morning in February, when she presented herself at Reception and was escorted to the nurses' home – another extension – everything seemed to go so smoothly that she almost began to wonder when the first snag would appear. But none did and eventually she lost her worries and fitted into hydro life as though it had been designed for her.

The key to the success of the new life, Isla decided, was almost certainly that everyone was so friendly – the nurses, the porters, Noreen Guthrie, the receptionist, Joan Elrick, Dr Lorne's secretary, Larry Telford, the lanky young man who occasionally helped Boyd. Even Matron, who was, as Boyd had said, 'not too tough', was quite helpful, while Sister Francis was as pleasant as she'd first appeared, and though the two staff nurses – Miller and Craddock – were a little stiff, they were friendly enough.

It was Sister Francis who came over to see Isla settled into the modern and comfortable nurses' home, showing her which bed was hers in the room she was to share with two others, where she could put her clothes, what time meals were in the staff dining room and so on.

'Such a shame that though you're an Edgemuir girl, you can't sleep at home,' she remarked, when she and Isla, now in her uniform, made their way to the treatment block. 'But you do understand, I'm sure, that Doctor Lorne, like many doctors, prefers to have his nursing staff readily available.'

'Oh, of course, Sister, it's the usual practice.'

'Exactly. Although we don't have acutely ill patients here – most are suffering from chronic diseases, arthritis, diabetes and asthma, that sort of thing – there are often those who need out-of-hours attention, and, of course, the occasional emergency. We must always be prepared.'

Sister Francis's long, sweet face brightened.

'But now you must prepare to meet your colleagues before the morning's work begins – needless to say, they're all dying to meet you!'

Faces. Names. How ever was Isla going to match them up? Yet the smiling faces were all distinctive; she guessed it wouldn't take too long, and sure enough, as the days had gone by, she'd mastered everyone's identity and had begun to make friends.

Special friends, in fact, of her room-mates – Sheana Fleming, blonde and bright-eyed, always willing to do more than she need, and Ellie Cumming, brown-haired and dark-eyed, the opposite of Sheana in nature, yet like her in energy and quickness to offer help. There'd been girls like them at Edinburgh Southern, and they'd been special friends, too, and a big miss at first for Isla, but Sheana and Ellie had filled the gap, helping to add to the pleasantness of her new life.

Visiting home on her first afternoon off, Isla was told by her mother that she must bring her new friends back for tea some time. And wasn't it one of the nicest things about her new job that she could do that so easily? No need to get a train or bus from Edinburgh now, which just showed that Isla had done the right thing in moving.

'And how about the work, then?' Nan went on to probe, slicing another piece of ginger cake for Isla, who said, no, no, but ate it anyway. 'You're no' finding it too strange? Working with all that water?'

'Oh, the work's fine, Ma! I love it. It's really quite varied, you see, with water being used in all sorts of ways, not just giving patients baths. That would be boring!'

'The thing is, I've no idea what you do. I mean, if it's not just giving folk baths, what is it?'

'Well, there are the sauna and steam baths – people really enjoy those, particularly the chest cases – they welcome the steam. And then there are the cold wraps with ice, or cold rubs with cloths, or complete wraps where the patient also has blankets. Massage is very important – sometimes underwater massage – or we might use douches of water for certain problems. Och, there are all sorts of variations of treatment, depending on patients' needs. The doctors decide.'

'Fancy. And are all the patients rich, like you thought?'

'They seem to be, but I've been told that Doctor Lorne has charity schemes so that he can reduce the fees for those who can't afford much.' Isla smiled a little. 'It would be like him to do that.'

'You admire him, eh?'

'Oh, yes, he's a very fine person.'

'And a widower,' Nan said thoughtfully, her eyes gazing into the distance, at which Isla shook her head at her and said she must be getting back.

'Thanks for the lovely cake, Ma. I'll be along again soon.'

'And won't that be grand!'

At the door, Nan spoke of Boyd: how pleased he'd been that Isla had followed up his idea of working at the hydro and that she was as happy there as he was himself.

'Oh, I know, he takes all the credit!' Isla laughed. 'And it's nice he's around – not that I see him much, except in the staff canteen. I don't get time to visit the gym – thought maybe I should get him to give me some exercises after all your cake, Ma!'

'I suppose one o' these days he's going to bring some young woman home, eh?'

Isla shrugged. 'Well, he did go out with a couple of the nurses at Lorne's a year or two back, if you remember. Never came to anything, did it? And they've both moved on.'

'As long as he finds Miss Right,' sighed Nan, and Isla, having kissed her goodbye and departed for the hydro, knew she wasn't too anxious for that to happen soon. As for herself, she was certainly not looking for a Mr Right. Maybe in the distant future, but for now she was happy in her new job.

Eleven

Although Isla had told her mother that some of the patients at the hydro were not rich and were only helped to stay there by Dr Lorne's charity, it had to be admitted that most of the clients were in fact 'pretty privileged', as Sheana put it. And didn't some of them show it!

'Only a few,' she'd told Isla in the early days. 'Most are really nice and uncomplaining, even if their arthritis is playing up, or whatever. But, oh Lord, some of the others – some of the women – it's fetch this, fetch the other, I need my hair done, where's my lipstick? You'd never think we were nurses at all. More like ladies' maids.'

'Oh, no,' Isla said, laughing. 'I can't see any nurses putting up with that!'

'Well, we don't, and I'm sure you won't, but you have to be patient, eh? With the men, too, the few that go on about not having a golf course here, and why are there no drinks on Sunday, et cetera. You've just got to make sure they accept their treatments – they've paid for 'em, after all.'

'Sister Francis said the hydro doesn't take acute patients, but I suppose the chronic problems can be bad enough.'

'Oh, sure. The asthmatics can really suffer, and, like I say, there are the arthritics – they're often in severe pain. There are also diabetics and folk with muscle problems, but worst of all, I reckon, are the nervy ones. They come here for peace and quiet and most get it, but some just create tension for themselves.'

Sheana had shaken her head. 'Och, I'd better shut up or I'll be putting you off. Most of the patients, like I say, are really very nice, and, of course, there's a good turnover anyway. You'll keep on seeing new faces all the time.'

★   ★   ★

To begin with, of course, for Isla, all the faces of the patients she met were new, but just as she'd learned to recognize the nurses she was to work with, so she learned to recognize those in her care. Just as Sheana had told her, there were the easy ones and the few who were difficult, but past experience helped Isla here, for she was used to coping with all kinds of people and never let anyone get her down; she always kept her patience, as Sheana had recommended, and soon became a general favourite.

'Happy?' Dr Lorne asked her once in passing, when she was on her way to supper, to which she was able to answer, quite genuinely, that she was.

'I certainly hear good reports of you, Nurse Scott. Well done.'

Thanking him, as he moved on, she felt quite warmly pleased. It was good to know that she was well thought of in this new life she'd opted for – so much could have gone wrong, but so far had not. Supposing she'd had regrets, wished herself back at Edinburgh Southern? But that hadn't happened; she'd had no regrets, no desire to return to her old hospital, even though she'd missed it at first.

The first person she saw at supper in the staff canteen was Boyd. There was a spare seat next to him and he waved to her to join him when she'd decided what to have at the self-service counter, the choice being between macaroni cheese and sausages and mash. No contest. She'd never liked sausages, but they were piled high on Boyd's plate, she noticed, when she took her place next to him. 'Heavens, Boyd, if you eat all those and that heap of potato, you'll be sure to put on weight! No advert for your gym!'

He smiled and said he never put on weight – he was like Isla and Ma – but it seemed to Isla that his attention was elsewhere. She asked if he was all right.

'Sure I'm all right. Why d'you ask?'

'I don't know. You seem sort of – elsewhere.'

'Elsewhere?' He began to eat, making great play with his knife and fork, as though finishing his meal was all that was on his mind. Finally, though, as he pushed away his plate, he turned to Isla and fixed her with his grey eyes, so like her own. 'Thing is, Isla – sounds a piece of nonsense, I know, but I've seen the most amazing girl. And she's right here, in the hydro!'

'Really?' she asked, trying to finish her macaroni.

'Yes, she's quite stunning. A new waitress for the patients' dining room; only started two days ago. And I saw her yesterday. Couldn't believe my eyes!'

Isla was mystified at his excitement. Hadn't he seen a pretty girl before?

'Why, what's so special, Boyd? You've seen good-looking girls at Lorne's before. Didn't you take a couple of 'em out?'

'Those two?' he leaned back, running his hand through his short fair hair. 'Well, they were all right, but not like Trina. That's her name – Trina Morris. There's something different about her. I can't describe it, but she's not just good-looking, you ken; she attracts you, draws you. It's like I say, you can't take your eyes off her. You must see her for yourself.'

'I intend to.' Isla had leaped to her feet. 'But now I'm going to get some tea. Do you want any?'

'No, no, thanks.'

'Well, listen, then, here's a piece of advice.' Isla sat down again. 'When you go home tonight, don't tell Ma about this girl. At least, don't talk about her the way you've talked to me. That would not go down well.'

He nodded, trying to smile.

'You're right, I won't say anything. I mean, I haven't even spoken to her yet, though, of course, I'm going to. But I'm sorry if I sounded like a fool to you just then.' He laughed shortly. 'Got a bit carried away, I guess.'

'I'd say so,' Isla said slowly. 'You didn't sound like the Boyd I know.'

'All right, I'm sorry. Listen, maybe I'll have some tea, after all – though I'd rather have a beer, if the truth were known. You sit there and I'll get tea for both of us.'

As he made his way to the buffet table, his head was high and he walked like the soldier he used to be, which went some way towards making Isla feel better. But maybe not far enough. She felt as though she'd taken two steps down instead of one, and that she'd seen a side to her brother that was still so strange she couldn't just accept it.

How was this sudden interest in an unknown girl going to develop? Even when Boyd came back with the tea and began to chat normally of this and that, and she was chatting back, she was feeling a strange apprehension of trouble ahead. As she drank her tea, she determined that, as soon as she could, she would see this stunning waitress for herself and try to understand why her sensible brother appeared to be in danger of quite losing his head.

Twelve

Next day, late morning, Isla managed to slip away from the treatment rooms and made her way to the patients' dining room. As it was not a place she needed to visit, she'd scarcely seen it since the day of her interview, but she knew it was quite grand, with white-clothed individual tables set with shining cutlery and flowers, and, of course, waiter service – all very different from where the staff had their meals.

Only to be expected, of course – the patients at Lorne's being used to dining out in good restaurants and probably counting the hydro's excellent food and pleasant surroundings as part of their cure. Certainly, no expense was spared in giving them what they wanted: a first rate chef Mr Paul, as he liked to be called – was employed in a modern kitchen, together with two assistants and several waiting staff, one of whom was the amazing Trina Morris.

Now that she thought about it, Isla vaguely remembered hearing that a waitress had left and a new one appointed, but she hadn't taken much notice of it at the time. Why should she? How could she have known that it would matter to her that a new waitress had arrived? Perhaps it still wouldn't, but all the signs pointed to her arrival mattering to Boyd. And what mattered to Boyd mattered to Isla.

Visiting the dining room at that time, Isla had hoped she'd find tables being set, and when she saw two young women busy with preparations, she knew she was in luck. One of them – bright and bouncy Daisy MacDuff – was known to her. The other – well, she must be Trina.

With a sinking heart, Isla took in the girl's undoubted beauty – the wide-apart dark eyes and well-cut black hair beneath a wisp of a cap, her wide scarlet mouth and pert, straight little nose. Wouldn't be turned up, would it? No, no, of course not. Everything about her was just right. Her slim figure in her black dress, her elegant

legs in her black stockings, her slender fingers laying out cutlery
. . . And the power to attract? To draw? Oh, God, that was there
all right. Even with no males in sight, even with only Isla approaching,
it was clear she liked to send out the charm like rays from the sun.
Poor Boyd didn't stand a chance.

'Hello, Isla!' Daisy was calling – dear, overweight Daisy, who
didn't seem in the least overpowered by her new colleague. 'Anything
we can do for you, pet?'

'No, no, I was just wondering if you'd seen one of my patients
– old Mr Gibson. He's always going missing; I thought he might
have come in here.'

'No, we haven't seen him – we'll tell him to get back to the
treatment rooms pronto, if we do. Oh, but you must meet Trina
– she's our new waitress, took over from Ruby, if you remember.
Trina, this is Nurse Scott – Isla to her friends.'

Isla and Trina shook hands, Trina smiling brightly, Isla less so.

'Nice to meet you,' said Isla, moving away.

'And you.'

'So, if you see Mr Gibson—'

'Don't worry, we know what to do.'

So that was that, Isla was thinking, when the door from the
kitchens flew open and one of the waiters came in, his gaze going
straight to Trina. As he went to her, continuing to fix her with
his eyes, Isla recognized him as Damon Duthie, known for creating
arguments and falling foul of Mr Paul, the chef, on a regular
basis. His own looks were not unlike Trina's, for his hair was
black and his eyes dark brown, but where she was certainly good-
looking, somehow he missed being handsome, perhaps because
his brows were inclined to meet too often and his smiles were
very rare.

'So, where've you been?' he now asked Trina, his voice truculent.
'I was going to show you round the grounds before we had to get
things ready. Where'd you go?'

'I asked Trina to help me with the tables,' Daisy told him pleasantly. 'There wasn't really time to look round the grounds, especially
when you know there's plenty to do anyway.'

'Sweet of you, Damon,' Trina said, her voice light but with an
undertone that said she was not going to argue. 'Thing is, I don't
want to get on the wrong side of Mr Paul. We can look at the
grounds later.'

'Look, you don't have to worry about that old windbag. Take it from me, he's past it, anyway . . .'

Leaving Damon still sounding off, Isla quietly slipped away, her mind racing as she tried to sort out what might happen if Boyd asked Trina to go out with him. On first seeing Damon, Isla had been encouraged that he might be enough to keep Boyd out of the running, but taking in his looks and his manner, it seemed obvious that Trina would prefer Boyd, which was exactly what Isla didn't want. Maybe she was being unfair – she didn't know the girl, she'd only just met her – but she remained certain in her own mind that Trina would be wrong for her brother.

Yet what was she doing, anyway, looking ahead, making assumptions, about something that wasn't really anything to do with her? Boyd was her brother, true, but he must work out his own problems, make his own decisions. Isla must just leave him to it.

But, oh, Lord, it was hard. He'd been through enough; she didn't want him hurt in any way again.

'Hello, Isla, there you are!' cried Ellie Cumming as Isla hurried into the treatment block, worrying that she would be late for her routine heat bath appointment with difficult Mrs Abbot who suffered from arthritis.

'Can't stop, Ellie, have to see Mrs Abbot.'

'That's why I wanted to speak to you. She sent a message that she doesn't feel up to the heat bath today. Would you go up and give her a massage?'

'Oh, I see. Well, yes. Just get my breath first.'

'You ought to have a cup of tea or something – you look a bit down. What's wrong?'

'Nothing, nothing at all. Just one of those days.'

'Well, to cheer you up, remember it'll soon be Easter and the days are getting longer. On the other hand, that means Doctor Lorne's daughter will be home from boarding school any day now, and is she difficult, or is she not?'

'That sweet little girl?'

'Sweet little girl? She's no little girl – she's leaving school this term. Going to a finishing school in Switzerland – typical!'

'But why is she so difficult?' Isla asked, turning to be on her way. 'Because Doctor Lorne spoils her, you mean?'

'That's right, so maybe it's not her fault, but she only thinks there's one person in the world who counts and that's her. Never has time for any of us. You'll see for yourself when she comes.'

'Maybe she'll have improved, now she's left school?'

Ellie laughed. 'And maybe she won't!'

Thirteen

After Isla's straight talking to him in the canteen, Boyd burned with anger – not with her, but with himself. He felt he had let himself down, speaking of Trina Morris in the extravagant way he had, as though he were some lovesick schoolboy. Isla had been right to show disappointment in him, and he only wished now that he'd kept his mouth shut about his feelings, even though, as he'd admitted to himself after he'd left her, they were real enough.

Yes, it was something he'd hardly been able to take in, the way he'd experienced an almost physical blow when he'd first set eyes on Trina. Was this what they called love at first sight? The sort of thing you saw acted out at the cinema, or the theatre. Romeo and Juliet, and all that sort of thing . . .

So, what did you do about it? If it felt unreal, try to make it real? Oh, God, yes. That's what he had to do. See Trina again. Ask her out – maybe not at first, but as soon as possible, certainly before the damned waiters she'd be working with got a chance. Damon Duthie, for instance, or Clive MacAlastair – two chaps Boyd had never had any time for, Damon being so fiery, Clive so boring. Surely Trina wouldn't be interested in either of them? No, he didn't believe so, but as he thought of another alternative, his heart almost missed a beat. Wasn't it more likely that a girl who looked like her would have a young man in her life already? Might even be engaged?

The only thing to do was to get along to the patients' dining room, find Trina and introduce himself. Take it from there. But what excuse could he have for being in the patients' dining room?

A better idea came to him. He'd pop into the kitchen – all very casually, of course – and pretend he was reminding Mr Paul to come in for his exercises. Trina would be sure to be in and out of the kitchen, and he would, again very casually, speak to her, welcome her to Lorne's, tell her who he was and what he did – and there it was – he'd have made himself known. They could progress from there, if they were to progress at all.

The following morning, he put a notice on the door of the gym – *Back in half an hour* – and having combed his hair and straightened the collar of his blue gym shirt, made for the kitchen. It was the time when morning coffee was being assembled for those patients in the lounge who had no treatments, and Mr Paul was reading the paper and smoking – strictly forbidden, except for himself – while his staff were filling silver-plated coffee pots and setting out biscuits.

No sign of Trina. That was the problem. Boyd, putting on a smile, approached the chef, a heavy man in whites, whose eyes were small and whose nose was large, and who now raised his eyebrows at Boyd.

'What brings you here, laddie?' he asked jovially. 'Come to cadge a cup of coffee?'

'No, thanks; just wanted to remind you about your exercises, Mr Paul. It's pretty important to keep up with 'em, you know, if you want to keep fit.'

'Hell, I've enough exercise here, if you ask me. Trying to get meals ready and keeping track of all these layabouts supposed to help me!'

'Layabouts, Mr Paul? That's a wee bit unfair!' cried skinny Clive MacAlastair, pausing in the doorway with a loaded tray.

'Well, where's Damon, then? Where's that new lassie?'

'Sorry, Mr Paul!' came Damon's voice, as he and Trina came sauntering in. 'I was just showing Trina here round the grounds – forgot the time, eh?'

'I'll say,' the chef snapped. 'Well, give the others a hand with the coffee, eh? You too, Trina. And remember when you work here, you work in the kitchen – looking round the grounds is for your own time, not mine!'

'Sorry, Mr Paul,' the new waitress murmured, echoing Damon but sweetening the apology with a charming smile which the chef couldn't help returning. Boyd stood aside, his rapt gaze on Trina.

'Hello, you're new, eh?' he asked in a low voice, moving closer to her. 'I'm Boyd Scott. I run the gymnasium. It's good to meet you.'

'Trina Morris,' she murmured, her dark eyes studying his handsome face with an appraising gaze he'd met often enough before. 'I didn't even know there was a gymnasium here. Not that I'm one for PE!'

'That's a shame.' He laughed lightly. 'We do have a ladies-only hour three times a week, when one of the nurses helps with the instruction. You might like to try that.'

'Ladies only? Not my style!' Trina's eyes were dancing. 'Who cares if women and men do PE together?'

'We just have to do what folk think is suitable,' Boyd said awkwardly. 'But it'd be grand if I could just show you round sometime.'

'OK, sometime I'll pop in. Nice to have met you, Mr Scott.'

'And for me to have met you, Miss Morris.'

'Trina,' she whispered, leaning towards him for a moment as Damon suddenly called her, his voice edgy and rough.

'You coming, Trina? We're supposed to be serving coffee!'

Shrugging her slim shoulders and taking a tray and a coffee pot, Trina favoured Boyd with a wide smile before following Damon and the other servers out of the kitchen.

'I'd better get back,' Boyd murmured, after standing in silence for a moment. 'Don't forget to come along for your PE, Mr Paul, when you've time.'

'Aye, when I've time.' The chef gave Boyd a grin. 'She's a looker, eh, our new lassie?'

'Miss Morris?' Boyd began to move to the door. 'Oh, yes, I suppose she is.'

'Reckon my dining room'll be more popular than ever, once the nobs have seen her.'

But Boyd was already gone.

Walking on air because he'd met Trina as he'd planned, he was almost back at the gym when he suddenly saw Isla making her way to the lift with a large bag of crushed ice. He called her name.

'Boyd?' She turned to meet him. 'What are you doing out of your gym?'

'What are you doing out of the treatment block?'

'I'm on my way upstairs to see a patient. She's here for diabetic treatment but sprained her ankle out walking – I'm giving her a cold pack.'

'I've just been to remind Mr Paul about his exercises.'

'In the kitchen?' Isla's eyes narrowed. 'You sure you saw Mr Paul?'

'OK, you win.' Boyd laughed. 'I did see Miss Morris as well. She said she wasn't one for PE but she's agreed to see my gymnasium.'

'Oh, Boyd!'

'No, it's all right, I'm not being an idiot this time – all very cool, calm and collected.'

Isla shook her head. 'Maybe. All I can say is, you be careful, Boyd; be sure what you're doing. But listen, I've just heard some really gloomy news. Doctor Woodville told us this morning he's leaving in April. Going to take over his father's practice as a GP in Edinburgh. Oh, he'll be such a loss, eh?'

'He will. That's bad news, all right. He's a great guy.'

'The next doctor won't be as nice, I bet you. But I'd better dash. Remember what I told you, Boyd.'

'Oh, yes,' he said carelessly and, as Isla's gaze followed him, continued on his way.

Fourteen

Some days later, seeing Dr Woodville on his own in his office, Isla decided on an impulse to tell him how much he was going to be missed. He wouldn't mind, would he? Of course he wouldn't. Dr Woodville never minded anything; that was what made him one to be missed.

'I haven't been here long but I feel the same as everyone else,' she said earnestly. 'It's just not going to be the same for us without you to cheer us on.'

'Oh, come,' he answered, flushing a little. 'I'm a very ordinary sort of guy, nothing special. But I certainly appreciate your kind words, Isla.'

Isla. His use of her first name saddened her, for she knew he wouldn't have done it if he hadn't soon been leaving. Dr Lorne preferred formality between members of staff at work; even after work, Isla had never heard anyone call Dr Woodville Bob, for instance.

'By the way,' he was continuing, 'we have a new patient arriving tomorrow who'll be staying several weeks, possibly more, as he really wants to give the treatment a chance to work. As he's also a bit depressed at present, I'm asking everyone to take a very positive attitude with him, reassure him that all will be well, and that sort of thing.'

'Oh, of course we will,' Isla agreed. 'What's his complaint?'

'Chronic bronchitis.'

'He's elderly, then?'

'Hope not.' Dr Woodville smiled. 'He's twenty-nine – my age.'

'Oh, I'm sorry, I didn't mean . . .' Isla blushed. 'It's just that most patients I've met who have chronic bronchitis have been older people. Maybe after having had a lot of acute bronchitis over the years.'

'That's usually the case, but for Mark Kinnaird, our patient, the acute attacks came early on in childhood. We went to school together, before he went into his father's law firm and I chose medicine, and I remember him often being ill as a boy. It's no surprise to me that he's developed the chronic form. Now he's always breathless, always coughing, and he's desperate for us to provide some relief. Nothing's worked for him so far in conventional medicine.'

'Poor chap – I hope we can help him.'

'Well, we've had plenty of success with chest patients. I think there's every chance. He's arriving about two tomorrow. Perhaps you'd see him settled in?'

'Certainly, I will, Doctor Woodville.'

'Look out for him, then, if you would.' Dr Woodville hesitated. 'Just one more thing – I think you'll all be happy with my replacement. Doctor Lorne says he's a very good doctor and will fit in here very well.'

Isla's eyes widened. 'You mean, Doctor Lorne's already chosen a new doctor? But there haven't been any interviews, have there?'

'Wasn't necessary. Doctor Lorne already knew of Doctor Revie, who's the son of a medical friend and has been working at a hydro in the Highlands. He's got the experience and was interested in a move here, so when Doctor Lorne offered him the job, he accepted. Should be ideal.'

'I thought there always had to be interviews for jobs. Seems fairer.'

'Maybe, but if you know the right man for the post, I don't see why you shouldn't just go for him. He would probably have been the best at an interview anyway.'

'I suppose so. Think I'd better get on, Doctor Woodville. I won't forget about the new patient.'

'Thanks, Isla.

They exchanged smiles and separated, Dr Woodville to make for the lift to see an upstairs patient, Isla to snatch a cup of coffee with Sheana before her next appointment. They discussed the surprising news that a new doctor had already been appointed and agreed he'd be no match for Dr Woodville, whatever he was like, though Sheana remarked that maybe they were being unfair.

'Should always keep an open mind, eh? Though you needn't keep one about our young madam arriving tomorrow. It'll not take you two minutes to see what she's like!'

'You're talking about Doctor Lorne's daughter? Coming tomorrow?'

'That's right. Day before Good Friday. Finished with one school, starting another in Switzerland. All right for some, eh?'

'I think I should keep an open mind, anyway,' Isla said, laughing. 'You folks sound prejudiced.'

'Och, it's just that she's just not interested in anybody but herself. See what you think, anyway, when you meet her.'

Also see what the poor new patient is like, thought Isla, rising to rinse her cup. Cheering him from his depression obviously would not be easy unless they were successful with his treatment, and that would not be known for a while. They would just have to do their best for him, seeing as he'd been so unlucky. A comfortable background, maybe, but so little chance to enjoy it. Poor Mr Kinnaird.

Fifteen

Having a little time to spare before she need expect to see Mr Kinnaird on the following day, Isla looked in on Boyd. It was quiet in the gym – patients were finishing lunch, after which they might rest or have appointments – and she found Boyd busy with his paperwork, a job he disliked and put off when he could. For some days, she'd thought he must be keeping out of her way, for she hadn't seen him around, but now he leaped up with alacrity and seemed delighted to see her.

'Isla! Nice to see you! I was just going cross-eyed, doing my books. Fancy a go on the parallel bars?'

'No, thanks. I just came in for a minute – to see how things were.'

'By which you mean has Trina been to look round the gym?' He gave a wry smile. 'The answer is, yes, she has. Thought it was grand.'

'I was just, you know, wondering what was happening.' Isla hesitated. 'Have you asked her out or anything?'

'Or anything? No, I . . . well, I wanted to, but I didn't have the nerve.'

'Didn't have the nerve? I thought sure you'd have fixed to take her out somewhere, before Damon beat you to it.'

'Don't think I've forgotten him. She never mentioned him, though, and I did find out that she has no other young man around at the moment. No sweetheart, you might say.' Boyd shook his head. 'Apart from me being chicken, the other snag was that there were too many people about when she came, which was about five o'clock – a popular time. I just couldn't speak to her on her own.'

'So you'll try some other time?'

'You bet I will. Whatever you think, Isla, I know Trina's the one for me and I'm not going to lose her. Even if Damon Duthie thinks he's a rival, I'll be the one she wants.'

'You think so?'

'Yes, I do.' Boyd's look was defiant. 'I do think so.'

'Well, I'll have to keep out of it, I suppose.' Isla glanced at the watch pinned to her uniform. 'But now I've got to go. Boyd, just be careful, eh? Don't get too worked up and maybe disappointed.'

'Don't worry, I know what I'm doing.' He gave her a long level look. 'Just leave my life to me, all right?'

She nodded, sighing, and hurried away, anxious not to be late in greeting Mr Kinnaird.

In fact, when she reached Reception, he still hadn't arrived, but from the long windows next to the desk, she could see Dr Lorne's car drawing up and, a moment later, saw him get out and open the door for his passenger, a beaming smile on his kindly face.

'Miss Guthrie,' Isla whispered, 'is that Miss Lorne arriving?'

'Where, let me see!'

Noreen Guthrie was swinging round, her eyes excited.

'Oh, yes, that's Magda, all right. Goodness, her school blazer's a bit small for her, isn't it? Bet she can't wait to get out of that. Watch out – they're coming in.'

'Here we are, my dear,' Isla could hear Dr Lorne saying, as he entered the hall with the tall young girl spinning her Panama hat in her fingers at this side. 'Back home again!'

'Not for long,' she replied coolly, standing just inside the door, her eyes slowly moving over the wide reception hall, taking in Miss Guthrie at her desk and Isla in her uniform, before finally returning to her father.

Isla, fascinated, was aware that she was staring at the new arrival but couldn't seem to look away. Such a lovely girl, with eyes of vivid green, an imperious little nose – straight, of course – and glossy dark hair, expertly cut. There was no doubt that she was very like the photo of her mother, with just a trace of her childish looks, but so composed, so sure of herself, she seemed hardly like the schoolgirl she had so recently been. Was she as careless of others as Sheana had reported?

Seemed so, for when Dr Lorne introduced Isla to her, she scarcely bothered to produce a smile and let her green eyes wander. Even when her father told her that Isla's brother was the young man who'd once shown her round the gymnasium, she merely nodded, though after a moment did remark that she was surprised.

'Is he still here? I should have thought he would have moved on by now.'

'Why should he?' asked Isla. 'He likes it here.'

'Oh, well.' Magda Lorne, making no effort to elaborate, shrugged and began to walk away, as her father arranged with Miss Guthrie to have Tam, the porter, move his daughter's luggage to his flat at the rear of the building.

'Nice to have met you,' Magda suddenly called over her shoulder.

Isla was so astonished, she took a moment or two to call back, 'And nice to have met you, Miss Lorne!'

'You waiting for a patient, Miss Scott?' Dr Lorne asked, pausing for a moment.

'Yes, Doctor Lorne. Mr Kinnaird.'

'Ah, yes. Doctor Woodville told me about him. As a matter of fact, I think I see his taxi now.' Dr Lorne was beginning to hurry after his daughter. 'I'll leave him in your good hands, then, Nurse Scott.'

As a tall, thin young man wearing a dark suit but no hat paid off his driver and turned to look up at the hydro's façade, Isla ran to open the door for him. Mr Mark Kinnaird had arrived.

Sixteen

His eyes were a warm brown, his features strongly defined, his smile pleasing, yet there were signs of strain obvious to Isla's practised gaze. Clearly, the new patient was having trouble with his breathing, even as he arrived.

'Mr Kinnaird?' Isla took his case. 'Welcome to Lorne's Hydro. I'm Nurse Scott and will take you up to your room. There is a lift – no need to worry.'

'I don't mind stairs,' he answered quickly, his Edinburgh accent most agreeable. 'But, here, do let me take that.'

'Oh, it's no trouble – we'll be using the lift, anyway. Miss Guthrie, will you let Doctor Woodville know Mr Kinnaird is here?'

'Of course, Nurse Scott.'

'Thanks so much. This way, Mr Kinnaird. The lift's just across the hall.'

Walking at his pace, Isla and the patient made their way to the lift where, as she pressed the button, Isla gave an encouraging smile.

'You're on the third floor; it would have been a long way up by the stairs, you see. But you have a nice view of the Edgemuir hills.'

As the lift came fast and they were able to take their places, he gave a rough, hacking cough and took out his handkerchief. 'Sounds . . . nice.'

They didn't speak again until they were in his comfortable room, where he had a beautifully made bed, a wardrobe, chest of drawers, an easy chair and a wash basin, as well as the view to the hills Isla had promised. This at once drew the new patient to the windows and brought another smile to his face as he turned back to her.

'This is splendid, really splendid.'

'Glad you like it, but please, Mr Kinnaird, take a seat and rest while I unpack your case. The doctor won't be long.'

'I'm not so good today,' he murmured, coughing again and wiping his lips with his handkerchief. 'Have good days and bad days. Too many bad days, maybe.'

'You're going to get better here,' she told him firmly. 'You must believe that.'

'I have high hopes.'

For a little while, they were silent as Mr Kinnaird sat in his chair, watching Isla deftly put away his clothes, hang up his dressing gown and place his toiletries in a cupboard beneath the wash basin.

'The bathroom's just next door, Mr Kinnaird,' she finally said. 'Not far to go, but if you'd prefer it, we could move you to a room with bathroom attached.'

'No, this will be fine, thank you,' he was replying when a knock sounded on his door and Dr Woodville breezed in, his hair on end, his smile wide as he bent to shake his patient's hand.

'Mark, how are you? It's good to see you.'

'Nice to see you too, Bob.'

Mark Kinnaird made to rise from his chair, but the doctor gently made him sit again.

'Don't get up, please. I'll just perch on the bed – don't report me, Nurse Scott! – and have a chat about your treatments. First, a word or two about your medical history – I know all about your early symptoms and I have your own doctor's report on your present symptoms, but I see he also mentions smoking being a contributory factor. You have, I hope, given that up?'

'Oh, yes, Bob.' Mark Kinnaird's expression was rueful. 'I suppose I should have realized it wasn't going to do me any good, but you know how it was in the war – I only had a desk job, but everyone around me smoked and I did, too.'

'I understand.' Dr Woodville shook his head. 'Had to have something to get us through it, and we were the lucky ones; we did come through. But smoking's past history now, eh?'

'Certainly is.'

'Right, well, I don't suppose you know what we do here, but for chest cases, we find that water as steam can be very successful. You know how a steaming kettle helps you? Well, it works on the same principle, loosens everything up. So, we'll be looking at saunas for you, Mark, plus moist warm wraps, massage and hot fomentations, and see how we go. OK?'

'Oh, yes, the steam idea sounds just the thing.'

'Right, well, next we'll take you down to meet Sister Francis who's the head nurse in the treatment rooms, and the routines will be explained and you'll be given a conducted tour. After that, it'll be time for a cup of tea!'

'Sounds excellent.' Mark slowly rose from his chair. 'Can't tell you how it helps to have someone I know explaining everything to me.'

'Unfortunately, I'm leaving soon – taking over Dad's practice as he's not up to it now.'

'Oh.' Mark's face fell. 'That's a blow.'

'It is,' Isla said with feeling. 'We're all so sad.'

'Enough of that!' Dr Woodville cried. 'Let's just get to the lift.'

Seventeen

While Mark Kinnaird was enjoying a rest and a cup of tea after his conducted tours, Boyd was still trying to think of a way to get Trina on her own and ask her out. He had to know where he stood, what hope there was for him, and, if none, how he would adjust. Maybe he wouldn't adjust at all, which was a crazy idea when he remembered what he'd had to face during the war – things so terrible he couldn't speak of them. What was being rejected compared with that? Somehow, though he felt bad about it, he knew that to ask that question wouldn't help at all.

In the end, he decided, as Isla had decided before him, that the way to catch Trina was before a meal in the patients' dining room when she would be setting the tables. The waiters didn't do that, which meant Damon wouldn't be around, and as dinner was not too far away, it was possible she was busy in the dining room at that very moment. Too bad if Daisy or someone else was there – as long as it wasn't Damon, he could successfully snatch a few words with her. Enough to seal his fate.

As Larry was busy with his steam baths, Boyd couldn't ask him to stand in for him, but he hung another of his notices on the door of the gym – *Back in Twenty Minutes* – which was optimistic but would have to do, and with his heart in his mouth, he left for the patients' dining room.

He put his head round the door. Was she there? Oh, God, she was, Daisy as well, both chatting as they flitted about, setting out cutlery and water jugs, putting fresh flowers into little vases to brighten each table.

Go in, he told himself, *for God's sake, get it over! Never mind what Daisy thinks*. This was his chance – better not mess it up!

'Hello there!' he called, striding in, hoping to look confident. 'Daisy – Trina.'

As Daisy stared and Trina smiled, he went on quite openly, 'Trina, could I have a word?'

She turned her great eyes on Daisy and gave a little shrug, as Daisy moved away, concealing a laugh

'Don't mind me! I've work to do.'

'Me, too,' said Trina. 'What is it, Boyd?'

'Just wondering . . .' His lips were so dry when he spoke, it seemed to him that he was mumbling and he cleared his throat. 'I was just wondering . . . if you'd care to . . . go to the pictures with me sometime? In Edinburgh?'

'Go to the pictures? You mean, in the evening?' She raised her fine brows. 'Not easy, Boyd, seeing as I work here in the evenings.'

'Not every evening.'

'True, we've a rota for our evenings off.'

'We could fix something up, then.'

'What about you? Don't you work in the evenings, too?'

'I have one free every week. We could make sure we got the same one. If you want to, that is. You haven't said yet.'

'Well, there might be a problem. With someone.'

His eyes never leaving her face, he braced himself for the name, then spoke it aloud himself.

'You mean Damon Duthie?'

'He has asked me out, too.'

'And did you go?'

'Oh, yes.' She smiled. 'We managed Sunday afternoon together. Went for a walk.'

Determined not to let her see the effect her words had had on him, he laughed.

'Sounds exciting.'

'It was very pleasant.'

'So pleasant that you don't want to go out with me?'

'Oh, I wouldn't say that. But there are the difficulties. I mean, arranging a time.'

If he hadn't wanted to let her see the pain she had caused, he didn't mind letting her see the relief, which he knew must be showing in his eyes.

Grasping her hand, he said huskily, 'Don't worry about that. We'll work it out and I'll speak to you again. All right?'

'If you'll just let go of my hand, Boyd. I do have to get on with my work. Look at poor Daisy, having to do it all!'

'Oh, yes, poor Daisy. Sorry.' Turning away and keeping the smile from his face with effort, he called to her. 'Sorry, Daisy!'

'That's all right, I understand.'

And I bet she does, too, he thought, not minding, not caring – about anything, really, except that Trina had not turned him down.

'I've to get back to the gym,' he declared, moving to the door, taking one last look at Trina, who was already setting another table, not watching him go, which didn't matter to him in the slightest. She wouldn't say she didn't want to see him, which meant, of course, that she did, and that was all that mattered. All the way back to the gym, everywhere seemed full of sunshine, and even when he found an irate retired general fuming over being kept waiting outside, there were no clouds in Boyd's sky.

Eighteen

The days began to speed away, bringing Dr Woodville's departure nearer, as well as Dr Revie's arrival, which was only a worry. It was unlikely that he would have the personality of the man they were all going to miss, and might make so many changes at the hydro that the nursing staff wouldn't know where they were. Of course, Dr Lorne would have to approve of all he did, but the new broom might still be able to raise too much dust.

So thought Sheana and Ellie, though Sheana did admit that they must just wait and see how things turned out – there was little point in trying to look into the future. At least, they could be grateful that Magda had departed for Switzerland, so they'd be free of seeing her about the place and knowing she didn't even know who they were.

'Poor Doctor Lorne,' sighed Ellie. 'He's going to miss not having her for the Easter holidays this year.'

'Just like Joan Elrick's going to miss Doctor Woodville,' said Sheana with a mischievous glint in her eye, causing Isla to stare in surprise.

'Whatever do you mean, Sheana? Aren't we all going to miss him?'

'Oh, not like Joan. She's had her hopes of him ever since he came, they say, but here he is, going, and has never made a sign!'

'I really don't know how you can know what she feels,' Isla declared. 'She's never shown anything when I've seen her with him.'

'Ah, you've just not been looking!' cried Sheana. 'But you know what they say – love and a cold can never be hid?'

Sheana's comment turned Isla's thoughts to Boyd. He can't mention Trina's name without his mouth beginning to smile, and after he'd taken her to the pictures, which he'd told Isla he was planning to do, he would probably be worse. Better not ask him about it, Isla decided, just in case things didn't go well.

There was probably no way they could have gone as well as Boyd had hoped, for his idea that spending time with Trina in a darkened cinema would be unalloyed bliss was never very realistic. Of course, at first, he'd been confident that what they were to see would be of no interest to either of them. He'd never found that watching a screen with people mouthing words you couldn't hear was anything but odd, and no doubt Trina would feel the same. There might be subtitles and a pianist thundering away in the pit, but she'd find them simply irritating, as he did, just something to be disregarded like the picture itself, while the main thing was that she and he could be together.

To his dismay, however, Trina seemed truly lost in another world, as she stared up at the screen showing *The Pleasure Garden*, an Alfred Hitchcock film about the loves and setbacks of two chorus girls, scarcely seeming even to notice when Boyd took her hand. This so doused his joy at being with her that he let her hand go and sat like a stone until the film ended.

'Oh, wasn't it lovely?' Trina cried, her beautiful eyes blinking, as the lights went up. 'Didn't you think Virginia Valli was wonderful? She's American, you know – a very famous star.'

'Is she? I didn't notice her particularly. Which one was she?'

'Why, Pat, of course! Surely you knew that?' Trina was looking round the crowded cinema, fanning herself with her handkerchief, while Boyd's intent gaze stayed on her face.

'What's up?' she asked at last, 'You seem in a mood.'

'Not really. It's just that you seem more interested in the picture than you are in me.'

'We did come to see the picture, eh?'

'You know I came to be with you. But if you'd rather see a picture, or be with Damon Duthie, maybe you'd better say so.'

'Boyd, I do want to be with you. But I'm not going to say I don't want to see Damon as well. Why should I have to choose?'

Boyd, his heart so heavy it seemed to weigh down his chest, shook his head. 'I thought you might have wanted to,' he said in a low voice. 'And chosen me.'

'We've only just met, Boyd.'

'Same with you and Damon.'

'Yes, so let's just say I'll see you both. No more arguments. The lights are going down; it's time for the second picture.'

'You want to see it?' he groaned.

'Oh, yes, I always watch everything.'

As he stared at the credits coming up for whatever the second picture was, he still felt pain around his heart, until Trina slipped her hand into his and suddenly there was hope again; he knew he'd take whatever she offered, even if it meant sharing her with Damon Duthie. Not to do that would mean to lose her altogether, and the way he felt, that was not something he could face.

'That's the way it's going to be,' he told Isla next day. 'Trina's seeing both of us.'

'You think Damon will put up with that?'

'He'll have to, if he wants to keep seeing Trina.'

'Seems to me it will lead to trouble. Damon will never accept sharing her with you. How could he? And how can you accept that she'll be seeing him as well as you?'

'It's all I've got, Isla. I have to take it. He'll take it, too. As I say, he'll have to.'

'I wonder.' Isla's worried eyes searched Boyd's face. 'I see storm clouds ahead.'

'I can manage whatever he comes up with,' Boyd said firmly. 'And I'm sure, in the end, Trina will choose me. I know it, Isla, I feel it.'

'Well, just don't tell Ma about this,' she warned. 'And watch your step. Doctor Lorne won't want any trouble.'

'There'll be no trouble,' said Boyd.

Nineteen

Although Mark Kinnaird had complained to Isla more than once that he was very disappointed about not having Bob, as he called Dr Woodville, to superintend his care much longer, the news was that his treatment did seem to be doing some good.

'I believe it's the sauna and the steam baths,' he told Isla, while she had been giving him his moist wrapping treatment. 'It's just as Bob said: the steam from them acts in the same way as my kettle at home, but it's much more efficient and far-reaching, and lasts longer, too. I must admit, though, I was a bit worried about the sauna at first.'

'You would be when it's something you're not familiar with,' Isla commented, as she took up a blanket to cover him. 'But Larry Telford's very experienced; he knows just what to do.'

'Of course, but the first time when I had to strip down and sit on the bench in the cubicle, I felt – I don't know – very vulnerable, and when this fellow came in and started throwing water at the stove and on the floor – well, I'd no idea what was coming next.'

'He has to create the steam somehow,' Isla said, laughing. 'And you've just said how much better it's made you feel.'

'That's true, and now, of course, I'm only too grateful to Larry and the hydro and everyone. The Finns, too, for inventing the sauna. I was telling my father all about it when he came to visit me.' Mark grinned. 'He's all for me trying anything that'll help, but still has his suspicions of the water cure. Very conventional man, my father.'

Isla smiled. Having met Mr Kinnaird, she knew Mark was right about him, but, like his son, he was courteous and pleasant, even if not quite as handsome.

'People usually come round to it in the end. The main thing is that we break the cycle of your symptoms, you see, and we're hoping that you'll find we have. Now, I'll leave you for an hour or so.'

'Thank you,' he said earnestly, his dark eyes resting on her with clear sincerity. 'You're always so kind, Nurse Scott.'

'It's just my job,' she told him.

He shook his head. 'I think you know you do more than your job.'

'Just rest, Mr Kinnaird. I'll see you soon.'

At the door, she looked back, glad to see that those fine eyes of his were closing, and relieved that they'd earlier been free of the strange blankness she had sometimes seen in them. Once or twice, when she'd come to check on him in his room, she'd found him sitting in his chair, his eyes on the hills, yet not, she guessed, seeing them. Seeing instead – what? Something in himself that stopped him from enjoying the moment? He'd been depressed, of course, facing a future in which he thought he'd never get better, but now that he was feeling better, could that be the end of the dark times for him?

As an experienced nurse, she knew that it was still too early to say. There could be setbacks – often were – and he might be disappointed, but at least there had been some progress, and she would cling on to that, realizing Mark's progress meant a lot to her. Although it was not her way to have 'special' patients, she had to admit he was becoming rather an exception.

Not because she was attracted to him, or believed that he was attracted to her, but just feeling . . . a sort of affinity with him that she couldn't remember having had for a patient before. And he felt it, too – she knew he did – and without going any further into it, as she moved on to other duties, she was happy about it.

'There you are, Miss Scott!' She heard someone calling and looked round to see Miss Elrick hurrying towards her, a sheet of paper in her hand.

'I thought I'd just catch you,' she said breathlessly. 'So difficult with all you nurses being so busy.'

'How can I help?' asked Isla.

'Well, I've been asked by Doctor Lorne to collect for Doctor Woodville's leaving present and I'm wondering if I could put you down for something? Say, half a crown?'

Did Miss Elrick hesitate a moment over Dr Woodville's name? Isla thought perhaps she did, but then was annoyed with herself, for the thought had probably only come because of what Sheana had said.

'Oh, yes, I want to contribute!' she cried eagerly. 'Half a crown would be fine, though I haven't any money on me now.'

'That's all right; you can give it to me later. I'm just taking names at the moment.'

As Miss Elrick pencilled in Isla's contribution, she smiled and said softly, 'Doctor Lorne's thinking a clock would be nice. He knows a very good Edinburgh shop and is sure we'll have enough money to get something quite handsome. I'm sure, too. Doctor Woodville is so popular, isn't he?'

'Everyone likes him,' Isla agreed. 'He'll be hard to follow.'

'The new doctor?' Miss Elrick laughed. 'He doesn't stand a chance!'

Oh, Lord, it looked as if Sheana was right about her, after all. Watching the doctor's secretary moving quickly away, her high heels clicking on the polished floor, Isla found herself suddenly feeling sorry for her. Why should that be? For all she knew, there might already be an understanding between Joan Elrick and Dr Woodville. They might be going to make some sort of declaration at the doctor's leaving ceremony, mightn't they? Just hope they do, was Isla's prayer, just hope they do. Observing Boyd's rocky path towards true love was more than enough for her, and certainly did not inspire her to want some sort of love affair for herself.

Twenty

True love. Boyd himself did not care to question whether or not he would ever get such a thing from Trina. It was what he wanted; there was no way he could settle for doing without it, and therefore he wouldn't let himself even imagine it wouldn't come. Yet on their second evening out, if he'd had the courage to be honest, he would have had to admit that Trina didn't yet feel as he did. She would, though, she would: he had to believe it. When they'd spent more time together, everything would be different. He clung on to that.

For their second meeting, he had taken her for a meal at an Edinburgh fish restaurant – nothing grand, and for that reason popular with younger people, something that found approval with Trina, who was looking so stunning in a short pink dress and matching stole that Boyd could not tear his eyes from her.

'Good choice, Boyd,' she commented. 'Just my sort of place.'

'Glad you like it,' he murmured, hoping he was off to a good start.

'In fact, I think you know what to do to please folk, don't you? Or should I say, please girls? I bet you've been out with plenty, eh?'

He hesitated as the waiter came to take their orders, only saying, when he'd gone, that there'd been no more than a couple of girls in his life so far.

'Nurses, were they? I bet they were nurses.'

'All right, they were.'

'Oh, Boyd, you should never go out with nurses! They only care about their patients and the doctors.'

'What's wrong with that?'

'Well, with patients, they like to put on their Florence Nightingale act, have everyone so grateful, saying they're so kind and such.'

'My sister's not like that!'

'Must be the exception.'

Trina drank a little water and dabbed at her deeply rouged lips as Boyd continued to stare at her in fascination.

'So, what about the doctors?' he asked, after a moment.

'Oh, of course, every nurse secretly wants to marry a doctor, and why not? They've got everything, eh? Money and position and folk thinking they're gods. I wouldn't mind marrying a doctor myself!'

His heart missing a beat, Boyd finally looked away.

'I bet you could, if you wanted to,' he said hoarsely. 'Bit late for Doctor Woodville, but there's a new doctor coming – maybe he'll do?'

'Why, Boyd, I think you're jealous!' Trina laughed. 'Oh, my, you don't need to be. Not over doctors, anyway. Did you ever hear of a doctor marrying a waitress? But here comes our fish! That's good – I'm starving.'

'What did you mean?' Boyd asked, after they'd begun to eat. 'What did you mean when you said "Not over doctors, anyway"? Were you saying I should be jealous of someone else? Damon Duthie, for instance?'

'Well, he's there, eh? In my life. I can't deny it.'

'He's only in your life the same as I am, Trina. Why should I be jealous, when he sees you no more than I do?'

Trina shrugged and loosened her stole, revealing her fine shoulders, which drew attention from numerous male eyes in the restaurant and caused Boyd to rest his gaze on them as though hypnotized.

'The thing is,' she said, continuing to eat, 'I'm just not sure what he'll do when he finds out about that.'

'When he finds out?'

A tightness of anxiety was beginning to grip Boyd as he took in what she was saying. He laid down his knife and fork and leaned towards her.

'You haven't told him yet, Trina? You haven't said you were seeing me as well as him?'

'Not yet. But I've only been out with you once. Well, twice, counting tonight.' She shrugged. 'I'm certainly going to tell him, but what's he going to do about it, anyway? It's not as if I'm engaged to him, or anything. Plenty of girls have more than one – you know – admirer.'

'Oh, Trina.' Boyd ran his hand through his hair and shook his head. 'I did think it was odd he hadn't come tearing round to face me, but I thought he knew. I thought he'd accepted he couldn't see you any other way.'

'I expect he will come to see you,' she said casually, as she finished eating and placed her knife and fork together. 'Just tell him what to do, eh? Listen, I think the waiter's coming with the menus again. Are we going to have a sweet?'

When they left the restaurant some time later, it was already late evening, yet the skies were as clear as day, almost seeming as though they would never darken.

'I hate these white nights you get in the summer,' Boyd muttered, scowling, as he and Trina sat together in the bus for Edgemuir. 'You don't know where you are with them.'

'You just don't want to be seen kissing,' she whispered in his ear, which sent a flush to his cheekbones. At the look on his face, she drew back, smiling. 'Don't say you weren't thinking of it, Boyd!'

'I . . . well, I was maybe hoping.'

'Come on, you didn't ask me out just to have a fish supper with me, eh?'

'I asked you out because I wanted to be with you, Trina.' He glanced round at the other passengers and lowered his voice. 'If there'll be kisses as well, they'll be a bonus.'

'Have to watch out for you-know-who. He was on duty this evening, but afterwards he said he was going to the pub with Clive. Better not see us together, eh? Not till I've told him about you.'

Boyd was looking stricken. 'For God's sake, Trina, this isn't a

game we're playing! You've got to get it sorted out. We can't go on
like this!'

'Ssh, folk are listening,' she told him. 'Let's talk later.'

They did not speak again until they'd left the bus and were walking
up the main street of Edgemuir towards the hydro, where the late-
evening light was shining on the windows and there still seemed no
hope of darkness.

'Don't be cross,' Trina said lightly. 'Damon probably won't be
back yet; we needn't worry.'

'But you will tell him?'

'I said so, eh?'

Trina paused at the entrance to an alleyway leading from the
street, where shadows had gathered.

'Look, it's nearly dark there, Boyd, and there's no one around.
Come on, it's our only chance.'

Before he'd had time to speak, she'd pulled him with her into
the alleyway and was pressing her lips to his in the sort of kiss he'd
dreamed about but had never thought would happen. When it was
over and she'd stepped back, perhaps trying to see its effect, he
caught her to him and began kissing her himself, only letting her
go when she'd given him a little push and said they must be away.
But in the semi-darkness of the alleyway, he could see her eyes
shining and guessed she'd enjoyed their little kissing session – maybe
not in the same way that he had, for her first kiss had come out of
the blue – but in her own way, yes, as much. Which meant she
must surely want to see him again.

'I'm not supposed to be too late back,' she told him, as they
returned to the main street. 'Doctor Lorne says while we're part of
his live-in staff, he feels responsible for us. A piece of nonsense, of
course, but there it is. I've got to go.'

'You share a room with Daisy and Junie?'

'Yes, worse luck. They're nice lassies, though Junie's always
moaning, but I'd love to be on my own. You're so lucky, going to
your own home.'

'With my folks knowing just when I come in?'

Trina laughed. 'Maybe not. But here we are, Boyd. I'll sneak in
the side door and up the back stairs.' She put her hand in his and
pressed it. 'Grand night out, eh? Thanks ever so much.'

'And we'll go out again?'

'Oh, sure. Yes, I'll see you again.'

Letting her hand go, he looked into her lovely eyes. 'And you'll speak to Damon?'

'Oh, Boyd, don't keep on! I've said I will, so leave it to me.'

'Sorry. Yes, I know you'll take care of it. Goodnight, then, Trina. We'll meet to fix up another evening?'

'Goodnight, Boyd,' she said firmly and vanished though the side door – far away from him, he felt already, and there was nothing he could do. After a moment, he turned and began his short walk home, suddenly remembering that he'd forgotten to look out for Damon. Well, he was nowhere around, that was for sure, or he'd have made himself felt, and though Boyd was confident he could deal with Damon whatever he did, he was relieved there was to be no showdown that night. Now it was up to Trina to sort the situation out; all Boyd could do was hope that she would.

Twenty-One

The money had been collected, the clock had been bought, and the chef had made two tremendous cakes for the farewell tea party for Dr Woodville. All that had to happen now was for the new doctor to arrive and spend a day or so being shown around to learn something of his new duties, and then it would be time for the actual farewell.

'Oh, I can't bear to think about it,' Sheana wailed to Isla, as they and other nurses were drinking tea at break time. 'It'll be the end of an era, eh?'

'We've still got Doctor Lorne,' Isla replied. 'And he's the main one here.'

'Yes, and a lovely man, but he's always got so much on; it's the doctor who works in the treatment rooms who matters to us. Isn't that right?'

'Yes, it is,' Isla agreed sadly. 'And that's why we'll feel the change most. The new man can't be the same.'

'Watch out,' murmured Ellie, 'here comes Sister Francis, all of a flutter. What's happening?'

What was happening was that a bevy of doctors was being piloted into the nurses' centre by the excited Sister Francis – Dr Lorne, Dr

Woodville and a dark-haired young man in a grey suit who could only be Dr Revie. The nurses put down their cups and stared.

'Oh, my,' whispered Sheana, 'he's arrived!'

'Everyone, gather round!' Sister Francis was calling. 'Doctor Lorne is here and wants to speak to you!'

'To introduce you to our new member of staff, Doctor Revie,' Dr Lorne said genially, as the dark-haired young man bowed his head politely, and Dr Woodville looked on, with a broad smile, his hair on end as usual.

Like everyone else, Isla was studying the new man, already admitting to herself that he was something of surprise. He wasn't at all as she'd expected him to be. Someone older, she'd thought, someone faceless; someone who might want to start changing things the minute he stepped through the door.

Whatever her picture of him had been, it was nothing like the reality of the actual man smiling round at the faces watching him, for Dr Revie was young, not old, and handsome in a most definite way, his features regular, his eyes a remarkable blue. Cornflower, would you say? Very fine, anyway, and a great contributor to the charm and self-assurance he was demonstrating at that moment, as Dr Lorne presented him with all the pride of a parent showing off a favoured child.

Heavens, what would the patients think of their new doctor, then? Particularly the lady patients? One look from those blue eyes and they'd follow any instructions he cared to give, with the staff reacting in a similar way, judging from the looks on their faces when Isla glanced quickly around at them.

As for her, she wasn't sure what she thought of handsome Dr Revie. A bit too sure of himself, wasn't he? A bit too used to the reaction of people to his looks? See him now, turning his gaze on Sister Francis, who was saying a few words to welcome him to Lorne's and telling him how much they were all looking forward to working with him. His smile, his manner, was so exactly right, as was his response to all the kind words in a little speech of his own.

'Thank you so much for your kind words, Sister Francis,' he began – see how he'd remembered her name – 'I can certainly say that I am myself looking forward to working with everyone here in this splendid hydro, and extend my thanks to you, Doctor Lorne, for giving me the opportunity. May I also thank you, Doctor Woodville, in advance, for showing me something of the work I'll be doing, and give my thanks again for the warm welcome I've received. I hope I may do it justice.'

'No doubt of that, Doctor Revie,' Dr Lorne declared and, shaking the new doctor's hand, he told him he'd leave him in Dr Woodville's care and see him in his office later, after which everyone dispersed to their duties.

'Would you ever have believed the new doctor'd be like him?' Sheana whispered, as she and others hurried down the corridor to their appointments. 'I mean, such a handsome man, eh?'

'He wasn't what we'd expected,' Ellie agreed. 'Though I'm not sure now what I did expect.'

'Snap,' said Isla. 'I never thought the new chap'd be quite such a charmer. Maybe too much of one. I prefer Doctor Woodville.'

'Not *quite* so much talking, girls!' came Staff Nurse Miller's hissing whisper at their shoulders. 'I know you think you've got plenty to talk about, but keep it for your own time. The patients have a right to be seen as the centre of interest, eh?'

'Sorry, Staff,' they murmured, colouring and exchanging glances.

'See you at supper,' Isla said, vowing to herself not to be caught out like that again. What a gaggle of silly girls they were to be bowled over by a pair of blue eyes! But as she attended to haughty Mrs Winter-Smithson and smiled sympathetically as she listened to her patient's usual string of complaints, she was already deciding she'd take no bets on the whole hydro's falling under Dr Revie's spell in no time at all.

Twenty-Two

Not a great deal was seen of Dr Woodville and Dr Revie in the next couple of days, as it was known they were closeted together, doing what was known as a 'hand-over'. When they did surface, it was for Dr Woodville's farewell. This was still, in spite of the excitement caused by Dr Revie's arrival, a matter of particular gloom for the staff of Lorne's, and for patients, too – one being, of course, Mark Kinnaird.

On the afternoon of the farewell tea party, which was to be

attended by all staff and patients, Isla had looked in on Mark to stock up on his medication, as Dr Woodville had ordered.

'You see,' she said with a smile, 'his last thought is of you, Mr Kinnaird. He wants to be sure that you have what you need before he goes, though, of course, Doctor Revie will be checking on you soon and making his own decisions.'

'I suppose so,' Mark said coldly. At the look in his eyes, Isla was dismayed to see the old blankness that had been absent for some time.

'Oh, don't look like that!' she cried quickly. 'Doctor Revie's a very good doctor; you'll be in excellent hands.'

'If you say so.'

'Don't you like him?'

'Don't know him yet, do I?'

'You've met him, though.'

'Oh, yes.' Mark shrugged. 'Looks like an actor.'

'I wouldn't say that.'

'You like him, then?'

Although she had her reservations about the new doctor, somehow Isla didn't want to put them into words for Mark; knew, in fact, that she shouldn't be discussing a doctor with a patient at all.

'It's not a question of liking,' she said carefully. 'I go by Doctor Lorne, and Doctor Lorne thinks highly of him.'

'Oh, well, then, I should be satisfied, shouldn't I?'

'Mr Kinnaird, you are coming to Doctor Woodville's farewell tea party, aren't you? It's almost time.'

'Of course I'm coming.' Mark left his chair without breaking into a cough and gave a sudden smile. 'Nurse Scott, I'm sorry – please forgive me for being such a miserable old so-and-so. It's just that I'm feeling so much better, and with Doctor Woodville gone, I can't help worrying I won't do as well.'

'You will, you will!' she cried, her smile radiant. 'It's the treatment, Mr Kinnaird; you're one of our successes! Don't worry about not staying well – you are well.'

'Almost, maybe. But I promise not to do any more complaining. Let's go down to say goodbye to Bob, then.'

The day being so fine and warm, the French windows of the large lounge had been opened to the terrace, and it had been suggested that following tea and speeches, everyone might like to stroll or sit out there.

'While *we* clear everything up, I suppose,' Damon muttered to his colleagues, his expression mutinous. 'After we've served the damned tea in the first place. Why are we the only ones working, eh?'

'Oh, stop moaning!' cried Junie, the waitress Trina had accused of moaning herself, but who didn't like Damon and enjoyed finding fault with him. 'We're the obvious folk to serve and clear away, eh? It's our job.'

'Aye, just like it's the job o' thae doctors to treat the patients, but they're all taking time off today, I notice. It's like I always say: if you're a doctor, you can get away with anything.'

'Come on, Damon, this is just a one-off for that nice Doctor Woodville,' Trina said lightly. 'Put up with it and try to be pleasant. I want to see the new chap – Doctor Revie. I was out when he came in to meet us, but they say he's very good-looking.'

'Who says?' Damon asked sharply. 'Didn't look anything special to me.'

'If you folk can stop your chatting, maybe you can serve some of these cups of tea I'm pouring out!' cried Mr Paul, already scarlet in the face from his work behind the long white-clothed table that had been set up to carry his scones, tiny sandwiches and the two large iced cakes that were in pride of place.

'And give everybody a plate!' he added. 'Starting with Doctor Lorne and serving the patients before the rest of the staff. Then take round the sandwiches.'

'Yes, Mr Paul!' they cried, scattering to follow his orders. Trina was the first away with her tray of tea and made directly for the doctors who were standing together.

'Why, thanks so much,' Dr Revie said as he took his tea, his blue eyes meeting Trina's dark gaze. 'I don't believe I've seen you before, have I?'

'You'd have remembered,' Dr Woodville put in cheerfully. 'This is Trina Morris, Grant. A new recruit to our dining staff.'

'Enjoying being at the hydro?' Dr Lorne asked.

'Oh, yes, Doctor Lorne,' she answered brightly, but as she turned aside to make way for Daisy arriving with plates and sandwiches, she shrugged a little. The new doctor was certainly as handsome as everyone said, but she knew – for she always knew – that he was not going to be one of her followers. How she knew, she couldn't say, but she was never wrong, so it was

back to Damon for her. Or maybe Boyd Scott, the other handsome fellow at the hydro, who was definitely one willing to
follow her anywhere. She'd better not speak to him now, though
– not while Damon was around.

Twenty-Three

With the cutting and handing round of Mr Paul's splendid cakes
and compliments to make him beam, tea finally came to an end and
Dr Lorne could make his farewell speech to Bob Woodville. Short,
but well phrased, it strongly conveyed his genuine appreciation of
the younger doctor's qualities – his sympathy, good humour and
patience, quite apart from his medical expertise, of course. While
understanding his reasons for leaving, Dr Lorne ended by saying
how much Dr Woodville would be missed and wishing him well
for the future on behalf of everyone at the hydro.

'Come back and see us, Bob, won't you?' he asked, using a first
name at last. 'Don't forget us, anyway.'

'No fear of that!'

Bob Woodville, who had been sitting with his eyes modestly cast
down during Dr Lorne's speech, now leaped to his feet and gave
one of his broad grins around the watching faces.

'I can't tell you how much you'll all be in my thoughts,' he told
them. 'Working here has meant a great deal to me and I really appreciate all I've learned, not just on the medical side but the human side,
too, from staff and patients – my whole experience, you might say. I
can't deny I'm going to miss my life here, or that there'll be a lot to
learn in running my father's practice, but I'm hoping I'll be able to
give my patients the sort of service they should have – especially as
I shall have my fiancée's help as soon as she's qualified.'

Fiancée? The little world of the hydro seemed to rock. Had Dr
Woodville said it? Had he said *fiancée?*

At the intake of breath, followed by the staff's stunned silence,
Bob's grin faded and he paused, seeming uncertain how to continue.

It was left to Dr Lorne to say after a long moment, 'Why, Doctor
Woodville – Bob – we had no idea you were engaged! We must
give you our congratulations.'

'It's only just happened, Doctor Lorne,' Bob said hastily. 'I can't actually believe it myself – I'm so happy. Eleanor – Miss Reynolds – is a medical student, taking finals at Edinburgh next year. She's the daughter of a doctor my family knows well, so we've known each other for some time, and when I managed to pop the question, she said yes – so, there we are.' He gave a sigh of obvious contentment. 'We're planning to marry after she qualifies, and then she'll come and work at the practice.'

'Well, we couldn't be more pleased for you,' Dr Lorne said warmly, reaching across to shake Bob's hand. 'And I know I'll be speaking for all when I say we wish you every happiness in the future.'

Speaking for all? Except Miss Elrick?

As cries of agreement met the doctor's words, Isla, who happened to be standing with Mark next to Miss Elrick, hardly dared to look at the secretary's face.

When she did, it was, as she had expected, stricken. At first, very pale – paper-white, in fact – but gradually turning scarlet over the cheekbones, a colour that looked as though it would never fade, while the eyes above seemed to have no colour whatever.

Oh, no, thought Isla. Oh, God, poor Miss Elrick – poor Joan – what would happen now? How would she get through the rest of the day – congratulating him, wishing him every happiness – when all she'd want to do would be to run away and hide? If only she could be comforted. But even as she stretched out her hand to touch Miss Elrick's, Isla realized that it would be the last thing the secretary wanted – someone knowing how she felt, feeling sorry for her – and she let her hand fall. There was nothing she could do.

'Oh, Miss Elrick!' she was startled to hear Dr Lorne's voice call. 'May we have the box, please?'

The box? What was he talking about? Isla didn't know, but Miss Elrick apparently did, for, moving very slowly, she bent down to pick up a wrapped box at her feet that Isla hadn't noticed. Her flush subsiding, thank heaven, she turned towards Dr Lorne, who immediately came forward to take it himself, resting it on a small table in front of Bob Woodville, while Miss Elrick took a step backwards.

'I have scissors in my bag,' she whispered, without looking at Dr Woodville. 'If you would like them to cut the paper.'

'This is for me?'

'Oh, yes, indeed,' Dr Lorne told him, smiling. 'From everyone at the hydro, as a small token of our appreciation.'

'Oh, no, oh, Lord, you shouldn't have – I don't know what to say. Miss Elrick, may I take you up on your offer of scissors?'

When she had impassively handed him the scissors, and he had removed the paper and opened the elegant box revealed, he gave a little gasp before lifting out, for all to see, a most handsome carriage clock that called forth loud murmurs of approval and much clapping of hands.

'Doctor Lorne – everyone – I really don't know what to say,' Bob said, looking around at his listeners as silence fell. 'It's too kind, honestly, and I'm so touched. I can't thank you enough. And Eleanor will want to thank you, too – she'll love it!'

'So we made the right choice,' Dr Lorne said cheerfully. 'Well, it was mainly Miss Elrick's, though it had my vote, too.'

'It will look wonderful in our drawing room and be a reminder always of Lorne's Hydro,' Bob said earnestly. 'My thanks to you, Doctor Lorne, and to Miss Elrick for her choice, and to everyone for a most generous gift.'

'So glad you like it,' Miss Elrick said, lifting her head at last and fixing the young doctor with a long, long gaze, before turning aside and looking at no one. Certainly not at Isla, who was thinking, *How brave she is! She's rallying, when she has to. But how will it be for her when she is alone?*

It was as though, for Isla, the summer's day had suddenly grown cold and she thought, as she'd thought before, that if love could bring so much heartache, she wanted no part in it.

The ceremony at an end, people began to drift away, and as Mark Kinnaird went to speak to Bob, and Isla was thinking of finding Boyd, a voice said her name and she turned to find Dr Revie. He had been such a quiet watcher at the presentation that she had scarcely noticed him, but now she found herself receiving the full battery of those blue eyes in a way she had not experienced before.

'That went well, didn't it?' he asked. 'Made me realize just what sort of chap I have to follow.' He laughed. 'Not leaving too many broken hearts behind, is he?'

'Broken hearts?' she cried sharply. 'Of course not! Doctor Woodville is engaged to be married.'

'Oh, I thought that wasn't known until today – sorry.'

'None of us ever thought of him in that way,' Isla said hastily, taking care not to look round to see where Miss Elrick might be. 'I can promise you that.'

'I'm sorry.' His look was contrite. 'Actually, it was just a joke – a poor one, I agree. Am I forgiven?'

'Nothing to forgive. But will you excuse me, Doctor Revie? I want to say goodbye to Doctor Woodville and then find my brother.'

'Ah, yes, the good-looking young man who looks after the gym? Tell him, I'm going to be keeping fit there as soon as I get settled in. And perhaps I could tell you that I'm looking forward to working with you – and all the staff?'

'We're all looking forward to working together,' she answered, finding a smile, somehow aware that his fine eyes were watching her as she walked away.

Twenty-Four

As everyone had predicted, it didn't take long after Bob Woodville's departure for Grant Revie to take his place as general favourite at the hydro, to send hearts fluttering among the female patients and sometimes a sigh or two of regret for the passing of time and lost youth. Nurses, too, were more excited than they cared to say about the new man in the treatment rooms, but one thing no one denied was that he was an excellent doctor. Even Isla, who had been holding herself apart from all the fuss, along with the subdued Miss Elrick, was willing to admit that.

Not only was he good at his work, he was also quick to suggest improvements. For instance, the hydro saunas gave patients only one bench where they could sit to absorb the steam, whereas a second bench at a higher level would mean differences in temperatures could be obtained, which would be beneficial. And music, he also pointed out, could be of great help as therapy, with gramophone records being played when patients were resting after wraps or massage treatment.

Dr Lorne, having listened carefully to all Dr Revie's suggestions, expressed himself very pleased with his interest, agreeing that they should look into the use of music as therapy – he'd been thinking of that himself – and, of course, to put extra benches in the saunas was an excellent idea.

'Well done, Doctor Revie! I congratulate you on your eye for improvements – it's exactly what we need.'

'Thank you, Doctor Lorne. There's just one more thing I'd like to mention, if that's all right?'

'Certainly, certainly.'

'Well, quite a lot of hydros these days do offer evening entertainment for their clients. You know the sort of thing – song and piano recitals, competitions, games. I wonder if we could do something in that direction?'

Dr Lorne hesitated. 'They already have bridge,' he replied at last. 'I don't know if our sort of client would welcome competitions. As for recitals – who is to organize things of that sort?'

'A professional host, Doctor Lorne. Often a lady, who is experienced in organization and perhaps a performer herself – in fact, where I last worked we had such a lady who was a tremendous asset.'

Dr Lorne at once shook his head. 'I'm sorry, but I really don't think that we need anyone to provide that sort of thing for us. Other hydros might be keen, but most of our people just like a quiet evening after dinner, with a little bridge, or conversation – you do understand?'

'Yes, indeed.' Dr Revie was pleasant and relaxed. 'I absolutely accept that here you know best – it was just an idea. Hope I haven't come up with too many.'

'Of course not!' Dr Lorne was opening his door for Dr Revie to depart. 'As I told you, I'm grateful for all your suggestions, and I've no hesitation in telling you that I think we are going to make an excellent team.'

'That's good to know, Doctor Lorne, very good indeed. Thank you for your interest.'

Looking suitably serious, Dr Revie took his leave as Dr Lorne called in Miss Elrick to take some letters.

'All right?' he asked her, when she had taken her seat, her pencil and notebook in her hand. 'You're looking a little pale. In fact, you've seemed off colour just lately. Perhaps you'd like to take some holiday?'

'No, no, thank you, Doctor Lorne,' she answered quickly, sitting up straight in her chair. 'I'm quite well.'

He studied her for a moment. 'That's good, then, but feel free, whenever you need, to take some time off. And if you should ever want, you know, to have a talk about anything that might be worrying you, don't hesitate to come to me.'

'That's very kind of you, Doctor Lorne, but I'm really quite all right.'

'Fine.'

As she sat with her pencil poised over her notebook, his smile, as kind as usual, made her smile back, and for a moment her spirits lifted. Only for that moment, though.

Twenty-Five

For some time, Boyd had been worried at hearing nothing from Damon Duthie, which might have been a reason for feeling relieved, except that Boyd knew it could only be the calm before the storm. Trina hadn't yet told him of her bizarre idea of seeing Boyd as well as him: that could be the only explanation for his not flying round to confront Boyd. Every day, Boyd had been gearing himself up to meeting him, and every day he had not appeared, leaving Boyd's nerves jangling.

It was never easy for him and Trina to meet, or even to catch her in the kitchen or dining room without Damon or others around, which meant he hadn't been able to ask her about the situation. When they finally managed another trip to the cinema and he spoke to her on the way home, she admitted at once that she hadn't got round to it yet.

'Trina, you know you must – we have to get this thing straight!' Boyd cried. 'What's stopping you? You can't be afraid of him – not you?'

'Of course I'm not afraid! It's just that – well, he'll make such a fuss, that's all.' She smiled at Boyd, widening her eyes at him, making his heart turn over. 'He can be difficult.'

Boyd gave a groan. 'We have to tell him the truth, Trina. Promise me you'll tell him tomorrow. Then I can be prepared to deal with him.'

'Oh, my, that sounds drastic!'

'Well, we'll have to have it out; you know we will.'

'All right, I promise. But let's not talk about it any more. Don't we have better things to do?'

'Oh, God, yes,' he whispered as they made their way down their dark alley and fell into each other's arms.

Even though Trina had promised to speak to Damon, Boyd still didn't believe she would do it. Which was why he was totally unprepared the following day, when he was alone in the gym at lunchtime, to see the door being thrown open and Damon standing before him.

Putting aside the ham sandwich he had been eating, Boyd slowly rose to his feet.

'Hello, Damon,' he said, with a good attempt at calmness.

'Don't speak to me!' Damon cried, breathing hard. 'Don't say a word!'

He slammed the door shut behind him and, having turned the key in the lock, advanced towards Boyd, his dark eyes smouldering, his hands at his sides jerking, while Boyd threw aside his sandwich and fixed Damon with a long cold stare.

'It's lunchtime – shouldn't you be on duty in the dining room?'

'To hell with that!' Damon tossed back his thick black hair. 'And I told you not to speak to me. I'm the one who's talking and you know why. You know what you've done. As though you could get away with it! You must be crazy – out of your mind. As though I'd let any man take my girl away from me!'

'I haven't taken your girl away from you, Damon, because she's not your girl and never was. She sees you, she goes out with you, but she wants to go out with me, too. That makes her nobody's girl in my book – until she makes up her mind which of us she wants.'

'You think I'm going to share Trina with you? I tell you, you're mad, Boyd Scott, because she doesn't want you; she wants me – she's made that clear. Don't think you can come muscling in, confusing her, playing the "big noise" – it's got to stop and I'll tell you how.'

'Oh, yes, how exactly?' Boyd asked, smiling. 'Damon, so long as Trina wants to go out with me, you'll have to grin and bear it. Will you now get out of my way so that I can unlock the door and finish my sandwich?'

A dark red colour had risen to Damon's brow and drops of sweat were trickling down his face as he bunched his fists and stepped so close to Boyd that they might have been preparing to dance. Instead, it was clear to Boyd that they were preparing to fight – at least, Damon was, while Boyd, the taller and stronger of the two, knew he'd have to stop him.

'Don't be an idiot,' he snapped. 'This is childish. You can't solve anything with your fists, and if you try, I'll prove it.'

For answer, Damon punched him on the chin with such force that Boyd was taken quite off guard and stepped back, his hand to his mouth, his look astonished, then furious.

'If that's what you want, it's what you'll get!' he shouted, and returned the blow, at which Damon only laughed. But then the two of them were suddenly grappling, moving round the floor, breathing hard, each well matched, it seemed, and getting nowhere, until Boyd suddenly straightened up and seized Damon in an iron grip.

'Let's finish this once and for all,' he muttered and, releasing Damon, gave him one last blow which sent him back to the floor. Where he lay without moving.

As Boyd stood staring down at him, his hand returning to his mouth, there came a rattling of the door and voices, one Trina's, the other Isla's, crying his name.

'Boyd, Boyd, are you there? Boyd, will you open the door? What's going on? Is Damon with you? Let us in, let us in!'

Walking stiffly to the door, Boyd unlocked it and stood aside as the girls burst in, staring only for a second or two at him before running to Damon on the floor.

'Oh, God, Boyd, what have you done?' Trina cried, stooping over Damon, whose eyes were closed. 'Oh, he looks awful!'

'He attacked me!' Boyd cried angrily. 'Came in here like a madman, hit me in the face. What was I supposed to do? Just stand there?'

'Trina, let me look at Damon,' Isla ordered. 'He shouldn't be lying there like that.'

Kneeling beside him, she bent to listen to his heart, then folded back an eyelid to examine his eye before springing to her feet, her face anxious as she looked at her brother.

'Boyd, I'm going to get Doctor Revie. I don't know what you did to Damon, but I think he's got concussion. Stay with him till I get back.'

'Of course we'll stay,' whispered Trina, moving to stand near Boyd. 'But I can't believe what's been happening. I mean, I never really expected it, you two fighting' – she lowered her voice – 'over me.'

'I'll be back as soon as I can,' Isla said coldly, and ran.

Twenty-Six

'It's very good of you to help us, Doctor Revie,' Isla told him as the two of them moved fast towards the gym. 'I feel so bad – something like this happening and involving my brother.'

'These things happen,' the doctor said cheerfully, his eyes on her. 'And, of course, I want to help – it's my job. I was only doing my paperwork, anyway. You say the chap who's injured is one of the waiters? Not that fiery, black-haired fellow – looks like an Italian?'

'Damon Duthie, yes. He's not Italian, he's Scottish.'

'But fiery. And he had a row with your brother? Over a woman, I bet. And I think I know which one.'

They had reached the door of the gym, but instead of opening it, Isla hesitated, her grey eyes on the doctor filled with apprehension. 'I'd . . . I'd be very grateful if . . . if you wouldn't—'

'Tell Doctor Lorne? Don't worry, my lips are sealed. Come on, let's see the patient.'

The little tableau was much as Isla had left it, with Boyd and Trina staring down at Damon still on the floor, the only difference being that now his large dark eyes were open. What they were seeing was unclear, though, for they seemed unfocussed.

'Ah, he's come round!' Dr Revie cried, kneeling down beside Damon and opening his bag. 'That's good, that's encouraging.'

'I don't think he knows where he is,' Trina whispered, moving closer to Boyd, whose face was stricken as he looked down at Damon.

'I didn't mean to hit him so hard,' he said in a low voice. 'But he met the floor with an almighty crack and just went out like a light.'

'Shaken the brain – that's what happens with a bad blow to the head.' Dr Revie took out his torch. 'I'll just examine his eyes.'

After some moments studying Damon's eyes, Grant looked up. 'I think he's been lucky – his pupils are fine and he's now beginning to focus properly. That's encouraging again.'

Turning back to Damon, Dr Revie held up his hand. 'Damon, it's Doctor Revie. Are you able to hear me?'

'I . . . hear you,' Damon answered hoarsely after a long pause.

'If I hold up my hand, how many fingers can you see?'

'Er – three.'

'Excellent! Three it is! You're doing well.' The doctor got to his feet. 'Which means, I think, that we're going to get you up now. Just see if you can stand and if we can check your balance. Boyd, will you give me a hand?'

Even before her brother had taken a step forward, Isla, knowing how little Damon would want Boyd to help him, said swiftly, 'I will.'

'Are you sure?' Dr Revie asked dubiously, but when she only raised her eyebrows, he laughed and briefly touched her arm.

'Sorry, Nurse Scott, I know how often you have to help patients – let's get Damon up then.'

Still looking very pale and somewhat lost, he finally stood between them, their arms supporting him, until Dr Revie told him to try a step or two if he felt able. Just to check his balance.

'It's my head,' Damon muttered. 'Feels like it'll float away.'

'Very understandable – you'll certainly have a headache for a time. But can you move?'

'Think so.'

After a long moment of hesitation, Damon did succeed in taking a few steps without mishap, after which Dr Revie called for a chair and, settling his patient into it, again told him he'd done well.

'I don't think you need worry too much, Damon. You have a slight concussion which will respond to painkillers, but I would like you to rest in bed for the next twenty-four hours. You really should be monitored for that length of time.' Dr Revie glanced at Trina. 'Could you inform Mr Paul that Damon will not be available for work just yet? I'm going to organize a bed for him in our special monitoring section.'

'Tell Mr Paul?' Trina repeated. 'He'll be furious.'

'Too bad, it can't be helped. Say Damon had an accident – slipped in the gym.'

'He'll never believe it. He's already cross because Damon didn't turn up to serve the lunches.'

'I don't want to go to bed,' Damon suddenly declared with surprising strength. 'I'd rather go back to work.'

'Just do as the doctor says,' Isla said sharply. 'He knows what's best for you. Boyd, have you still got that old wheelchair in the back cupboard? I expect you'd like me to push Damon back to the treatment rooms, Doctor?'

'There speaks the practical one! Yes, that would be best. We'll take him over now, and leave you, Boyd, to put some cold water on your lip – it's swelling badly.'

'Oh, God,' groaned Boyd, only brightening when Trina said she'd help him, even though the look that Damon then directed towards him boded nothing but ill for the future.

Twenty-Seven

As soon as Trina began delicately to bathe his swollen lip and chin, Boyd forgot Damon anyway and kept his eyes fixed on her face so close to his, praying that no patients would arrive until she'd finished. By the gymnasium clock, it was just after two, which seemed unbelievable, for surely it was hours after that? The fact remained that the patients' lunch was over, and one or two who didn't want to rest might soon be arriving at his now open door, which meant he'd have to keep Trina out of sight and pretend everything was normal. Normal? Oh, God, with his job on the line?

'I didn't mean to hit Damon so hard,' he told Trina earnestly as she finished dabbing at his lip. 'You know that, don't you?'

'Oh, sure. It's just like Damon to cause trouble, eh? I've had enough of him.'

Enough of him? Enough of Damon? Boyd's heart leaped as he took in what she'd said.

'Trina, what are you saying?'

She gave him an enchanting smile. 'I'm saying it's too difficult, what I've been trying to do. Seeing two fellows – I've decided it's not for me.'

'So, if you have to choose one . . .'

Her eyes were sparkling. 'I choose the winner.'

'Trina!' He tried to take her in his arms, but she wriggled away, shaking her head at him.

'Boyd, I've got to go. I have to tell Mr Paul what's happened to

Damon, and I have to be all apologetic for skipping off after lunch and not helping to clear up.'

Her face suddenly serious, she touched Boyd's swollen face.

'I was worried, you know. Damon was in such a state after I'd told him about going out with you as well as him; I was scared he'd do something terrible. That's why I got your sister to come with me to the gym to see what was happening. And you know what we found.'

'He's going to be all right; the doctor said so.'

'Yes, but you'd sorted him out, hadn't you?'

She laughed a little and suddenly kissed Boyd on the lips. 'Let's go out together, soon as we can, eh? Let's forget all this nonsense. Come to the kitchen tomorrow and we'll fix it up.'

'But you're going to have to tell Damon what you've decided, Trina, as soon as he's better. And then there'll be more trouble.'

'I don't think so; I think he's learned his lesson. Oh, there's your door – you have a customer, Boyd.' She blew him a kiss. 'I'll away. See you tomorrow.'

'Tomorrow,' he answered dazedly, as she slipped out and tall, thin Mr Weston came in, smiling, until he noticed Boyd's swollen lip.

'Oh, my, laddie, what's happened to you? Got the toothache?'

'Just a bit of a knock, Mr Weston. Nothing to worry about.'

And now that Trina had made her amazing decision, that was true for Boyd. Job or no job, Damon or no Damon, she had chosen him. He felt he need never worry again.

With Damon unwillingly settled into bed and already beginning to drift into sleep, Dr Revie suggested that he and Isla had deserved a small break and a cup of tea, and led the way to his office.

'I can get some tea for us, but I have a patient to see very soon,' said Isla, refusing the chair he offered. 'First, though, I want to thank you again, Doctor Revie, for all your help. You were wonderful.'

'Please, spare my blushes, I didn't do a damn thing that was special,' he said quietly, his blue gaze on her so direct that she felt she must look away. 'But do you really have a patient? I was looking forward to a little time with you.'

'Time with me?'

'Why not? Can't doctors talk to nurses?'

'I'll get the tea,' she said quickly, feeling she was suddenly venturing into unknown waters. Before she could leave, though, he lightly took her wrist and held it.

'Never mind the tea. If time's so limited, Isla, just let me get my plea in before you have to go.'

At the look on her face when he used her first name, he smiled.

'Oh, yes, I know the rule here about first names at work, but just at this moment we are not at work, so you are Isla, and I am Grant. And my plea to you, Isla, is this: will you let me take you out to some other non-work situation? A restaurant in Edinburgh, for instance?'

For a moment, she could only stare. What was he saying? He wanted to take her out? To some non-work situation, as he put it? A restaurant in Edinburgh? Her mind was reeling.

Even though she'd noticed his eyes often on her and had had a sort of feeling he might be interested in her, she'd still remained aloof and felt no interest in him. Or so she'd thought, letting the thought stay on the surface. But beneath the surface, what would she have found if she'd allowed herself to look?

After his coming to the rescue over what had happened in Boyd's gym, it was true she'd seen a different side to him – one of less charm, more genuine feeling. And now he'd actually asked her out, what was she to do? Look beneath the surface at last? Discover if there was something there?

'Isla?'

As she met those amazing eyes of his and saw in them such serious intent, this time she did not look away.

'Thank you, Doctor Revie—'

'Grant, please.'

'Grant. I'd like to come, if it's possible.'

'Possible? Why shouldn't it be possible?'

'Well – you know – finding a time that suits.'

'It's simple: I can fit in with you. When's your evening off next week?'

'Wednesday.'

'Right, Wednesday it is. Shall we say we'll meet at six thirty? Away from the gate, if you're worried about people seeing us?' He grinned. 'And I expect you will be.'

'It'd be easier, if folk didn't see.'

'That's what we'll do, then. On Wednesday evening, I'll be just beyond the gate, in my car.'

'Oh, yes, you have a car – I was forgetting.'

So few people she knew had cars that it was not something she ever expected to find. And impressive? Oh, yes!

'Now I'd better let you go to your patient,' he murmured, releasing her wrist. 'Till Wednesday, Isla. Or, as we're returning to work, perhaps I'd better say Nurse Scott.'

'Till Wednesday, Doctor Revie.'

Their eyes met again just for an instant, and then she was gone, hurrying to her patient, crusty old Colonel Ferguson, due for a cold rubbing. Luckily if he thought she was abstracted over something as she attended to him, he was far too much of a gentleman to mention it.

Twenty-Eight

Till Wednesday. Would the days ever pass? Isla, on duty as usual, couldn't be sure whether she wanted them to or not; didn't know precisely how she was feeling over her coming date with Dr Revie. Of course, she had to be flattered that he'd asked her, had singled her out from all his admirers, when she hadn't been an admirer at all, until the episode of Damon's concussion. Maybe he'd sensed that and been attracted to her because she was different? Was she different still?

Immediate concerns were what to wear and who to tell. Not her mother – she'd only read too much into Isla's going out with a doctor. Best say nothing, for the moment, anyhow. And the same went for Boyd who might possibly not approve. Not that it was any of his business, of course, but she didn't feel like getting into an argument at this stage.

Anyway, though he claimed not to be worried, he probably had enough to think about, wondering how Damon would take the news that Trina was giving him up. Even if he was not afraid of anything Damon might do, Boyd, like Isla herself, must be wishing to see the whole situation settled.

As for telling any of her colleagues of her dinner date with Dr Revie, it would be better, as she had told him, if they didn't see her leaving with him, meaning, in fact, that they should know nothing about it. Certainly, it was not her intention to tell any of them – what on earth would they say?

She was soon to find out, from two of them at least, for when Wednesday evening finally came and she was in her room, wearing her best dark-green dress and jacket, and confident that Sheana and Ellie were down in the canteen, they came in and found her.

'Hey, look at you, all dressed up!' cried Sheana, her eyes alight with interest. 'Where are you going, then, dark horse?'

'Somewhere special, from the look of it,' Ellie chimed in. 'Haven't seen you in that outfit before, have we?'

'As a matter of fact, I'm going out for dinner,' Isla answered with a sinking heart. Pretending to be unconcerned, she put a comb and handkerchief into her evening bag, and took a last look at herself in the dressing table mirror. 'See you later, girls.'

'Oh, no, no, you're not going to get away with that!' Sheana said firmly. 'Who's the lucky man?'

'Do we know him?' asked Ellie.

Looking away from the two faces so intent on hers, Isla knew she was going to have to tell them, ask them not to say anything, keep it under their hats . . .

'Look,' she said slowly, 'it doesn't mean anything, it's nothing special, but just keep it to yourselves, eh?'

'OK, OK, you can count on us,' Sheana replied impatiently. 'But you've got to tell us who it is, Isla.'

'All right.' Isla moved to the door. 'It's Doctor Revie.'

There was a stunned silence. Although she kept her eyes down, Isla knew what she would have seen if she'd looked up – amazement, shock and disbelief written all over their faces. *Why Isla?* they would be wondering. *Why Isla, when Dr Revie could have chosen anyone he liked?* He must know beautiful girls from his own circle; he didn't have to choose one of the nurses at Lorne's, and he certainly didn't have to choose Isla.

Finally raising her eyes to her two friends, Isla read in theirs exactly what she'd expected to find, and even though what she saw was painful, she understood it. Yes, she was a pretty girl, but no prettier than others at the hydro, no prettier than Sheana and Ellie, as they might already be thinking. They were friends of hers, they liked her, but – well – there was no way they could conceal their feelings at her news.

'I can see you're surprised,' she said in a low voice. 'I am myself, but it's just like I say: it doesn't mean anything.'

'Oh, come on!' Sheana's eyes were bright. 'Going out with the most eligible man around and it doesn't mean anything? Maybe not to him, but it will to you, eh? Don't tell us you're not thrilled to bits!'

'I don't know what I am!' Isla snapped, suddenly annoyed at their attitude, even if she did understand it.

'All I know is I'm due out now and I'm going, and that's that.'

As they opened their mouths to speak, and even as Ellie put out a placating hand, Isla opened the door and went out, banging it behind her. Oh, what bad luck they'd come up early from their tea! Now she'd have to try to forget that they knew she was going out with Dr Revie, forget that they hadn't spoiled everything, which wasn't going to be easy . . .

In fact, it turned out to be astonishingly easy. As soon as she saw Grant Revie standing beside his open-topped two-seater, dressed in a smart lightweight suit, his dark hair blowing in the evening breeze, his blue eyes on her, all thought of Sheana and Ellie went quite out of her head. And as he held the door for her and she slipped into her seat, she felt strangely, wonderfully at ease, wonderfully light-hearted. Whether or not this evening was going to mean anything to him, whether or not it was just a one-off and not to be explained, she decided she was going to enjoy it!

Twenty-Nine

'All right to have the top down?' Grant asked, giving her a quick glance as they bowled away. 'You're not wearing a hat – might get your hair blown about.'

'Oh, no, it'll be fine, thanks.'

'If you're sure. You have such pretty hair, Isla.'

'It's red,' she said flatly.

'What's wrong with red for a woman? I'll admit, some think red-headed men are not so attractive. I expect that good-looking brother of yours is glad he's blond.'

'He doesn't think about his looks.'

'Sensible fellow.' Grant smiled, then gave Isla another quick side-long glance. 'But let's get back to you. You're happy now?'

Her eyes widened. 'Happy? Yes, why not?'

'I thought you looked worried, as you came down the steps. As though you might be having second thoughts.'

'Oh, no, that's not true. Did I look worried?' She laughed – convincingly, she hoped. 'I'm not at all worried.' Which was true *now*, anyway.

'That's all right, then.' Turning his eyes back to the road, Grant seemed satisfied, and Isla, feeling free to look at him, thought how handsome he was in profile, his straight nose so elegant in a straight classical line from his brow, his chin and lips so finely moulded. Though not obviously alike, the symmetry of his looks reminded her of Boyd, and, as so often when she thought of him, she found herself wanting to smooth down her turned-up nose. Whatever did Grant Revie see in her? she wondered. But she decided not to dwell on it.

'I've booked us in at Flair's restaurant,' Grant told her, as they soon covered the miles to Edinburgh. 'It's in Bruntsfield – don't know if you know it?'

'I've heard of it, never been there.'

Or to many other Edinburgh restaurants, Isla added to herself.

'Well, it's nothing grand but they've a roof terrace where you can eat. Should be OK this evening.'

'Sounds lovely.'

'Yes, you can look out over the Bruntsfield Links. There's a great old pub there – one of my favourites.' Grant gave Isla a quick grin. 'But I thought Flair's would be more your style.'

'I don't think I've got a style,' she retorted, laughing, but he shook his head.

'All women have style.'

'Even redheads?'

'Especially redheads.'

Leaving the centre of the city, packed with evening traffic, Grant drove out to the Bruntsfield area. He seemed to spin his car just where he wanted it to go, easily impressing Isla, even though she knew nothing about either cars or driving. She did wonder, though, if he might be showing off. No, she decided, just demonstrating another example of his efficiency. How comforting to be out with a man who always knew what to do!

'Here we are!' he exclaimed, parking the roadster between two larger vehicles outside the modern, stone-built building that was Flair's. It had glass entrance doors, open to the warm air, long sash windows, also open, and a small strip of paving where a few customers were having dinner.

'Good job we booked,' Grant whispered in Isla's ear. 'Looks as if they're already overflowing!'

But of course he'd booked, and of course they had a fine table on the roof terrace with excellent views over the old golf course, Bruntsfield Links, where Grant said his father had played at one time. He'd been a member of the Royal Burgess Golf Club in his Edinburgh days, but had moved to Glasgow to set up a medical practice even before his marriage to Grant's mother.

'So, you're a Glasgow man,' Isla commented as they ate their first course of shrimp salad.

'Hope you'll forgive me, if you're an Edinburgh girl.'

'I'm not from Edinburgh. I'm from Edgemuir – I thought you knew.'

'Why, no, I only knew you lived in with other nurses at the hydro. And I supposed your brother must be in lodgings.' Grant shook his head. 'I certainly never realized you came from Edgemuir. Just shows how I need you to tell me about yourself.' He raised a hand. 'Please don't say there's nothing to tell!'

'Well, there isn't much.'

'Let's have some wine first, anyway. The waiter's on his way.'

'Oh, honestly, Grant, I'd rather not.' Isla's tone was earnest. 'It really doesn't mean anything to me and I'm not used to it.'

'One glass? A few sips?' Grant touched her hand lightly. 'That's all I'm having. I've got this funny idea no one else believes that alcohol affects driving, so I'm very careful. Unless I'm a pedestrian.'

Smiling, she agreed to one glass and sipped a little as she told him about her father at the woollen mill, her mother at the tweed shop, and how she'd decided to be a nurse and trained and worked in Edinburgh, eventually moving to Lorne's.

'Why Lorne's?' asked Grant. 'What made you chuck up a splendid hospital like Edinburgh Southern for the hydro?'

'You don't think Lorne's is a splendid hospital?'

'Oh, I do. I'm genuinely keen on all it stands for, but it's not everyone's cup of tea. What made it yours?'

'Well, when Boyd wanted me to apply, I sort of got interested, and then I was interviewed by Doctor Lorne. He was the one who clinched it – he really made me want to work at the hydro.'

'Ah, yes, Doctor Lorne.' Grant sat back a little, and drank some of his wine as their salad plates were removed. 'He could sell hydropathy to anyone, I sometimes think. Not that he's interested in selling, of course.'

'Are you?' asked Isla.

'Nurse Scott, I am just a dedicated doctor!' Grant laughed. 'But I'll admit, I am interested in making money – put it that way.'

Isla was silent for a little while until their main course of chicken arrived, when she told Grant it was his turn to talk about himself. All she knew was that he'd been brought up in Glasgow.

'Well, I have two sisters, both married and away from Scotland. My parents are very active, with Dad running his practice and Mother running umpteen charities. I qualified in Glasgow, worked in a couple of places before going to the Highlands hydro where I got interested in the water cure. The rest, I think, you know.'

'I know Doctor Lorne wanted you to replace Doctor Woodville,' said Isla, 'but why did you want to come when you already had a good job in a hydro?'

'Remember what you said about Doctor Lorne? How he clinched it for you? He clinched it for me, too. I knew his reputation, I knew it would be good for me to work with him, and so it is.' Grant gave Isla a long steady look. 'I'm glad I made the move.'

He leaned forward, his gaze holding hers.

'You wouldn't like to say you're glad, too?'

Her colour rose, as she tried to look away, only succeeding when she made great play of drinking a little more wine.

'Why would I not say that?' she asked at last, setting down the glass.

'Well, I wasn't exactly your favourite guy when I first arrived, was I? I couldn't help noticing that you weren't one of the welcoming party.'

'Oh, that's unfair! When did I make you feel unwelcome?'

'I don't say you went as far as that, but I definitely got the feeling that when other people seemed glad I'd come, you were . . . just polite.'

For a few minutes, they continued eating, while Isla wondered what she could say. It was not easy to deny what he'd just said when it happened to be true. If she didn't deny it, what would happen to their evening? Looked like being short and not very sweet, and however she had felt towards him once, she knew now she didn't want that.

'I'm . . . sorry if I gave you that impression,' she said at last, laying down her knife and fork. 'That was wrong.'

'It's all right,' he answered easily. 'I didn't mind about it. I just thought you might be thinking I was a poor substitute for Bob Woodville.'

'I was very sorry to see Doctor Woodville go, that's true, but I wouldn't have made you feel unwelcome because of that.'

So, why had she made him feel unwelcome? Because she'd at first thought him rather too full of himself? She wasn't, of course, going to tell him that.

'Maybe not,' he said with a wry smile. 'Maybe you just didn't like me. No, no, don't say any more, Isla. Actually, it wasn't exactly true when I said I didn't mind about your feelings towards me. I did mind, because I liked you and I wanted you to like me.' He laughed. 'Fell completely under your spell, as a matter of fact – it was your little nose that did it.'

'My what?'

'Your turned-up nose, Isla. It makes you so attractive. Has no one told you that before?'

She wanted to laugh – or maybe cry. After all the years of wanting to change her nose, here was a man – and a handsome man, too – saying he admired it? What could you ever be sure of in this world? Nothing, it seemed, but sometimes good things could happen and surprise you. Nice to think that.

'You're looking so happy now,' he said softly, 'but there'd already been a change in your feelings, hadn't there? I knew at once when it happened. After Damon's injury. The way you looked at me, talked to me – I began to think I could ask you out and you might say yes.'

'I wanted to come,' she said breathlessly. 'I did.'

'And I'm glad you did,' he was beginning, when the waiter appeared to remove their plates and place the pudding menu before them, which meant their eyes had to go over all the creams and gateaux, the jellies and whips, when all they wanted was to be on their way.

'Just want coffee?' Grant asked.

'No coffee, thanks.'

'The bill, then, please,' he told the waiter, and they both rose to go.

Thirty

The sky was still light when they drove out of the city, though a few violet streaks breaking the blue showed there would eventually be darkness. But not until after they'd arrived back at Edgemuir, Isla thought, rather wishing she could have run into the hydro under cover of night. She would have agreed with Boyd, had she heard his comment, that the white nights of the Scottish summer did not suit everyone. Certainly not Isla, who was wondering now how Grant would want to say goodnight on this their first date, and as he drove fast and well down the country roads to Edgemuir, she found her hands on her bag trembling.

'Won't be long before we're back,' Grant remarked, giving her one of his snatched looks. 'You'll be in good time if you've a curfew. I'm afraid I should know, but don't, whether they make you girls in the nurses' home come back at a certain time.'

'They're not too bad, but they like you to be in by half past eleven at the latest – preferably eleven. Unless you've been to a dance. You can get special permission for that, but I don't know anyone who goes dancing.'

'We could go to one sometime, if you like. The hotels have good dinner dances.'

'That would be nice.'

Would he really take her to a dinner dance? What would she wear?

'Anyway, tonight you won't be late, so would you mind if we took a slight detour?' Grant's tone was very light, very casual. 'Then we can be nicely alone for a bit – without me driving.'

'I don't mind,' she answered, equally casually, but her hands were trembling even more and her heart was thumping. This is it, was the thought going through her mind, this would be when he would kiss her. And how would she respond? She'd only kissed one or two young men – boys, really – and that was ages ago, before she'd started nursing. To think of them in comparison with Grant was impossible, though she'd been quite excited at the time, she remembered.

'Where's the detour?' she asked, as though she were simply asking directions.

'Just down this lane on the left – spotted it the other day.'

Grant turned into the lane he pointed out, and in moments was stopping the car, turning off the engine and looking at Isla.

'There's no one around,' he whispered, 'just you and me. All you can hear is an owl who thinks it should be night-time.'

'It's not dark yet.'

'No, but we're surrounded by trees and foliage – feels quite private, doesn't it?'

He took her hands and gently pulled her towards him.

'You'll let me kiss you?' he asked, his face close to hers. 'I couldn't say goodnight to you without a kiss. I've been thinking about it for so long.'

'How long?' As though it mattered . . . She hadn't allowed herself to think during the evening of their eventual parting, but, of course, it must have been at the back of her mind. Just getting out of the car back at the hydro and saying 'thank you very much' didn't really seem likely.

'Don't ask,' he answered and, taking her in his arms, kissed her long and gently, gradually increasing in strength as he sensed her pleasure, and not letting her go until they both had to take breath.

'All right?' he whispered. 'You didn't mind?'

'Mind?' She could hardly speak for the feelings the kiss had called up within her, the intense delight, the longing to return the passion she sensed in him, as all memory of those boys she had kissed long ago faded from her mind. 'Oh, Grant, do you need to ask me that?'

She'd thought he would be sure to kiss her again, but instead he said, reluctantly, that they'd better get back. Time was getting on – she wouldn't want to be late.

'I'm not even thinking about it.'

'Well, we have to keep everybody happy, don't we?' he asked, as he turned the car round and drove slowly back to the main road. 'I see no reason why you and I shouldn't see each other away from Lorne's, but there are those who think it's bad for efficiency – you know – to have relationships. Maybe if we keep ours to ourselves, it would be best.'

'And if I'm late back, you think I'll have to explain where I was and that might not be a good idea?'

Although she had not wanted anyone at the hydro to know she

and Grant were meeting, it worried her that he didn't want that either. So there must be secrets? Well, of course, there was no point in minding when she'd wanted secrecy herself.

'It's just that I don't know Doctor Lorne's views,' Grant explained as they returned to the empty and now darkening road home. 'As I say, it might be best not to make our meetings public.'

'I'm afraid two people already know,' Isla said slowly. 'Sheana and Ellie made me tell them where I was going, but they've promised not to say anything. I'm sure they won't.'

'It's not the end of the world if they do,' Grant answered after a pause, 'but remind them again when you see them.'

'I'll see them tonight. We share a room.'

'Oh, yes, well – don't worry about it.' Grant's smile was wide and unforced. 'Just think about being with me.'

He didn't need to tell her that; since his kiss, she knew she would be thinking of him anyway. When they pulled up some way from the hydro, they sat without moving or speaking, gazing into each other's faces, until Grant finally made a move and left the car to open Isla's passenger door.

'Goodnight, Isla,' he said softly, his eyes glinting in the dusk, as she left her seat. 'We'll soon meet again.'

'Goodnight, Grant – and thank you. It was a wonderful evening.'

'Glad you enjoyed it.'

For a moment or two they lingered, then Isla turned away and began to walk swiftly back to the hydro, looking back only once when Grant raised his hand to her. She smiled and walked on.

It took only a few minutes for her to be back in her room, back to her old life, which could not be the same, and having to face Sheana and Ellie, both in their nightgowns, both with interested eyes trained on her.

'Isla, how'd it go?' cried Sheana.

'You were cutting it fine, getting back,' remarked Ellie.

'It's not half past yet,' Isla told her, taking off her jacket and flopping on to her bed. 'And it all went well. I enjoyed it.'

'Anybody'd think it was a Sunday school treat,' said Sheana shortly. 'Where'd you go for dinner?'

'Flair's. It was very good. They have a roof terrace.'

There was a silence as the two nurses watched Isla get up and take off her dress which she shook out and hung on a hanger on the back of the door. She appeared to be quite calm, quite in control, but their experienced eyes told them she was, in fact, so full of nerves she might have been strung on a wire. After a moment or two, she put on a cotton dressing gown and turned to face her watchers.

'There's something I'd like to say—' she began, but Sheana cut her short.

'It's all right, Isla, we know what you want and we won't say anything – isn't that right, Ellie?'

'Quite right,' Ellie agreed. 'In fact, we're sorry now that we weren't, you know, nicer, when you first told us about seeing Doctor Revie. I mean, it was none of our business.'

Isla's large grey eyes softened.

'Thanks, girls. I'm really grateful. It's not that we want secrets, but you can imagine what it'd be like, what everyone would say—'

'Just don't worry about it,' Sheana said robustly. 'You can count on us.'

'A big relief.' Isla turned to the door. 'Well, I'll just pop along to the bathroom. Goodnight, girls.'

'Goodnight, Isla.'

Alone in the bathroom, Isla relaxed, almost sagged, with the relief of strain, but now was her time to think again of Grant, to go over, as though she must study it, every aspect of their evening together. There was no doubt that it had been one of the most important evenings in her life, something she would always remember, the first time she realized she was in love.

And she was in love – she definitely was – as she had certainly never expected to be with Grant Revie. Even if she hadn't felt the sharp arrow of love when he'd praised her nose, there was no question over the acuteness of her feeling when he'd kissed her. That kiss had been the turning point in their new relationship, revealing to her what true passion might be, and what other people had known about while she had not.

Next day, she decided, she would tell Boyd about her evening out with Grant, for even if she did not want anyone else at the hydro to know, she felt she had to tell him. Oh, not about her feelings, of course. No, just that Grant had so amazingly chosen her from everyone else, and that they'd had a lovely evening. Maybe she should have been telling Ma, not Boyd, but she still felt unwilling to face her mother's interrogation and decided to leave it for the time being. Maybe if Grant asked her out again – she was sure he would – she'd tell Ma, but tomorrow she'd tell Boyd.

When she finally returned to her room, it was to find Sheana and Ellie in bed and asleep, but as she climbed into her own bed, she really wasn't expecting to sleep at all. Nor did she, for quite some time.

Thirty-One

At one o'clock the following day, Isla was ringing the bell at the door of the gym, which Boyd usually locked when he was having a sandwich at lunch time.

'Only me,' she called when he came to let her in. 'Sorry to interrupt your lunch – just wanted a word.'

'Come on through, I'm in the office. Want one of my ham rolls?'

'No, thanks, I've had a sandwich.'

Studying him in his little office, she thought he looked rather strained, though he hadn't lost his appetite and was now finishing his ham rolls himself.

'Are you OK?' she asked, filling his kettle for tea. 'You look a bit worried.'

'Not really. It's just been a bit of a shock, what's happened, you see, and Trina's upset, anyway.'

'What has happened, then?'

'Haven't you heard?' Boyd raised his eyebrows. 'Damon's gone.'

'Gone? Gone where?'

'I don't know. Maybe Moffat – he comes from there. He's left the hydro, anyway. Told Mr Paul yesterday, the day he started back at work again, that he wasn't giving any notice and didn't care what they said – he was on his way.'

'That's crazy!' Isla cried. 'What's got into him? I'd heard he was better and going back to work, and now he's away – doesn't make sense.'

Suddenly, however, the explanation came to her and she put her hand on her brother's arm.

'Oh, I think I see – Trina's told him about choosing you over him, hasn't she? I suppose he went wild.'

'You can say that again,' Boyd answered grimly. 'The things he said to her don't bear repeating – and she'd waited specially to tell him till he was better before she said anything. I just wish I'd been there when he threw his tantrum. I'd have known what to do!'

'Boyd, you wouldn't have hit him again! That would have been wrong; he's been ill!'

'Yes, but you don't know what names he called her – harlot was one, and streetwalker – said she was no better than girls like that and he wanted nothing more to do with her, never wanted to see her again – I tell you, she was in a state.'

'Oh, Boyd, I'm sorry.' As the kettle began to whistle, Isla turned aside to make the tea and took a couple of mugs from Boyd's cupboard. 'But it was pretty well expected that he'd be like that, wasn't it? You were worried about what he might do.'

'I never thought he'd speak to Trina in that way. She said it was awful. At one point, she really thought he might hit her, but in the end he didn't. Probably afraid of what would happen to him when I found out.'

'Oh, how I hate all this talk of violence!' Isla sighed, as she poured the tea and passed Boyd a mug. 'I think it's a relief he's gone. You'll be able to relax, be happy with Trina, and that's all you want, isn't it?'

A quick, radiant smile answered her, and he nodded.

'If we've really seen the last of him, yes, I'll be happy. Won't be able to believe my luck, in fact. The good thing is that now Trina's found out what he's really like, she says she never wants to see him again.'

'You're the one she wants to see, Boyd. I'm very pleased for you.' Isla set down her mug. 'But I should be getting back and I haven't told you my news yet.'

'What news?'

'Well . . .' She hesitated, blushing a little. 'It's not earth-shattering, just nice. The thing is Doctor Revie took me out for a meal last evening. To Flair's – that's a restaurant near Bruntsfield Links – it's lovely.'

She had lowered her eyes, but when she raised them, she saw that Boyd's smile had vanished and his face was stony.

'You went out with Doctor Revie?' he asked tightly. 'What did you think you were playing at? I never dreamed you'd be like all the rest, fawning around him, sighing over his blue eyes and I don't know what. I'm surprised at you, Isla, I'm very, very surprised!'

For a moment, she was too stunned to speak. To hear her brother speak to her in that way? How could he?

'How can you talk to me like that?' she cried, her face turning a deeper scarlet. 'What right have you to tell me what I should and shouldn't do?'

'You're quick enough to tell me what to do, Isla. And I've every right to question what you're doing now – going out with a guy like Doctor Revie, who'll be wining and dining you and throwing money about. And then what? I've met men like him in the army – all charm and soft soap, and never to be trusted. I'd like to know what Ma thinks about it. Have you told her?'

'No! We've only been out once – if we go out again, I'll tell her then. Not that it's any of your business! Probably we will go out again and why shouldn't we? You can't stop us. And why do you want to, anyway? Don't you remember how kind Doctor Revie was when he treated Damon? He's not like those men you were talking about – he's a good doctor, he works for others . . . he's genuine.'

'He may be a good doctor, but don't tell me Doctor Lorne and Matron will be happy about you going out with him. Do they know, in fact?'

'As I say, we've only been out once, Boyd. We haven't gone around telling everybody in the hydro!'

'I bet you haven't. Your Doctor Revie'll be keeping it dark, and if going out with you damages his career, he'll drop you like a hot potato. I don't want to be unkind, Isla, but he's the sort who'll only want somebody who'll be a help to him – and what can *you* offer? Break this off now, please, for your own sake!'

'How can you be so cruel?' she whispered, her eyes filling with tears. 'I never thought you could be so hurtful, to me, your own sister!'

'I'm not cruel, Isla. I'm not trying to hurt you! I just don't want you to be hurt by him, that's all – can't you see that?'

Boyd tried to catch at Isla's hand, but she wrenched it away and ran to the door, which Boyd had again locked.

'Please unlock this. I have to go, I have a patient waiting—'

'Isla, wait! Don't go like that – hating me when I swear I never meant to hurt you.'

'Just unlock the door, please.'

As soon as he'd turned the key, she left him without a backward glance, and with two patients coming into view, there was nothing he could do but let her go.

Thirty-Two

Isla's patient was Mark Kinnaird, who was resting in his room after a slight setback. He'd picked up what was described as a summer cold, but it had been bad enough to bring back some of his symptoms that had been waning, and Dr Revie had decided to suspend treatment until it was over. Still necessary, however, was Isla's general check, though the last thing she wanted as she approached Mark's room was to see him or anyone, when she felt so vanquished by the scene with Boyd.

'Nurse Scott, how nice to see you!' Mark cried, after she'd tapped on his door and entered, and she thought for a moment that he seemed better than when she'd seen him the day before. But then he coughed, and it was the same racking cough of old, accompanied by the same rustling of mucous in his chest, and her spirits that were low enough sank even further. Always did when a patient who had been doing well had a relapse.

'Your cold's improving,' she said as cheerfully as possible, 'but you've a bit of the old trouble back again. Don't worry, it will pass, as soon as we get you back to treatment.'

Mark wiped his lips, not looking at her. 'Shows the cure isn't permanent though, doesn't it?'

'You mustn't think on those lines. You were doing well – really well – it's just a wee setback because of the cold.'

He shrugged, let his eyes at last rest on her, and his look changed. 'But how are you? Are you all right? You seem – I don't know – not sickening for my cold, I hope?'

'Oh, no!' she answered, intending to laugh, but the words came out with a totally unexpected sob and, to her horror, she was soon crying in earnest, while her patient appeared stricken.

'What is it?' he asked. 'What's wrong? Please, tell me, let me help—'

'Thank you, it's kind of you, but I'm all right – I mean, I will be . . .' She found a handkerchief in her uniform pocket and blew her nose. 'It's just that . . . it's just that I . . . I've fallen out with my brother.'

'With Boyd? Oh, but why? You two get on so well – much better than brothers and sisters usually get on, I'm sure.'

Mark Kinnaird's gaze was so full of sympathy that it made her want to cry again, but she mastered her tears and, looking at him with drenched eyes, said, 'You see, it's so unfair. What he said, it's unfair, and not true.'

'I'm sure he didn't mean to upset you, whatever he said—'

'Oh, no, he didn't – that only made it worse. It was supposed to be for my own good, because he didn't want me to get hurt.' Giving a final wipe to her eyes, she sat up straight and gazed seriously into her patient's face.

'As though Doctor Revie would hurt me, Mr Kinnaird! I've only been out with him once, but I know he's kind and genuine, and he wouldn't do that. Boyd had no right to say I shouldn't see him again, had he? You see that, don't you?'

'You've been out with Doctor Revie?' he asked quietly. 'I didn't know.'

'Well, we didn't really want to tell anybody, you know; we thought it'd be easier . . .'

Suddenly, Isla's eyes grew large and she put her hand to her lips in consternation.

'Oh, Lord, and now I've told you, haven't I? Mr Kinnaird, I'm sorry, I shouldn't have done that. It's absolutely wrong; I shouldn't have dragged you in—'

'You have no need to worry,' he said gently. 'I wouldn't dream of discussing your private life with anyone, believe me.'

'Of course you wouldn't. Please forgive me. I've been very remiss – very unprofessional – I'm sorry, I really am. Oh, look, can we start again? Let me take your pulse and temperature, which is what I came for. Please forget all my nonsense.'

'Nurse Scott – Isla – will you let me call you Isla, just for now? You haven't been talking nonsense; you've been genuinely upset, and I hope you'll be able to sort things out with your brother as soon as you can. He's probably tackled it badly, but he has your interests at heart. It is your right to go out with anyone you please, and I'm sure he'll see that. Try him, eh? As soon as you can?'

At his smile, she almost broke down again, but when she'd completed her checks and rose to go, she knew he'd made her feel a little better.

'And even if you can only use it in my room, my name, by the way, is Mark,' he told her as he walked with her to his door. 'Please tell me how you get on – promise?'

'I will . . . Mark,' she answered, and managed a smile. 'I'll see you again later, and we'll soon have you back to where you were, I promise you.'

'Hope so. I was thinking of going home soon.'

Going home.

Returning to the treatment rooms, Isla thought how pleasant the words sounded. Another satisfied client, Dr Lorne would no doubt think. So why should she feel so sad?

It was evening and supper time before she saw Boyd again, but as soon as they met, she knew it was going to be all right. Words were hanging on their lips, words they couldn't really get out, until Boyd finally managed to say, 'Isla, I'm sorry. I was like a bull in a china shop, stamping all over your feelings. Can you forgive me?'

'Boyd, I'm sorry, too. I didn't want to quarrel. I know you were thinking of me, but it's my life, you see, and I have to make my own decisions. You do see that?'

'I do. As you say, it's your life; you should do what you want to do. And for all I know, I'm completely wrong about – och, let's not say who. All I want is for us to be friends again.'

'Me, too.' They exchanged smiles and went together to serve themselves with something to eat.

'What'll it be to celebrate?' asked Isla. 'Toad in the hole?'

'You bet! My favourite. This is my lucky day.'

'Mine, too,' she agreed, thinking of how Mark would be pleased. She must tell him soon of her reconciliation with Boyd, and tell Ma about Grant – when he asked her out again. As she knew he would.

Thirty-Three

And Grant did ask her out again – this time to the Queen's Theatre in Edinburgh to see *Chu Chin Chow*, a London musical comedy on tour.

'Sort of thing I like,' he told Isla. 'Something I can really relax with – I've enough to worry about without being sunk in gloom by some dismal play.'

'Enough to worry about? You never give the impression of being worried.'

'Any doctor is worried. It's the responsibility, you understand. I know Doctor Lorne has the ultimate responsibility, of course, and the cases aren't usually life-threatening at the hydro. But I have to get the treatments right, I have to see everyone gets what they should have, especially as there's money involved. People want what they pay for.'

'I do understand, Grant. So let's see *Chu Chin Chow* and forget all our worries!'

'Let's!' he agreed, his eyes dancing, and she knew he would have kissed her, except that they were in his office, where she'd made a pretence of taking a supply order he had to sign, and couldn't risk someone else walking in. That was a worry if you like, thought Isla, who minded very much that she and Grant could usually only meet at work when surrounded by other people, or carried the risk, if they tried to be alone, that someone would find them.

Even arranging the theatre visit was not easy, as matching their free evenings meant one of them having to change to suit the other, and for Grant to do that involved getting Dr Lorne to cover for him.

'Next time, it's your turn to arrange a swap,' Grant told Isla. 'We don't want to alert Doctor Lorne's suspicions, do we?'

'I'm beginning to think I'd just like to bring it all out into the open,' she murmured, but Grant shook his head.

'No, it'll be best if we don't, believe me.'

'If you say so.'

Isla gave a sigh, but made no mention of her own particular worry, which was that she must, now that she was going out again with Grant, tell her mother. And how her mother would respond, she could make a good guess.

She was right, too, for as soon as she mentioned Grant's name, her mother's face lit up!'

'Going out with the doctor!' she cried. 'That new one you said was so handsome? Isla, that's grand! He's a catch, eh? A doctor, and good-looking, too?'

'Ma, I'm not getting engaged. We're only going to the theatre.'

'But he's asked you, Isla, he's chosen you. Now don't tell me that doesn't mean something. Will, don't you agree?'

As it was a Sunday afternoon when Isla had been able to look in on her parents, her father was reading the Sunday paper which he now put down as he raised his eyes to his wife's.

'Now, don't ask me, Nan. Young folks today – they've different ideas from you and me.'

'Some things stay the same,' Nan declared. 'And when a man takes a girl out, it's because he's interested. I always knew Isla would catch someone's eye, but, of course, I never thought about the new doctor.'

She laughed a little as she gave Isla more tea. 'And it's about time one or other of my children got themselves married, eh? There's Boyd got some young lady he won't even bring to see me, though he keeps promising. Seemingly, she's a waitress at the hydro – very good-looking. Well, you'll know more about her than I do, Isla.'

'Yes, Trina is certainly very pretty, but I don't think Boyd's got as far as thinking about marriage,' Isla answered, her fingers tightly crossed against her lie, for she was sure Boyd would marry Trina tomorrow if he could. 'You'll just have to give him time, Ma. As for me, I'm only going to the theatre, so don't start ringing any wedding bells for me, eh?'

She finished her tea and said she must fly. Lovely to see them . . . quick, give her a hug, and she'd be in touch.

'You'll tell me all about this theatre visit?' asked Nan, at the door, as Isla prepared to leave.

'Yes, but don't mention it to anyone will you, Ma? We're keeping it under our hats, at present.'

'Oh?' Nan's expression was dubious. 'Well, of course I won't say a word, if that's what you want. Your dad won't either. But what's this you're going to see, then?'

'It's really a musical comedy – *Chu Chin Chow*.'

'Read about that,' said Will. 'Very successful in London, but silly, if you ask me. Based on Ali Baba.'

'Fancy a doctor wanting to see something like that!' Nan cried. 'You'd think he'd want something more serious.'

'Wants to relax,' said Isla, finally getting away.

She hurried back to the hydro, rather wishing she was able to relax herself, longing with all her heart for the theatre evening to arrive. Being surrounded by other people in the audience might seem the same as their work situation, but it was really quite different. They would be able to feel alone – for no one in the audience would know who they were.

Thirty-Four

The theatre evening was a great success, for if *Chu Chin Chow* was a bit silly in its plot, the songs were catchy and the chorus was splendid – better even than the principals. Truth was, though, Isla wouldn't have cared what she was watching, as long as she was next to Grant, as long as they were holding hands and exchanging glances, as long as there was the drive home to look forward to, with the usual detour.

That dalliance in the comfort of the car in the lane Grant had found was for Isla quite rapturous. She'd never realized, until she experienced it, just how much pleasure could come from being kissed and kissing in return, from being held and caressed, and realizing Grant's power over her, as well as her power over him.

As they sank back in their seats, exchanging smiles in the dusk, their passionate kissing over, she couldn't help wondering what it would be like to make love. Could it be that the ordinary people you saw all around were secretly feeling as she did now, only more so? She couldn't believe it, yet that's how it must be. Even her parents must have – well, she wouldn't go into that. People could never imagine their parents making love, but she was beginning to imagine it for herself. With Grant, of course. If they were married.

'Oh, God, Isla,' he was murmuring now, softly touching her cheek, 'if only – if only—'

'Only what?' she whispered.

'No point in thinking about it. Let's get back.'

At their stopping point outside the hydro, he turned to look at her.

'When can we meet again?' he asked quietly.

'We'll have to work it out. If only it wasn't so difficult!'

'Difficult or not, we'll have to manage it.' He laughed. 'Can't go too long without seeing you away from work!'

Her eyes shone as they snatched a last kiss.

'Don't worry; if we both want to meet, it will happen.'

'I want to meet, all right.'

'And so do I.'

★   ★   ★

And meet they did, whenever they could, spending the long evenings at the end of July and early August driving somewhere, maybe just to the country for a meal at a small hotel – no pubs, of course – or to a city cinema where they sat as close as possible to each other, but kept their heads down when the lights went up, in case anyone they knew was around.

So far they'd been lucky in that respect. No one at Lorne's seemed to have any suspicions at all that there was anything between them – perhaps because to most people it would have seemed so unlikely. Sheana and Ellie had obviously kept their promise to say nothing, and of the few others who knew – Isla's parents, Mark Kinnaird and Boyd – none would breathe a word.

Sometimes Isla would ask Boyd how things were between him and Trina, but really she didn't feel she needed to, when one look at his face showed how happy he was.

'I'm up in the clouds,' he told her once. 'Never thought it could work out like this for me, but that's fate, eh? Can never tell what's ahead.'

'How about taking Trina to see the folks, then?' Isla asked him. 'You know Ma's dying to meet her.'

'Ma expects a wedding,' Boyd muttered. 'I don't want her going on to Trina, maybe putting her off, or something. I mean, obviously, we haven't got to that stage.'

'Putting her off? Surely, if you're the one for Trina, she'll want to be married to you, won't she?'

The one for Trina . . . He wished he knew if that were true.

'You might say that of you and Doctor Revie,' he said after a moment. 'Don't you want to get married?'

'We haven't known each other very long,' Isla said quickly. 'I haven't got that far yet.'

'Not heard that Ma and Dad got engaged three weeks after they'd met?'

'Grant and I aren't Ma and Dad. I suppose neither are you and Trina.'

'Very true,' said Boyd, with a sharp little stab about his heart that he immediately denied to himself.

It was all very well for Isla to tell Boyd to take Trina to meet their parents, but she was taken by surprise when Nan demanded that she should do the same with Grant.

'Ma, it's not very easy,' she protested. 'I mean, he wouldn't expect it – we're not an engaged couple.'

'He's never said anything?'

'We've only been going out since June.'

'Been seeing him a lot, though. And your dad and me, we didn't waste any time. We'd only—'

'I know, I know, you'd only known each other three weeks. Well, it's not the same with Grant and me.'

'You could still bring him round for a cup o' tea. Tell him you'd like him to look in on Sunday if he can, just for an hour or so. I won't put on a big tea – just maybe do my Victoria sandwich cake, eh?'

'I'll see what he says, Ma. He's very busy.'

'Yes, but he'll understand. He's been seeing our daughter a lot and we just want to say hello. Put it that way.'

It was with some trepidation that Isla did ask Grant to visit her parents on the following Sunday, when he was free for the afternoon and she could manage an hour or two away from the hydro. Why she felt so nervous, asking him, was her fear that he might see the invitation as an attempt to make him seem her fiancé – which he wasn't, whatever her mother was hoping.

But it was all right. He didn't seem to mind being asked, and said of course he would be delighted to come – Dr Lorne would be on call, anyway, so no problems there.

'Poor old Doctor Lorne,' he added casually. 'Seems like he's disappointed in his daughter.'

'In Magda?' Isla asked with interest. 'Why, she's in Switzerland – what's she done?'

'Postponed coming home straight away for the holidays, he told me – gone to stay instead with a school friend in Paris.'

'Oh, dear, and he does so miss her! When is she coming home, then?'

'Later on in August, if it's of any interest.' Grant shrugged. 'Sounds a spoiled little madam, if you ask me.'

'Nobody at the hydro will argue with that!' Isla smiled. 'So, you'll come, then, on Sunday? I'll give you the address and directions later. Shall we say half past three?'

'I'll look forward to it,' he said gallantly, which should have relieved her mind but instead brought back worries. If he was so much the charmer with her mother, mightn't she become even more convinced that he was the perfect one for Isla? It was only what Isla thought herself, but she didn't dare to hope that he would soon propose and didn't want to spoil what she had with expectations. In her heart, she was sure he loved her and that they would one day be married, but men had to make their own decisions and mustn't think they were being pressurized – especially not by match-making mothers.

'Till Sunday,' she whispered, as she prepared to leave his office and he quickly pressed her hand.

'Till Sunday, dear Isla.'

Thirty-Five

As Isla had known would happen, number forty-six had been swept, washed and polished even more than usual in honour of Sunday's visitor. He was special, of course, being Isla's young man *and* a doctor, but Nan would have done the same for any visitor, or even to please herself. As for spring cleaning, Will always said he got his overtime in then, home not being the most comfortable place, with no curtains up, everything you touched being wet from washing, and not much ready in the way of tea. At least things were better on that Sunday afternoon when Dr Revie was expected.

Isla felt she'd been swept and polished, too, for she'd had to rush home to wash and change out of her uniform into a pretty blouse and skirt before Grant's arrival, adding some lipstick and brushing her red hair to a shine.

'Very nice,' her mother said when she presented herself in the parlour, 'that blouse suits you.'

'You're looking very smart yourself, Ma, though really Grant won't expect all this preparation, you know. He's only having a cup of tea.'

Smoothing the skirt of her Sunday dress, Nan frowned and said, whatever the situation, you must do your best and look your best.

'Quite right,' said Will, handsome in his Scottish woollen cardigan and tweed trousers. 'Now, isn't that the door, Isla? Your young man's on time, eh?'

Flying to let him in, Isla's hands were trembling as she drew him into the hallway, for it had come to her afresh how important this meeting could be. A great deal might depend on it, though, of course, she would have to pretend that wasn't so.

'You're looking very smart,' she told him, though in fact he was looking the same as usual, in a dark checked sports coat, white shirt and grey flannels, for the truth was he always looked smart, always looked handsome, and Isla knew her parents would be impressed.

'Do my best,' he said cheerfully, and from behind his back produced a bunch of pink and white roses. 'For your mother, Isla.'

'Grant, she'll be thrilled! Oh, you must give them to her yourself. Please, come this way.'

In the parlour, where tea was laid on a small table, Will was standing very stiff and straight beside his chair, as though he were on inspection, and Nan was moving forward, hand outstretched, until she saw Grant's bouquet, when she gave a little cry.

'Oh, my, will you look at those roses!'

'For you, Mrs Scott,' Grant said, slightly bowing his head, as Isla stepped forward to make the introductions. Nan, taking the flowers, though clearly surprised, remained in command.

'For me, Doctor Revie? Well, I'm sure I don't know what to say, but how kind, eh? How very kind. Thank you, then, thank you very much. I'll just away to put them in water. Will, look after the doctor.'

'Take a seat, Doctor,' Will responded, placing a chair, while Isla said she'd just be putting the kettle on.

'That's all right,' Grant said easily. 'Your father can be telling me about the woollen mill. I'm afraid I haven't any idea how such wonderful clothes are made from the fleece of sheep!'

'Aren't they lovely, Ma?' Isla asked, as her mother placed the roses in a vase of water. 'I never knew Grant was going to bring you flowers.'

'I'm sure he needn't have gone to such trouble,' Nan said, gazing at her arrangement. 'I wonder why he did?'

'Why, to give you pleasure, Ma!'

'Or he wanted to make me think he was a nice generous chap and right to be going out with you.'

'I'm sure he never thought of any such thing!' Isla retorted. 'Ma, don't you like him?'

'What a question! I've only just met him. Better put that kettle on, Isla. I've got the scones all buttered.'

'Scones? I thought we were just having cake.'

'Your dad likes a scone on a Sunday. I'm sure Doctor Revie will like one, too.'

'His name's Grant,' Isla said shortly.

'We're not ready for first names yet,' said Nan.

*   *   *

The tea went well. Grant said he hadn't enjoyed anything so much for some time.

'Home cooking, you can't beat it, and I don't get much of it.'

'A shame,' Will remarked, taking a second scone. 'Now our Boyd thinks the same as you, Doctor Revie – he has to have a lot o' meals at the hydro, but he always says his ma's food is best.'

'A pity he's not here today,' sighed Nan, slicing her sandwich cake, as Isla kept her head down, knowing Boyd, who'd made an excuse not to attend the tea, was probably out with Trina, as patients' lunches would be over. Maybe her mother guessed that, too, but was not admitting it.

'I expect he's busy,' Nan was continuing. You'll know our son, Doctor Revie? He runs the gymnasium at Lorne's.'

'Oh, of course I know him, Mrs Scott. A splendid young man – he's very highly thought of.'

'Was in the war, you know,' said Will. 'Doesn't like to talk about it.'

'None of us do, Mr Scott.'

'You were in the war yourself?'

'Royal Highland Fusiliers. I'd done three years at medical school when I joined up, but I wanted to see some action, didn't want to be an army medic.' Grant shrugged. 'In the end, I was invalided out with a head injury in 1916, and went back to my studies – not exactly a hero.'

'I think you were!' Isla cried, 'You did your bit, Grant!'

'That's true, Doctor Revie,' said Will, and Nan nodded in agreement, at which Isla's spirits lightened. Surely her mother must be seeing Grant's good points now!

A little later, with tea over, it was time for leave taking, with smiles, handshakes and thanks all round.

'I've very much enjoyed meeting you, Mrs Scott – Mr Scott,' Grant declared on the doorstep. 'And I must thank you for a most delicious tea.'

'Well, I want to thank you for the lovely flowers,' said Nan. 'They were much appreciated. Isla, you'll see us when you can?'

'That's right, Ma. And thanks for everything. Sorry to leave you with the washing-up.'

'Och, get on with you, there's only a few tea things.'

There were last smiles and waves, and then Isla and Grant were walking back to the hydro, not speaking until they were in the High Street, not feeling, it seemed to Isla, quite at ease.

'I think that went well, don't you?' Grant asked at last. 'Your parents made me very welcome.'

'It was sweet of you to give my mother the roses.'

'My pleasure,' he answered rather distractedly, and when Isla noticed he was beginning to look around at the passers-by, it came to her that this was the first time they had been in the town where they could be seen together.

'You're worrying if anyone's around?' she asked quickly. 'Most will be at work.'

'Might be somebody with time off.'

'You want us to split up?'

'Might be best.' He gave an apologetic smile. 'Sorry it has to be like this.'

'I'll go on first, then,' she told him, not with coldness, rather just regret that things had to be the way they were. When would they be able to declare themselves, let the world know of their love? In the beginning, she herself hadn't wanted others to know about her seeing Dr Revie, but now – well, now it was different. What they had was no longer casual; it had come to mean something, it was the real thing. Soon – she felt it deep in her heart – it must be admitted to everyone.

'I'll follow,' Grant said quietly, and that was how they parted, returning to the hydro as though they had never been to tea at Meredith Street, as though all there could ever be between them was the formality between colleagues, when one colleague was officially superior to the other.

There must be a change, Isla decided, putting on her uniform. They couldn't go on like this. Or could they?

Thirty-Six

For some days, Isla was on tenterhooks, waiting to find out what her parents thought of Grant, or, rather, what her mother thought. It was only at the end of the week that she managed to meet Nan at the café in the High Street and could finally, when they'd been served with their teapot and a plate of fancy cakes, ask the question that had been tormenting her since Sunday.

'Well, Ma, what did you and Dad think of Grant? It was nice of him, eh, to bring you the roses?'

For some moments, Nan busied herself pouring the tea and passing the cake plate, while Isla looked on, slightly leaning forward, lips parted, grey eyes anxious.

'The roses were very nice,' Nan said at last. 'What about a cake, then?'

'I don't want anything, thanks.'

'No? I think I'll have one o' the Madeira buns.'

'Ma, will you answer me?' Isla asked in a furious whisper. 'What's all this playing about?'

'I'm not wanting to upset you.'

'Upset me?' Isla sat back, a heavy sensation seeming to occupy her chest. 'You mean, you didn't like him?'

'He's very charming, knows what to say and all that, and I'm sure he's a very good doctor, but he's not for you, Isla.'

'What do you mean, not for me?'

'I mean, he'll never marry you.'

Two red spots began to burn in Isla's cheeks as she stared at her mother, whose grey eyes resolutely returned her gaze. Both then drank some tea, as though they had to, and Nan very deliberately began to eat her Madeira bun.

'We've only been going out a few weeks, Ma; why should I be thinking about marriage?' Isla asked, attempting calmness. 'Not everyone's like you and Dad, knowing what you wanted so soon.'

'Every girl, when she starts going out with somebody and is keen like you, is thinking of marriage,' Nan replied firmly. 'I know you've got your nursing, but you won't want to end up an old maid doing that, eh? You'll want a home of your own and children, and you won't get them without a husband. That's all there is to it. It's the way things are.'

'Well, it shouldn't be,' Isla said sharply. 'Women shouldn't have to be so dependent on men. But what you seem to have forgotten, Ma, is that I'm not looking to Grant for what he can provide. I happen to . . . to care for him. In fact, I love him, and I think he loves me. Why shouldn't he want to marry me, anyway?'

Nan sighed and poured more tea.

'He's very good-looking, eh? Very attractive to women. And the sort to want a girlfriend wherever he happens to be. How many's he had, I wonder?'

'I've never asked him,' Isla answered coldly. 'They're in the past. I'm the one he wants now, and whatever you say, I'm not giving him up. You were all excited when I first told you about him – what's gone wrong?'

'We've met him,' Nan answered simply. 'I'm saying no more, except that if you keep on seeing him, it'll all end in tears. Believe me, Isla, it will.'

In fact, tears were already filling Isla's eyes, just as they had when she'd quarrelled with Boyd, and for the same reason, but she dashed them away and, rising, said she'd get the bill.

'Got to go,' she told her mother curtly outside the café. 'I'm not sure when I'll be round.'

'Oh, Isla, don't say that, don't say you won't be coming round!' Nan was near to tears herself. 'I'll be that upset – well, I'm upset now, canna bear to see you unhappy—'

'I'm not saying I won't be round, just don't know when. Don't worry about me, I'm all right.'

'I wish I'd not said anything, but I had to, eh? I had to tell you what your dad and me believe?'

'Goodbye, Ma. I've really got to go.'

After a quick peck at her mother's cheek, Isla was on her way, her face set, her eyes still blurred with tears.

When she got back to the hydro, she knew she'd better wash her face to make it suitable to present to her little world, Grant included, and made such a successful job of it that no one noticed anything amiss.

Not even Grant, whose fine eyes sent their usual message when they met in the treatment rooms, and who contrived to pass her a quick note under cover of a patient's chart.

How about the flicks next Wednesday? it read. *See what you can do to meet me as usual.*

Again, Isla's world was filled with sunshine, and as she went about her duties, all her mother's words of gloom faded from her mind.

Thirty-Seven

On a sultry afternoon in mid-August, Boyd was in his gymnasium, instructing a patient, Mr Newman, on the use of the dumb-bells to improve upper body muscles, when the door opened and a young woman came sauntering in.

'Another customer?' gasped Mr Newman, who was middle-aged, overweight and already sweating. 'If you want to speak to her, I think I'll just take a break, if you don't mind.'

'Certainly, Mr Newman, we never want anyone to be over-stretched,' Boyd replied. 'Take a seat and rest for a moment while I have a word with Miss Lorne.'

For he had recognized her, though in her white silk shirt and short summer skirt, she looked even more grown-up than he remembered, and she never had seemed like a school girl. Of course, she'd left ordinary school now, anyway, hadn't she? Gone to some grand finishing place in Switzerland. What she was doing in his gymnasium, he couldn't imagine, being certain she wasn't interested in exercise.

'You know who I am?' she asked, moving her green-eyed gaze from a survey of the gym to a survey of Boyd, while Mr Newman sat down, rubbing his face with a towel and gratefully sighing. 'I didn't think you would.'

'Certainly, I know who you are, Miss Lorne,' Boyd told her easily. 'But what can I do for you?'

'Oh, well, as you can see, I'm back, and as there's so little to do here, I thought I might try out your gym – you know – get nice and fit?' She laughed, showing her perfect teeth, and put back a lock of her dark hair from her brow.

'That's a very good idea, Miss Lorne. I'd recommend everyone to do that, no matter how they feel, or how young or old. You'd certainly be very welcome here.'

'Lovely – when do I start?'

Boyd hesitated, glancing back to Mr Newman who was now happily reading a newspaper, before turning back, reassured, to Miss Lorne.

'Our ladies' sessions are three times a week on Mondays, Wednesdays and Fridays, taken by Nurse Henley. Just come along to one of the sessions – they start at three.'

His gaze on her was encouraging, his smile welcoming, but Magda Lorne's response was to raise her dark eyebrows and frown.

'You mean it's an all-women's thing?' she asked coldly. 'And taken by a nurse? If you're in charge of the gym, why aren't you taking the class?'

'I'm afraid it's what the ladies prefer,' Boyd answered, remembering having a similar conversation with Trina, who also hadn't favoured the idea of a women's-only class.

'You mean it's what my father thinks they'd prefer!' Magda snapped. 'Why, it's absurd to separate men and women like that – I'm going to speak to him about it.'

'I'd rather you didn't, Miss Lorne. The system's worked very well up till now, and I think we shouldn't change it. I really think you'd enjoy the ladies' class. Nurse Henley is very good and I'm always on hand – you know – to give advice and so on.'

Still frowning, and with her bright lips pursed in disapproval, Magda shrugged. 'I'll think about it, then, see how I feel.'

'I hope you'll decide to come along; you won't regret it. Now, if you'll excuse me, I must attend to my client.'

After studying him for a moment, she turned to go, then with a sudden smile, put out her hand for him to shake.

'Thank you, Mr Scott, you've been very kind – now I'll let you get on.'

'Hope we'll see you here soon, Miss Lorne.'

At the door she seemed to hesitate – someone else was coming through – and when Boyd saw who it was, his heart leaped. For it was Trina, looking in as she often did when the patients' lunches were over. Trina, whose large dark eyes were meeting the green eyes of Miss Lorne with no great pleasure. Trina, who, as Miss Lorne advanced and went out, the door swinging behind her, made straight for Boyd.

'What was *she* doing here?' she demanded. Boyd shook his head at her and gestured towards Mr Newman who was looking up with interest from his paper.

'Ssh,' murmured Boyd. 'I have a patient here.'

'Well, just tell me what Doctor Lorne's daughter is doing here, Boyd. Only came back yesterday from abroad and she comes round to your gym? Don't tell me she wants to use the dumb-bells!'

'She does want to do some exercises here – I've told her about the women's classes.'

'And she'd be thrilled about them, eh? Och, you go and see to your chap – I'll make some tea.'

Shrugging, Trina flounced away to Boyd's office, while Mr Newman stood up and said apologetically that he was a wee bit tired, he'd missed his nap, might call it a day, if Mr Scott didn't mind . . .

'Not at all, Mr Newman, but please don't think that I won't want to instruct you because I have a visitor. It's my job to help you and that's what I want to do.'

'No, no, that's quite all right. I know you want to help, Mr Scott. I'll come tomorrow – maybe a bit later – have my rest first.' Mr Newman smiled. 'Now you have your cup of tea with Miss Morris – everyone's favourite waitress, you know!'

When they were alone, Boyd said he'd no time for tea, for now that the naps were over, more patients would be arriving at any moment. Even so, he did have time to kiss Trina before she said she might as well go.

'Thought you might have got your sidekick in today and then we could've walked out somewhere,' she remarked, staring moodily at Boyd. 'But, of course, he's not here.'

'You know Larry's not here every day – he has the saunas to look after. We can't just go out when we want to.'

'Lucky for Miss Lorne, eh? That she could find you on your own? I tell you, she's got her eye on you, Boyd.'

'That's just a piece of nonsense, Trina. We've scarcely met. She'd be much more likely to be interested in somebody like Doctor Revie. He's more her style.'

'But he's spoken for already,' Trina said over her shoulder, as she moved out of the office. 'Don't try to deny it.'

'What do you mean?' Boyd asked quickly. 'Who are you talking about?'

'Why, your sister, of course! Now, don't pretend to look surprised. I've seen the way they look at each other – oh, Boyd, what a giveaway!'

'They don't want anyone to know,' Boyd said after a pause. 'Not yet, anyhow. You won't say anything, will you, Trina?'

'Not if you promise never to entertain Miss Lorne in your gym again!'

Her eyes sparkling, Trina was teasing and he knew it, but as he walked with her to the door, Boyd was feeling curiously low in spirits. Something to do with Isla, he guessed, something to do with her vulnerability that she always refused to recognize. But then maybe she was right about Grant Revie. Trina certainly believed he was in love and she seemed to know.

'See you tonight after we've cleared up?' Trina whispered, when the first of Boyd's expected clients for afternoon exercise came cheerfully into sight.

'Sure,' he whispered back, and Isla and her love affair melted from his mind.

Thirty-Eight

Isla was making herself an evening dress – sleeveless which was fashionable, but only ankle-length, nothing grand. Smart, though; made of dark blue taffeta with a pretty neckline, which she thought would suit her – should she ever get it finished. As she had to use her mother's sewing machine, the time she could spend on it was short, but at least she'd made up with Ma and that had to be a good thing. Neither had wanted any coldness between them, and as Nan had taken care not to voice her views on Grant again, so far their truce had held.

The problem with the slow progress on the dress was that Grant might come up with an invitation to a dinner dance before it was ready, which would mean asking Ma to take a hand. She was a good needlewoman, had made the most of Isla's clothes when she was young, and Isla would just have to hope that she wouldn't mind getting involved with something intended for Grant Revie's eyes. Although she'd said no more against him, it was clear enough that she'd be happier if Isla gave him up, but as that wasn't going to happen, she'd probably just hold her tongue and hope for the best. Wasn't that what Isla did, anyway?

As the days of August went by, though, it gradually dawned on Isla that she'd hardly seen Grant at all, even at work. Usually, there would be exchanged glances, smiles, notes passed under cover and definite dates arranged for meeting up. But just lately, it had been different; he always seemed to be disappearing into the distance, never had time to stop, and there'd been no special contact at all.

Strange, indeed. Although she was unwilling to speak to him about it, she began to feel she must. Especially when Sheana and Ellie kept asking where she was going next, and even Mark Kinnaird seemed to wonder what was planned, though he laughed when he asked and said it was no business of his.

'I just take vicarious pleasure in hearing about people going places in real life, Isla, while I'm still cooped up here,' he told her. She was taking his temperature in his room one evening, and she'd been able to say that he was so much better again that he'd be going home soon.

'Can't wait! You mean I might be going to a good restaurant myself, or even to a play or something?'

'Why not? You're not a permanent invalid, Mark. You have a condition that flares up, but it's better now.'

Isla smiled and, looking at the thermometer, waved it before Mark's eyes. 'You see? Normal!'

'I'm so grateful,' he said seriously. 'For all the care I've had in here. Specially your care, Isla.'

For a moment, he touched her hand, then immediately let it go.

'Tell me, how's that dress going? Didn't you say you were making a new one for dancing?'

'It's nearly finished.' She smiled again, in spite of the brief pang his words had given her. 'I think it will look all right.'

'Wish I could see you in it.'

What could she say? It wasn't at all likely he ever would. Glancing at her watch, she said she must fly and she'd see him in the morning. After she'd left him, though, she was overcome with a deep, strange sense of unease.

Some days ago, when she'd told Grant about the dress, she'd been quite happy, quite at ease, confident that she'd soon be wearing it to go dancing with him, or if that hadn't been arranged, to go with him elsewhere. One of the restaurants he liked, or the theatre – or something, anyway . . .

And then, of course, they'd be finishing up in their own special country lane, exchanging their rapturous kisses and caresses. Oh, there'd been no problem then.

Well, was there a problem now? She couldn't even be sure. Just because she hadn't seen Grant to speak to, it didn't mean he was avoiding her. He'd just been busy, and heaven knows, he was busy, with so many people with calls on his time, and meetings with Dr Lorne and Matron and all the rest of the routine at the hydro. Why should she be worrying?

She wasn't worrying. Not really. But tomorrow, maybe, she'd try to catch him. Perhaps in his office, when she could take something in as an excuse, and just say . . . Maybe she wouldn't decide what to say in advance. She'd just let the words come when she saw him. When she saw him, she would know what to say. Of course she would.

But that night, after she'd taken her decision what to do, she hardly slept at all.

Thirty-Nine

The following morning, when she arrived early for work and saw the door to Grant's office closed, Isla knew that this was the time. The time she'd been waiting for. The time to find out – whatever it was she must know.

Some sixth sense told her he was there, behind that closed door, probably doing some paperwork, probably not wanting to be disturbed – though only a short time ago, she knew she'd have had no qualms about disturbing him. She was different from the rest of the staff; he would never have turned her away. Yet that morning, with no real evidence of change, she found herself gazing at his closed door and feeling afraid to raise her hand to knock.

Come on, she told herself, *get on with it, will you?*

Folk will be arriving any minute to begin work – this is the time, the only time there might be. *Just knock on the door!* So easy, so hard. Strange, how much courage was needed to do something so usual, so routine!

'Trying to catch Doctor Revie, Nurse?' came the voice of Sister Francis, who had just come hurrying in. 'Ah, he's the elusive one!'

'Just want to ask him about Mr Kinnaird's leaving date, Sister, as I'm seeing Mr Kinnaird first thing—'

'Go ahead, then, I'm sure he won't mind. Always use an opportunity when it comes up, Nurse.'

'Yes, Sister,' said Isla, and with a sigh she hoped could not be heard, she finally tapped on Dr Revie's door.

'Come in!'

There was his voice, so mellow, so pleasant, a voice that had come to mean so much to her over the past weeks she suddenly could not believe that it would be used to say things she would not want to hear. She'd been wrong, must have been – there would be some simple explanation for their not meeting – *so go ahead,* she ordered her still reluctant self, *go in and find it!*

'Why, Isla!' he said, when she was standing before him, his door closed behind her, her gaze on his face, 'I didn't expect to see you.'

'Why not?' she asked huskily. 'I've often come to see you in your office.'

'Did you have something you wanted to ask me about?'

'You mean to do with work?'

'Well, yes, I suppose so.'

He was moving papers on his desk and, with sharpened gaze, she saw that his hands were very slightly trembling and knew he was nervous. It did not please her, for if he was nervous, there must be something for him to be nervous about, and with renewed apprehension, she guessed what it was. Just then, just hearing his voice, she'd had a little rush of confidence, let herself believe for a moment or two that she had nothing to worry about. But here was that same voice suggesting she wanted to see him about work.

About *work*?

Oh, no, she wanted to cry, *I don't want to see you about work. It's love I want to see you about; it's love we have to talk about!*

But she didn't say that, of course. Only cleared her throat and said, 'It's not about work, Grant, and I think you know that.'

'Isla, this isn't the time or place to—'

'Yes, it is. It's just the time and place.'

He waited a moment, still moving papers on his desk.

Then, without looking at her, he said, 'Look, I'm sorry I haven't been able to see you, but the thing is, I've had a lot to do – more than usual. Doctor Lorne's taking a few days off – not going away, but not working.' Grant hesitated and moved another paper on his desk. 'He wants to spend time with his daughter, you see. Miss Lorne is just home from abroad.'

Isla was silent, her eyes never leaving Grant's face, while her hands trembled like his and her heart increased its pace, as his words hung in the air between them.

Wants to spend time with his daughter, she seemed to hear again. *Miss Lorne is just home from abroad.*

Suddenly, everything was becoming plain; what had been dark and mystifying was now exposed and seen in a most powerful and terrible light.

Grant had stopped seeing her; Miss Lorne had come home.

Oh, so clearly, Isla could now understand how the two events were connected. Why had she not realized before what might have happened? What had, in fact, happened, just as Boyd had predicted, in words that had seemed so cruel at the time.

'He's the sort,' he had said of Grant, 'who'll only want someone who'll be of help to him. And what,' he had asked Isla, 'can *you* offer?'

What indeed? Compared with Magda, who was not only beautiful but the daughter of Dr Lorne, what had Isla to offer? Nothing at all. Dr Lorne was the director of the hydro; he had money and standing. As a father-in-law, he would be perfect for an ambitious young doctor. Whereas Isla could bring nothing from her own dear father; all she could offer was herself alone. Apart, of course, from her love, which she'd been foolish enough to think Grant might want. Already, her time of thinking that seemed very long ago.

As her thoughts flooded her being with an intensity she had never experienced before, she found herself trying desperately to clutch at a last straw. Supposing she'd been wrong? Supposing Grant was not after all making a play for Dr Lorne's daughter and was really genuinely too busy to see Isla? That he did care for her, after all?

'If Doctor Lorne's on holiday, I can see it's difficult for you, Grant,' she said, making a brave effort to sound as though her world was still intact and not crumbling around her ears. 'But you must get some time off. Couldn't we meet then?'

'It's not so easy, Isla. Doctor Lorne's arranged with Doctor Morgan to come in if I need him – he's the retired doctor Doctor Lorne knows locally – but he really hasn't much experience of hydropathy. I think I'd prefer to crack on myself.'

'Well, what about our lunch hour?' she asked desperately. 'Just so that we can talk – see each other. I miss that so much.'

For some moments, he looked down at his desk without speaking.

Finally, he raised his blue eyes to give her a fleeting glance before lowering them again.

'Oh, God, this is so difficult,' he said in a low voice. 'I don't really know how to put it.'

'What? Put what?'

'Well, I've really loved being with you, Isla – you must believe that. You're a very attractive girl and we've had some good times, haven't we? But it was never a permanent thing, was it? I mean, you probably realized that, just as much as I did – all good things come to an end, they say . . . and maybe, you know, we've got to that stage.'

The blue eyes were now looking everywhere, except at Isla's face which had turned very pale.

'That stage?' she repeated. 'You mean, saying goodbye? Is that what you're meaning, Grant?'

'Well, we'll still see each other around. We'll still be friends, won't we? I wouldn't want to lose you as a friend, Isla.'

Wouldn't want to lose her as a friend . . . She smiled a little, would have liked to laugh and throw back the offer in his face, except that any laugh might end in shameful tears. Even just realizing that the last straw she'd tried to clutch had broken in her grasp was a dangerous source of breaking down, and whatever happened, she wasn't going to break down in front of Grant Revie.

'I . . . think I'd better go,' she said, clearing her throat. 'I really only came in to ask about Mark Kinnaird.'

'Mark Kinnaird?' Grant repeated, rising from his desk and looking at her at last with amazed eyes. 'What about him?'

'He's very keen now to go home. Could you make an assessment some time? I'm seeing him this morning, if you want to fix a time.'

'Yes. Yes, do that.' Grant was still floundering at Isla's sudden change of subject from their love affair to work. 'It's true he does seem better, but, of course, we can't be sure how he'll be away from here. I'll have to explain to him that we've broken the cycle, but there may be a return of symptoms.'

'I'm sure he understands that. When will you see him, then?'

'Could you tell him . . . about eleven this morning?'

'I'll tell him.'

They faced each other for a long, tight moment, each holding themselves stiffly as though ordinary posture was not possible, scarcely seeming to breathe, until Isla turned and moved to the door.

'Isla,' Grant cried hoarsely, 'may I just say—' But she was already on her way, closing the door behind her, walking fast, not looking at anyone about, but straining every nerve to let no feelings show as she made for the lift and her waiting patient.

Forty

Mark was in his room, rising hastily to his feet when she came in, his eyes bright, his questions ready.

'Isla, good morning! Did you see him – Doctor Revie? Is he going to let me go?'

'Hello, Mark,' she replied, keeping her eyes down, as though that meant he wouldn't notice how she was looking. 'Let me get my breath.'

'Of course, of course. Sorry, I'm absurdly over-excited.'

'I did see him,' she began. Then she stopped, her face still lowered, her lips trembling. She'd had such good intentions, coming up here. No tears, no revelations, everything to be just as usual. Until she'd had to say she'd seen him, seen Grant, and the so-recent memory of what had passed between them was too much. Too much for her to hold back when it was Mark she was with, and not Sister Francis or any of her colleagues, for with him, in spite of herself, she could let go.

And she did let go. Not dissolving into tears, but beginning to shake like a leaf and losing all the self-control she'd managed to achieve on the way up to Mark's room, while he, horrified, put his arms around her and held her close.

'Isla, what is it?' he kept asking. 'What's upset you like this? What's happened?'

'You . . . asked me if I'd seen him,' she answered, catching her breath. 'Seen Doctor Revie. And I had.'

'Oh, God, Isla, you've had a row? Look, it's not worth being upset like this. It's not the end of the world—'

'There was no row.' Making a great effort, she left his arms. 'But you mustn't hold me. You're my patient.'

'I know, I'm sorry. It was just instinctive – I wanted to help.'

'You did help, you're helping now. I'm the one who should be saying sorry; I shouldn't have broken down the way I did. Look, I'd better get on with taking your temperature—'

'To hell with my temperature! Tell me what's happened, Isla.'

She swallowed, looked away, looked back and gave a slight shrug.

'Grant has given me up, that's all. That's all that's happened.'

'Isla, no!' Mark's eyes were so large on her face, so filled with sympathy, that she had to look away again. She resolutely shook down her thermometer.

'Open wide, Mark! We must stick to routine, even if you'll soon be away. Doctor Revie is coming to see you at eleven o'clock this morning; he might give you the all-clear to go. But there is a proviso.'

'Never mind about me, Isla; just tell me—'

'No, you must listen, Mark, it's important. The doctors think you are much better, but there's no guarantee that away from here the symptoms won't return.'

'I'm aware of that, I'm prepared,' he said impatiently. 'But I'm well at present and I want to get home. I can't stay here for ever. Now, will you tell me why Doctor Revie has done . . . what you say he has. I mean, why should he? I'd have said he did care for you very much. Just to see you together—'

'All moonshine, whatever you saw, Mark. Didn't mean anything. He loved being with me, he said, I was a very attractive girl, we had some good times . . . only we always knew, didn't we, it wasn't permanent? But we could still be friends, couldn't we?'

At the memory of the words, Isla's face twisted and Mark grasped her hand.

'How could he hurt you like that?' he murmured. 'How could he? He must have known how you felt about him.'

'Didn't want it, did he? Didn't want what I felt about him. But I am never going to be a friend of Grant Revie's, and he doesn't really want that either.'

'What the hell does he want?'

She paused, wondering whether to tell Mark of her thoughts about Grant and Miss Lorne, but decided against it. No need to go into something she didn't know for certain, even if she was sure in her own mind that it was so.

'Not me, anyway,' she said at last. 'But he can be sure I'm not staying around to see him every day. Not when I feel so bad, Mark – as though I've cheapened myself for wanting him when he doesn't want me. And everyone will be looking at me—'

'Surely very few people know about you and Grant, Isla? There won't be anyone looking at you.'

'Well, the thing is, just lately I've had the feeling that some folks did suspect there was something between him and me. These things come out, Mark, I don't know how.' Isla shook her head. 'But they'll all be sorry for me now, won't they? Thinking I've thought too much of myself, capturing Doctor Revie! Well, I'm not staying to see that, either. I can get a job in Edinburgh again; I needn't stay here.'

Mark suddenly tightened his grip on her hand.

'Isla, listen to me. What you must do now is weather this storm. Let people see you don't care as much as they might think. Keep going as though everything was normal. Before you know it, the whole thing will be forgotten.'

He smiled, keeping his eyes on hers, and pressed her hand, and she knew he was willing her to do as he wanted and that probably she should, but just the thought of it made her flinch and shake her head. It wasn't possible, she couldn't do it; the pain was too much.

'I know you think you can't,' he told her, 'but believe me, Isla, it will be best. Running away won't help – you'll only take it all with you and have to live with the knowledge that Grant has won. So look at me, and tell me that you still want to choose that.'

As she stared at him, amazed by the strength of his voice and his air of decision, it came to her that this was the real Mark, the one so often overshadowed by his illness, and through the mists of her misery, she decided to do as he said. It was right, anyway, that she should just weather the storm, as he put it, so that those around might even believe that the storm was of no importance. Lots of people had to face heartbreak – they just had to come through it, as poor Joan Elrick appeared recently to be doing. She was certainly looking better – but, oh God, how long before Isla herself could be like her?

Putting aside that inner cry and the dull ache that seemed now a part of her being, she said quietly, 'You're right, Mark, I shouldn't run away. I'll stick it out, however I feel.'

'Take one day at a time,' he told her. 'Each day, you'll feel a little better, until one day you'll be really better and the world will be yours again. That's the way it goes.'

'You know about these things?'

'I've had my share of disappointments.'

She stared in surprise for a moment, once again discovering

another facet of this man she didn't know as well as she'd thought, then relaxed and managed a smile.

'I'm going to miss you, Mark,' she said softly. 'I'll always be grateful for your support.'

'Haven't gone yet,' he answered cheerfully, releasing her hand. 'But if anyone's been supportive, it's been you, Isla. And I'm the grateful one.'

They exchanged long, thoughtful looks before Isla, remembering her duty, finally took his temperature.

'Normal,' she told him. 'That's good. I'm sure you'll be leaving us soon. Now, I've got to go.'

'You'll look in this evening?'

'Of course.' But her look was sombre. 'By then, I'll probably have seen Boyd. And some time, I must see my mother and my dad. Tell them my news . . .'

'They'll be very understanding.'

'They'll say, *I told you so.* Should have listened to them, shouldn't I?'

With last long looks, they moved to the door.

'Till this evening,' said Mark, and she smiled and was gone.

Forty-One

Sticking it out at the hydro, as Isla had agreed to do, proved no easier than she'd thought it would be, especially after Grant Revie had given his permission to Mark to return home. Not immediately, but for the following week, which meant that after only a few days, Isla would be without Mark's comforting presence.

Although both Boyd and her mother were truly sympathetic, with Boyd at one point threatening to punch the doctor's jaw, and neither of them actually saying *I told you so,* Isla couldn't help feeling a certain awkwardness with them, when they had been so right about Grant, and she had been so wrong. Which meant that though she always felt free to express her feelings to Mark, she tried to soft-pedal them to Nan and Boyd, especially in the case of Boyd when Trina was with him. For who would want to admit to being jilted in front of her pitying smile? Not Isla.

As for her colleagues, there had been no pitying smiles from them so far, but there were certainly plenty of thoughtful glances coming her way, and she still had her suspicions that they knew about her relationship with Grant. And now, somehow, its ending.

Anxious to know the truth, after she'd told Sheana and Ellie that it was all over between her and Grant, she did venture to ask if they'd ever let slip about the relationship to anyone else. Which, of course, only caused an immediate flare-up of denials and cries of disappointment that she should ever have thought such a thing.

'It's a bit hard you should ask that!' declared Sheana. 'Especially when we've been so careful, haven't we, Ellie?'

'Aye, and it was all for nothing, anyway, when it was Staff Miller who spilt the beans.'

'Staff Miller?' cried Isla. 'How did she know?'

'Seems she'd noticed little talks and smiles between you and Doctor Revie, and told Sister Francis she was sure something was going on. Said Sister should inform Doctor Lorne, but Sister said she wasn't even sure about it . . . but Kitty Brown had overheard it all, and you know what Kitty's like. Mouth as big as a letterbox for gossiping!'

'I'm surprised you never noticed folk looking at you, Isla,' remarked Sheana. 'The story was all over the hydro, anyway, though we said there was nothing in it, just to be helpful.'

'I did notice,' Isla said slowly. 'At least, I felt it. But I couldn't be sure.' She gave a small bitter smile. 'Anyway, it's true now, that there's nothing in it.'

'We do feel sorry, Isla,' said Ellie earnestly.

'We do,' agreed Sheana.

They were, thought Isla, but she couldn't help noticing that the expressions in their eyes had changed from when they saw her as the girl who was going out with Dr Revie. He'd been such a catch, hadn't he? With his looks and status, being so swooned over by so many lady patients, why had Isla been the one who'd caught him? That was the question she'd read in their eyes then. Now that she hadn't caught him, there was no longer any need for questions in her friends' eyes, only sympathy – and maybe a little satisfaction that things had righted themselves. Isla was just the same as everyone else, after all – only sadder, of course.

And those looks she now saw in the eyes of Sheana and Ellie were the same, she realized, as those she saw in the eyes of her other colleagues. Which proved that they knew what had happened, and it was just as she'd told Mark: they were all looking at her and feeling sorry for her. She'd been lucky for a while, but her luck had run out, and now she was the same as everyone else. Dr Revie would never come back to her.

Even if he were ever likely to do that, which he wasn't, Isla knew she wouldn't want him. Though still feeling the ache of the loss of his love, after what he'd put her through, she could never think the same of him as a person. Yet on one sunny morning, when she had taken an elderly lady to the terrace, his power still to hurt her struck her like an arrow to the heart.

For he, too, was on the terrace, wearing his white coat as though on duty, but certainly not with a patient. Oh, no, the person sitting with him was no patient, and he would never have been looking at a patient so intently, would never have been talking to a patient the way he was talking to the girl beside him now.

Magda Lorne.

Never had Isla thought she'd be so shocked to see Grant with her, when she'd already had her suspicions that he would try for the girl who was Dr Lorne's daughter. But now that her fears were realized, it seemed too terrible to accept that she'd been right, and that the man she'd loved – still hadn't stopped loving – was only interested in his own future and didn't care who got in his way.

'All right, dear?' came Mrs Noble's voice, cutting through the darkness of Isla's thoughts. With a start, Isla managed to smile and shake her head.

'Quite all right, thank you, Mrs Noble. But will you be happy here until lunchtime?'

'Oh, certainly,' the old lady told her, her faded blue eyes searching Isla's face. 'I just need you to put up my parasol, if you would? My hands, as you know, aren't much use these days, though, of course, my treatments are a help – a great help.'

'Of course I'll put up your parasol. The sun's quite strong this morning – you'll need it.'

Who is this talking so well? Isla asked herself, for she could hardly believe it was her, when all she wanted to do was go somewhere and never see the world again. But she wouldn't do that; she'd see her next patient, come back to wheel Mrs Noble to the dining room, then change and run down to see her mother in her own lunch hour. Not to tell her of seeing Grant and Magda together. No, not that. She had something else in mind.

★   ★   ★

'Well, this is a nice surprise!' Nan cried. You didn't say you'd be seeing me today.'

'Well, it's not one of your work days, so I thought I'd look in. Don't need much to eat – a sandwich will do.'

'Isla, Isla, you'll never get better if you don't eat properly. I could have done you a nice ham and egg pie or something if I'd known you were coming.'

'Get better? I'm not ill.'

'Is that right?' Nan pursed her lips. 'Well, I'll just put the kettle on and rustle something up. You sit down; you're as white as a sheet.'

'Something to do first, Ma. Where's that dress I was making? The evening dress?'

'The evening dress? It's in your wardrobe. As a matter of fact, I finished it for you; there wasn't much to do. Why'd you want it?'

'You shouldn't have bothered finishing it. I want you to put it in the bin.'

'Put it in the bin?' Nan's eyes were horrified. 'I'll do no such thing. It's a lovely dress – you'll get plenty of wear out if it.'

'I'll never wear it!' Isla's voice was trembling, her eyes full of tears. 'I don't even want even to see it again.'

'Now listen to me, Isla,' her mother said, using the tone of voice that Isla knew from childhood meant she would brook no arguments, 'you are going to keep that dress and one day you are going to wear it. For someone else, not Grant Revie. It was meant for a dinner dance, eh? But he never took you to one and you never wore it for him, so now it's got nothing to do with him. What you must do is keep it for the time when you can go dancing with someone else and never give him a thought. Are you listening to me, Isla?'

'Yes, Ma, but I'm not sure I can do what you say.'

'You can do what I say, because it makes sense, eh? Throwing that dress away would mean you're still letting him matter, and you don't want that, I'm sure!'

Wiping her eyes, Isla gave a long weary sigh.

'No, but it's hard, it's very hard, to believe he's so far from what I thought.' She raised her eyes to Nan. 'And I still sort of love him.'

'Aye, well, no one said it would be easy. These things take time. But at least you can show some sense and not go throwing out a perfectly good dress in the heat of the moment!' Nan stood up and rested her hand for a moment on Isla's shoulder. 'Poor lassie,' she said softly. 'Just take it one day at a time, eh?'

'Someone else said that,' Isla said, rising to fill the kettle. 'Must be good advice.'

As she buttered the bread her mother sliced, the thought of Mark, who had been the one to give her that advice, stayed with her and might have been comforting, except that soon she would have to prepare to say goodbye to him. Would he want to keep in touch? She had no idea, and after a while his image had faded and she was back to bearing her own particular burden.

Forty-Two

It was the day of Mark's departure. He had handed out his tips, his chocolates and his bottles of wine. He had made his farewells to the doctors, to the nurses, to everyone who'd looked after him, and now was back in his room, wearing his formal suit, to pick up his case before his father came to collect him.

'This is it, then,' he said quietly to Isla, who was to accompany him downstairs. 'This is goodbye.'

'I'm afraid so,' she answered lightly, making great play of checking around to see that nothing had been left. 'You must take a last view of the hills – you always liked to look at them, didn't you?'

He glanced at the armchair that had been his and soon would be someone else's, and nodded. 'Kept me sane, at times, that view.'

'Oh, don't say that, Mark! Things weren't so bad here, were they?'

'No, no, I didn't mean that. It's been marvellous, the help I've been given; I couldn't be more grateful. But sometimes in the early days, you know, I used to get so depressed – I just couldn't see an end to it.'

'And then the treatment began to work and you felt better?' Isla moved closer to him, her eyes searching his face. 'You did, didn't you?'

'You know I did. And, as I say, I had wonderful help. Particularly from you, Isla.' His gaze was as intense as hers. 'And I want to thank you.'

'Mark, I was just doing my job.'

'I know it's your job to help everyone, but what you don't realize is that from someone as dedicated as you, your help is special.' He hesitated. 'It always seemed very special to me, anyway.'

They were silent for a moment or two, each exchanging long, sad looks, until Isla glanced at her watch.

'Time's getting on, Mark. We'd better go down; your father will be here soon.'

'First, I've something for you. Just hang on – I'll get it out of my case.'

'You've already given us those beautiful chocolates, Mark; you shouldn't be giving me anything else—'

But he was already returning to her with a small elegant carrier bag which he put into her hand. At the name on the bag, her eyes widened.

'Logie's of Edinburgh? Oh, Mark, what is it?

'It's just some scent.' He was a little embarrassed. 'Well, it's French – something pretty new. I rang my father's receptionist and asked her to get it for me, and she said this one only came out last year. Hope it's all right.'

'All right? Oh, heavens, I'll say it's all right!'

Isla was taking the elegant glass bottle from the carrier and reading the magic name, which she'd only seen in magazines. Chanel. A French perfume. This was without doubt the most exciting present she'd ever received, and the one she would always cherish. If she ever used it all up, which she couldn't imagine doing, well, she'd have the bottle, wouldn't she? A bottle, a memory . . .

She raised astonished eyes to Mark, who was watching her with anxiety.

'You like it?' he asked.

'Mark, I do. I love it. I've never had anything like it before. The only thing is—'

'What? Tell me.'

'Well, I don't know if I can accept it. There's a sort of unwritten rule that we don't accept presents except for chocolates, or something small – and this is not really small.' She gave an apologetic smile.

Mark shook his head. 'Isla, all I wanted to do was show my appreciation. That can't be wrong, can it? It's not as though the scent's a pearl necklace or something. Please, won't you reconsider?'

'I'd like to, Mark . . .'

'Well, why not? Why tell Sister Francis, anyway? I know, as a lawyer, that's not the sort of thing I should suggest, but it's a damn silly rule you're worrying about, anyway.'

For a moment, he was silent, still keeping his eyes on her face, then he said quietly, 'It would give me a great deal of pleasure to give you something you liked, Isla.'

Oh, why not? she thought, *why not take it and stop making difficulties?* There weren't so many people in her life queueing up to give her something she liked, were there?

'Then I say thank you,' she told Mark. 'I'll keep your lovely present and thank you very much for thinking of me.'

He relaxed visibly and it seemed as though they might seal off her decision with – what? A hug? A kiss on the cheek? Isla, holding her present, found herself wanting to do that – to hug or kiss Mark in a friendly way – and almost made a move towards him. But years of training held her where she was. Nurses didn't kiss patients, even on the cheek. She must hold back.

'We'd better go down,' she said breathlessly. 'Let's fasten up your case again, shall we?'

'And say goodbye.'

'We can say goodbye downstairs, when we see your father.'

'No,' said Mark, 'now.'

And doing what she had failed to do, he moved towards her, bent his head and kissed her on the cheek.

'Goodbye, Isla, and thank you for everything,' he murmured, and turned to fasten his suitcase, leaving her once again astonished. Seemingly, if nurses shouldn't kiss patients, patients could certainly kiss nurses. Only with friendly kisses, of course, nothing romantic. And a friendly kiss was what she would have expected from Mark, for that was what they were, wasn't it? Friends?

Even so, when it came to saying another goodbye, this time also to Mark's father, who had arrived to drive him home, Mark didn't say they would keep in touch. Never asked her to write, for instance, or said he'd write himself; only told his father how well she and everyone had looked after him, and he was sure he was going to be all right now.

'I hope so,' sighed Mr Kinnaird. 'But many thanks, Nurse Scott – we'll see how things work out. Mark, shall we go?'

'I'm ready,' Mark said, smiling, and with a last long look for Isla and a wave of his hand, he turned to follow his father from the entrance hall, insisting that he carry his own case, as he had insisted when coming down from his room.

How well he looks, she thought, watching Mark as his father drove him slowly away; all they had to hope now was that he'd be all right away from the hydro. Fingers crossed, for that. Strange, he'd made no attempt to suggest that they might meet again – she'd thought he might, for they'd had such an affinity. Or she'd believed they had. But perhaps all along he'd realized that their friendship was for the confines of Lorne's, and that once he was back in his own life, it would wither and die?

She couldn't know the truth of it, but as she returned to duty, having first put her precious scent in her locker, she knew that before she could think of any kind of new relationship, she must first get over Grant Revie. And, as her mother had said, that was not going to be easy.

Take one day at a time. That was the thing. There could be no avoiding the pain of seeing Grant at work and knowing his thoughts were for Magda, just as there could be no more comforting talks with sympathetic Mark. From now on, she was on her own. Must stand straight, face the world and wait for time to do its work.

And work in itself was a help. Take that afternoon, for instance. While she was giving Captain Bonnymore his herbal bath, which he always complained about, especially if it was lavender, she had no time to think of anything else. And when he said again he felt such a cissy, coming out smelling like a woman, she even laughed, as she always did. That was something, eh? One day at a time . . . She'd come through, in the end.

Forty-Three

On a Saturday evening in mid-September, Boyd and Trina were at the Edinburgh Palace Theatre enjoying a variety show and feeling lucky they'd managed to wangle time off together – always so difficult, and for Boyd, when they failed, frustrating. It meant so much to him, to be with Trina, all time spent away from her seeming only a waste. Whether she felt the same, he could never be sure, the truth being that he could never be sure of her feelings, anyway.

She seemed to enjoy being with him, certainly enjoyed their love-making, as far as it went, but of more than that he just had no real knowledge. Maybe he should just relax, let things take their course, wait for her to feel as he did, if she didn't already. As though he could!

In the semi-darkness of the theatre, he found his eyes turning often from the stage to rest on Trina sitting close, taking pleasure in her obvious delight in the performance of the dancing girls, who had followed the stand-up comedian, the conjuror, the juggler and the other acts they'd already seen. Just look at the way her eyes were sparkling and her lips were parted, as she sat forward in her seat, clearly concentrating only on the stage, completely unaware of Boyd at her side, who was so very much aware of her. He didn't mind. He knew she loved the spectacle of the theatre – the costumes, the music, the atmosphere of being out of her ordinary world. She'd come back to him when the lights went up for the interval, and she would look at him with great, dazzled eyes before returning his smile, and then it would be his turn to take her attention.

'Like an ice?' he asked, when the interval came.

'Oh, yes, please. It's so hot, eh?' Trina fanned herself with her programme and rose in her seat. 'Think I'll just pop along to the ladies' first – better join the queue, eh?'

'Me, too,' said Boyd, eyeing the line already forming at the ice-cream seller's side.

By the time Trina came back, however, he had his two tubs of ice cream ready. As he tackled his own, he watched, fascinated, as she enjoyed hers, her tongue catching little drips on her scarlet mouth, her delighted shiver as the icy sweetness met her throat.

'Oh, that's grand!' she cried, placing her wooden spoon into her empty tub and putting it on the ashtray on the back of the seat in front of her. 'Don't you love ice cream, Boyd? I'm so glad somebody invented it. But listen – you'll never guess who I saw in the Dress Circle just now!'

'Dress Circle? I thought you went to the ladies'?'

'I did, but when you come out, you can see the whole auditorium so I just looked up at the Dress Circle and there they were!'

'Who?'

'Doctor Lorne's daughter and Doctor Revie!'

Boyd's face darkened. 'Are you sure, Trina?'

'Of course I am! I know what they look like. They were there in the front row of the best seats, all dressed up, with the doctor trying to get so close to Magda that he was practically on her lap!' Trina laughed loudly. 'And she was just sitting there, trying to read the programme!'

Looking into Boyd's face, which was still shadowed with anger, his fine mouth grim, his grey eyes cold, Trina's laughter ceased and she put her hand to her lip.

'Oh, Boyd, I'm sorry! Your poor sister, eh? Hasn't taken the doctor long to move on, has it?'

Trina took Boyd's hand.

'But don't look so angry, Boyd – she's well shot of Doctor Revie. It does no good to think about him.'

'It does me good,' Boyd said tightly. 'I think about him a lot – how much I'd like to knock his block off, and see him have to leave the hydro. Doctor Lorne would never want him around if he knew what had been going on.'

'He might think Doctor Revie's OK for his daughter, though. So handsome, eh? And ambitious. Everybody knows Doctor Revie's going places.'

'Doctor Lorne would never approve of the way he hurt Isla, Trina. He's a nice, decent chap.'

'Yes, but Doctor Revie would wriggle out of trouble somehow. He's the type. Make out it was all in your sister's imagination – he never meant what she thought he meant.' Trina squeezed Boyd's hand in hers. 'But come on, it's nearly time for curtain up; let's not spoil our evening, eh?'

'Let's not,' Boyd agreed, managing a smile. 'You're right, we shouldn't let him spoil our time together. It means so much, eh?'

'Oh, yes,' said Trina, her eyes on the stage as the theatre lights dimmed, the curtain went up and a high-kicking group of girls danced on to great applause. 'You bet I'm not going to let him spoil this show for me. I just love variety!'

Boyd didn't and, in between gazing at spellbound Trina, found his thoughts going to Isla and the damage Dr Revie had done to her. How he wished he could do something! He couldn't, of course, and by the time he and Trina were making for their own special place for saying goodnight, his sister had left his mind. At least, for the time being. Thank God the year had progressed and it was dark now when they approached their alleyway, for, like most lovers, Boyd was happier in the dark. No more white nights!

Even more than usual, Trina responded to his kisses and urgent caresses with a passion that filled him with rapture, so much so that when they finally had to make a move, he felt able to say the words he'd held back for so long.

'Trina, I love you,' he whispered.

When she sighed, but did not speak, he made her stop and turn towards him, so that he could make out her lovely face.

'You feel the same, don't you?' he asked gently. 'I know you do. We wouldn't have been together as we have, would we? If you didn't feel like me?'

'We have been together a good while,' she agreed, and laughed a little. 'Bit unusual – for me.'

'Proves what I said, Trina. Proves you feel the same as I do.' He pressed his hands to her shoulders. 'So, won't you say it, then?'

'Say what, Boyd?'

'That you love me. Come on, say, "I love you, Boyd". I have to hear you say it.'

'Oh.' She pulled his hands from her shoulders. 'All right, then. I love you, Boyd. But why do we have to put things into words?'

'Because words matter. If you mean them.'

Trina was silent, then sighed again. 'I must go, Boyd. You know the rules for us livers-in.'

'Yes, yes, I won't keep you. There was just one other thing I wanted to ask. As you know, my folks are very anxious to meet you and I said I'd see if you'd like to come round some time. Just for a cup of tea?'

'Your folks? You mean your mother?'

He could sense her stiffening, putting up defences.

'Yes, well – no, it's both of them. Look, it would just be a quick visit, nothing earth-shattering—'

'It's late, Boyd; you shouldn't have sprung it on me now. Let's say we'll think about it, eh?'

Quickly, she kissed his lips, then turned and waved and hurried away towards the back entrance of the hydro, leaving him to stand for some time, wondering if he was any more sure of her than before. Except that she had said it, hadn't she? She had said, 'I love you, Boyd'. With those words echoing so wonderfully in his mind, he slowly turned to make his way back home.

Forty-Four

Only two days after she'd been seen at the theatre, Magda Lorne returned to school in Switzerland.

'What a relief!' cried the staff at the hydro, glad to be free of the doctor's daughter for another few weeks. And what a relief for Boyd, too, for he was glad she was out of the reach of Grant Revie. It was nothing to do with Boyd who she went out with, but he didn't like to think that she would want to be involved with anyone like Revie.

He'd said nothing to Isla of Trina's sighting of Magda with Grant at the theatre, but he knew she'd already accepted that Magda was his next conquest and saw it as just one more nail in the coffin of her old feelings for him. He was not what she'd thought him, and if it took time to get over him, it would be worth it in the end.

In fact, as September moved into October, she told Boyd one lunchtime in the canteen that she was already feeling a little better: her pain not quite so raw, her opinion of herself for being such a fool not quite so low. Even when she saw Grant Revie in the course of duty, she no longer felt quite the same stab of regret, and some-times – it might be her imagination – it seemed that he himself was not looking so very happy.

'Guilty conscience, I expect,' Boyd commented. 'And you were never a fool over him. You'd a right to care for him, after the way he led you on, and I think you've been damned brave, the way you've coped.'

'I wouldn't say that, Boyd.'

'Yes, I mean it.' He shook his head. 'I know if Trina gave me the push, I wouldn't be able to face it the way you've faced what happened to you. I'm not proud of saying that, but it's the truth, so I might as well admit it.'

'There's no risk of it, though, is there?' Isla asked anxiously. 'She seems very happy with you.'

'No, there's no risk, thank God, except—' He hesitated, while Isla's eyes sharpened.

'Except what, Boyd? What's worrying you?'

'Nothing, really. It's just that Ma keeps saying she'd like to meet her, and Trina doesn't seem keen. She says her old aunt – and that's all she's got as family – isn't bothered about meeting me, so why should Ma be different?'

'That's ridiculous! She knows Ma is different – and Dad, too, come to that. They're right here in Edgemuir – it's the obvious thing for Trina to meet them. You tell her you want her to do it. If she cares for you, she will.'

'Maybe.' Boyd looked away. 'She does care for me, there's no question of that, but, well, she's probably just nervous – you know, about meeting Ma.'

Nervous? Trina? Isla could have smiled, but she kept a straight face as she said she'd better get back to work. And back at the treatment rooms, she was so worried about Boyd that she didn't feel like smiling; this business of Trina's refusing to meet their parents didn't bode well for the future, did it? Or, maybe Trina was one of those people who didn't care about families? That needn't matter at all, as long as she really cared for Boyd. Isla just wished she could be sure she did.

About to enter the lift on her way to collect an upstairs patient, she heard Sheana's voice calling, 'Hold the lift, Isla, I'm coming!'

'Hey, where's the fire?' Isla asked, smiling. 'I'm sure your patient'll wait for you, Sheana.'

'I'm not seeing a patient. I wanted to catch you – have a quick word.'

'What about?'

'Well, there's gossip going round that I don't think you've heard. Folk don't like to talk to you about Doctor Revie, you see, though this is news I say you'd want to hear.'

As the lift doors closed and they were whisked to the upper floor, Isla's face was blank of all expression. Not looking at Sheana, she said, coldly, 'If other people don't talk to me about Grant, it's because I don't want to talk about him.'

'But this is different!' Sheana cried, when the lift stopped and they emerged on to the upstairs corridor. 'Like I say, you'll want to hear it, because it's about him getting his comeuppance. We're all thrilled because, seemingly, he's been turned down flat by Doctor Lorne's daughter!'

'Magda?' Isla asked quickly.

'Yes, darling Magda!' Sheana's eyes were suddenly anxious. 'You did know about them, eh? I mean, going out together before she went back to Switzerland? They were seen around – never bothered to keep it secret.'

'I'd seen them together,' Isla answered after a pause. 'I didn't know how far it had gone.'

'Och, not far! Seemingly, before she went back to Switzerland, she told Kitty Brown she was going to tell him she wasn't interested. And from the way he's been looking lately, I bet she did tell him. Must have knocked him for six!'

'Kitty Brown?' Isla repeated. 'Why should Magda have talked to Kitty Brown?'

'Because she's the only one of us Magda's deigned to make a friend of, after they met in Edinburgh once. If you ask me, Magda's just fascinated by Kitty being such a chatterbox and so different from all the starchy folk she meets. And the very one to spread the news about Doctor Revie – if that's what Magda wanted.'

Sheana, watching Isla's face, smiled.

'Anyway, that's the story, Isla, and I thought you should know, seeing as it's time you enjoyed getting your own back on Doctor Revie!'

But Isla was shaking her head. 'I've got to go, Sheana. I'm late already for Mrs Noble.'

'Oh, but, Isla, aren't you interested in hearing about his downfall? I thought you'd be thrilled!'

'It doesn't help me,' Isla said slowly, 'that he's been given the push by Magda. He doesn't care for her the way I cared for him.'

'But his vanity's been hurt – that's what counts! You wouldn't be human if you didn't take a bit of satisfaction in that.'

'Maybe I do.' Isla heaved a great sigh. 'All I want is to be free of him altogether. But thanks, Sheana, for giving me the news; it's good of you to think of me. Now, I've got to run.'

'We all think of you!' Sheana cried after her.

And Isla, hurrying to Mrs Noble's door, found her heart suddenly lifting. Thank goodness she'd followed Mark's advice, she decided, and stayed on at the hydro. For, excluding Grant Revie, who had his own problems, it seemed she was among friends.

Forty-Five

To be among friends. That was good, and it certainly helped in what Isla was now regarding as her convalescence – in other words, her 'getting over' Grant Revie. Of course, things would be better if he weren't around, but as there was no possibility of that, she'd learned to keep out of his way, or, if that wasn't possible, to be polite and seem indifferent. Did it help that he'd lost some of his self-confidence after Magda had turned him down? Seemed, in fact, to be not quite the charmer he'd been? Not really, for as she'd said to Sheana, all she wanted was to be free of him, and there seemed no prospect of that.

Then, suddenly, he was gone.

It was a morning in November, grey and misty, the hills out of sight, leafless trees around the hydro dripping moisture, spiders' webs stretched on shrubs like pieces of damp, intricate lace.

'Oh, how I hate November!' cried Ellie, as the staff hurried into the treatment rooms to begin work.

'At least, it's warm in here—' Sheana was beginning, when silence suddenly fell on the nurses. Sister Francis had arrived and, with her, not only Dr Revie but Dr Lorne and the tall, bony figure of Dr Morgan who covered for the medical staff when required.

'What's going on?' Sheana whispered, but Sister Francis had already stepped forward to make an announcement. 'Please listen, everyone! Doctor Lorne would like to speak to you before you begin work.' She turned. 'Doctor Lorne?'

'Thank you, Sister.'

Appearing his usual calm self, the director let his gaze move over the watching faces before him and slightly raised his hand.

'Sad news, I'm afraid. I have to tell you that Doctor Revie will be leaving us today. Perhaps not permanently, but he will of course be a great loss. Fortunately, Doctor Morgan has agreed to take his place for the time being.'

With a brief smile, Dr Lorne turned to Dr Morgan, who politely bowed his head, while the nurses tried to conceal their gasps as their eyes moved to Dr Revie, standing a little apart. Tall and elegant in a dark suit, over which he wore no white coat, he now moved forward, his blue eyes still bright, though his face was strained. At Dr Lorne's request for him to speak, he immediately agreed.

'Certainly, Doctor Lorne, I'm glad to be able to tell the staff here how very sorry I am to be leaving the hydro, and how I hope I may be able to return one day. The sad news is that my father has been taken seriously ill and I'm needed in Glasgow, not to run his practice which will be in the charge of his partner, but to manage my father's care. As it happens, I've just been offered the temporary post of director of a nursing home, which I've accepted, as it will be convenient for me to see to my father from there.'

Here, Doctor Revie paused and gave a short sigh before continuing, 'You'll understand that I'm anxious to move to Glasgow as quickly as possible, and Doctor Lorne has been very kind in releasing me so soon. But I'll just say again how sorry I am to be leaving Lorne's and all my colleagues. May I thank you for all your cooperation, and wish you the very best for the future.'

At first, no one spoke and there was a slight awkwardness, until Dr Lorne expressed thanks to Dr Revie, after which Sister Francis hastily said a few words.

'We're all so sorry to hear about your father, Doctor Revie, and quite understand that you want to be near him. As Doctor Lorne said, you will be greatly missed, but we hope all goes well and that you'll be able to return to Lorne's in the future.'

'Thank you, Sister Francis,' Dr Revie replied gravely. 'You're very kind.'

'And now, we welcome you, Doctor Morgan,' she said, turning to him. 'So good of you to help us.'

'Indeed,' added Doctor Lorne, turning to leave. 'Doctor Morgan, if you'd like to accompany me to my office, we can finalize things. Doctor Revie, we'll leave you to say goodbye. You'll see me before you go?'

'Of course, Doctor Lorne.'

As soon as the two older doctors had left, Dr Revie, with a smile that revived some of his old charm, shook hands with Sister Francis and every one of the nurses, even Isla, who turned quite white as she felt his hand in hers. She could feel his gaze on her, though she had already lowered her eyes, and wished with all her heart that she need not have allowed him to take her hand. But what could she have done? To be the only one not to shake his hand would have marked her out in a way that would have been upsetting, and at least this goodbye would mark the end of him at the hydro for some time to come.

After he'd left them, she said as much to Sheana when they were making their way to the pool room, but Sheana only snorted with laughter.

'Oh, you're right, Isla, we won't be seeing him again any time soon, if ever. As for all that stuff he was spouting, I don't believe a word of it!'

'Why, what do you mean, Sheana?'

'I'd bet any money there's nothing wrong with his dad at all. He's just cooked up the story as the perfect excuse to make Doctor Lorne let him go to another job, even though he's only been in this one for five minutes. And don't worry about him coming back – as I say, I don't think we'll ever see him again.'

Sheana, smiling triumphantly, clapped Isla on the back. 'You'll see, that'll be the truth of it, Isla.'

'I don't believe it, Sheana. I don't believe even Grant Revie would pretend his father was ill just to get away from here. He's very fond of his family; he'd never tell lies about them.'

'Oh, Isla, Isla! Shows how much you know about people, eh?'

'I know about Grant. I'll never forgive him for the way he dumped me, but I don't think he'd do what you're suggesting.'

'At least, you'll be glad if he doesn't come back?'

A broad smile gradually lit up Isla's face and she heaved a long deep sigh of relief. 'Too right, I'll be glad,' she said softly, and as she went to find her patient, for the first time since Grant had given her up, she felt her burden of unrequited love and raw, painful regret lift from her shoulders and leave her free. So euphoric did this make her feel that she was inclined to believe that from then on everything would be fine – for her, for Boyd, for everyone. Oh, what a pleasant feeling that gave her!

Not for long, however.

Trying out a new café in the High Street, one lunchtime, she and Ellie were browsing the menu of soups, snacks on toast and sandwiches when a waiter came sauntering over to their table.

'Ready to order?' he asked throatily, and Isla, at once recognizing the voice, looked up with dread straight into the dark, hostile eyes of Damon Duthie.

Forty-Six

He recognized them, of course, but made no sign, even when Ellie, not fully aware of what his return might mean, pleasantly smiled at him as she gave him her order of soup and eggs on toast. When he turned to Isla, keeping his eyes on his note pad, she took a deep breath and spoke his name.

'Damon?'

He scribbled something on his pad, before slowly looking up, still avoiding her face.

'Yes?'

'How come you're back in Edgemuir? You wanted to get away, didn't you?'

'I've a right to move back if I like.'

'Oh, sure, but seemingly you've changed your mind.'

He leaned forward, his eyes taking on that fiery look she remembered too well.

'Listen, if you think I've come back to see that precious brother of yours, you can forget it. I'm not going to see him. I never want to see him again – ever! That clear?'

'Perfectly,' she answered, swallowing hard, while Ellie nervously looked on.

'So, what do you want to eat?' he asked, straightening up.

'Isla, we can go somewhere else,' Ellie whispered, but Isla shook her head.

'It's all right; we're here now, might as well stay. Damon, I'll have the same as Ellie, please. Soup and eggs on toast.'

Without speaking again, he stalked away as the two young women exchanged glances.

'Isla, shall we have to give him a tip?' asked Ellie, but Isla vehemently shook her head.

'I'm damned if I'll give him a tip, Ellie! He doesn't deserve one, the way he spoke to me.'

She looked across the café to where two young waitresses were taking trays of meals from a hatch. 'Anyway, my betting is that he won't serve us again. He'll ask one of those girls to see to us.'

And Isla was right. One of the waitresses did serve them, while Damon was nowhere to be seen, but Isla still could hardly eat her lunch for wondering why he had come back and hoping she didn't already know.

After their meal, Isla decided to try to see Boyd. She didn't want to tell him, but was sure he should know that Damon was back in town. He'd be alarmed, of course, thinking what Isla had been trying not to face, which was that Damon would try to see Trina. And wondering, too, if she would agree to see him? Surely not? Hadn't she chosen Boyd? Hadn't she been glad to see the back of Damon, who was so volatile, so dangerous?

Arriving at the gym, Isla felt strangely helpless; there was so little she could do to help here, except give Boyd her message and leave things to him. Only, of course, he was busy, his gym full of patients, some requiring help, so that he could only shake his head at Isla and say this wasn't the best time to chat.

'I'm sorry, Isla, as you can see I've got my hands full at the moment. What's up, anyway?'

In spite of his unwillingness, Isla pulled her brother out of earshot of his clients.

'All I want to tell you is that I've just seen Damon. He's got a job at the new café in the High Street. He says he doesn't want to see you, but I thought you should know he's here.'

Boyd's face had paled. He seemed incredulous.

'Damon? He can't have come back here. He wouldn't. You remember, he said he never wanted to see Trina again, and this is where she is.'

As he hastily looked back at the patient he'd left, Isla guessed Boyd was trying to convince himself that Damon really didn't want to see Trina again. But he would know in his heart that if Damon was back, it could only be to see her. Why else would he come?

'All he said to me,' Isla murmured 'was that he didn't want to see you again.'

'And we know why,' Boyd said grimly, turning back to her. 'But even if he has come back to see her, it won't do him any good. She won't want to see him. She said so, Isla, and she meant it.'

'Yes, Boyd, I know.'

'And if he does try to see her, he'll have me to reckon with,

because I won't let him bother her, and that's for sure.' Boyd ran his
hand across his brow. 'But thanks for telling me about this, Isla.
Forewarned is forearmed, eh? Now, I've to get back to Mr Donaldson.'

Forty-Seven

As soon as he'd closed the gym at the end of work, Boyd went
round to the kitchen to try to speak to Trina. It was not a good
time to look in when patients' dinners were being served, and Mr
Paul would probably throw him out, but if he could just fix up a
meeting with Trina, it would be all he wanted.

Just as he'd expected, the place seemed to be in chaos – organized
chaos, of course – and Mr Paul was storming around, giving orders,
while his staff were hurrying to obey. Only Trina herself seemed to
be unmoved. When she saw Boyd, she raised her eyebrows and
jerked her head towards Mr Paul, who was inspecting his Duchess
potatoes just out of the oven, but at the look on Boyd's face, she
came gliding over to see him.

'What on earth are you doing here?' she whispered. 'You'll get
shot, coming in at this time.'

'I have to see you, Trina. It's very important. Meet me at the
back vestibule as soon as you've finished here.'

'I want to wash my hair tonight, Boyd. Can't this wait?'

'No, I must see you. Please be there.'

'Boyd Scott, what the hell are you doing in my kitchen?' Mr Paul
suddenly hissed, appearing at Boyd's side. 'Get out – now – do you
hear me?'

'Yes, Mr Paul. I'm sorry, Mr Paul—'

'Trina, get your serving dish for the potatoes and make it snappy!'
the chef ordered, as Boyd left the kitchen with a last beseeching
look at Trina. He was pretty sure that she wouldn't let him down;
she'd come to the rear entrance and he could tell her that Damon
was back and she must prepare herself for trouble. Who knew what
that fellow would do, now that he was back in Edgemuir?

The November evening was dark and chill, not the time to go
walking, but Boyd, fastening his jacket and putting on his cap,

couldn't face going home, to pretend everything was all right when he had a terrible feeling in his stomach that everything could soon be all wrong. What to do? He let himself out of the hydro, leaving behind its warmth and comfort to face the wind that had risen and was gathering strength, and found himself making for the hills. Not a good idea in the darkness, but he didn't care where he went, as long as he was back by the time Trina's duties were over and he could see her and speak to her.

Up and up he went on a well-worn path, stopping once or twice to look back at the lights of the hydro and the town, glad of the wind against his face, eager to be struggling with nature rather than his thoughts, until he knew it was time to go back. Mustn't risk Trina going to meet him and leaving because he wasn't there. Oh, God, no!

He began to hurry, slipping down the hillside, lucky to stay upright in the wind, so grateful, when he reached the rear of the hydro, to find Trina just arriving, even though she was looking far from pleased.

'What's all this about?' she demanded, as they moved into the back vestibule used by staff for coats and storage. 'It's freezing here and I'm not staying long, I can tell you.' Taking a closer look at him in the poor light from a low-watt bulb, she frowned. 'And what's up with you, Boyd? You look as though you've been pulled through a hedge backwards.'

'I went up to the hills, waiting for you.'

'At this time of night? You're crazy. Just tell me what's so important and then we can go.'

'Trina, this *is* important. Damon's back in Edgemuir – he's working at the new café in the High Street. You have to watch out, in case he tries to see you.' Boyd held her hands fast in his. 'And you know what he's like. If anyone's crazy, it's him, so you must be careful.'

She stared at him, her dark eyes wide, then looked away. Boyd, watching closely, waited for her to say something, but she said nothing.

'You don't seem surprised,' he said at last.

'Well . . .' She gave a little laugh. 'I was going to tell you. The other day, I was just doing a bit of shopping after we'd done the lunches when I bumped into Damon. In the High Street. Talk about surprise!'

For a long moment, Boyd couldn't speak. He felt as though Trina had hit him, punched him with all the strength of a man, and though it was all imaginary, standing in front of her, he almost felt himself reeling.

'Bumped into him?' he got out, loosening her hands from his. 'The other day?'

'I really was going to tell you, Boyd.'

'But you didn't tell me.'

'Only because – well, I thought you'd make a fuss.'

'A fuss? Why wouldn't I make a fuss? Think about what he did, Trina. Picked a fight with me, nearly lost me my job, called you all the names under the sun – now he turns up again and you think I shouldn't make a fuss?'

'The thing is, Boyd, he was so nice. Honestly, he was. And he's sorry – really sorry for what he did.'

'*So nice?*' Boyd repeated. '*Sorry?* For God's sake, Trina, why are you defending him? When you know what he's like?'

Trina hesitated, her face very serious. 'I know he can be difficult, but at heart he doesn't mean to be, and I feel bad because it was just because of me that he caused all the trouble.' She put her hand on Boyd's arm. 'You can understand how he felt, eh?'

'Know what he told Isla, this good-at-heart fellow?' Boyd asked grimly. 'That he didn't want to see me. So, he's not apologizing to me, is he? He's not sorry he came round to the gym and would have beaten me up if I hadn't knocked him out. All he wants, Trina, is to be with you again, and that's not going to happen, is it?'

As Trina, not looking at him, removed her hand from his arm, Boyd snatched it back.

'Look at me, Trina! Tell me you told him you wouldn't see him again. You did, didn't you? Because you're with me now. You chose me, and you've said you love me, just like I love you. There's no place for Damon in our lives and he'd best get the hell out of Edgemuir before there's more trouble.'

'He didn't ask to see me again, Boyd.' She gave a quick shrug. 'So I didn't have to say anything to him. Mind if I go now? I'd really like to get on with things.' She ran her hand through her thick black hair. 'Don't get much time, you know.'

'That's all you have to say?' Boyd asked quietly.

'Why, what else is there? Let's not get all worked up about Damon, eh?' Reaching up, Trina pulled Boyd's head down and kissed him lightly before stepping back to the door. 'All right? I'll see you tomorrow. Goodnight, then.'

'Wait.'

It was his turn then to kiss her, but though it was passionate and she responded as she always did, it brought him no pleasure. All he could think of was that she had defended Damon Duthie and that he'd never expected it of her. Not after the way Damon had treated her before he left the hydro. She'd been so shocked, so surprised he could behave like that to her, that she'd obviously believed it when she'd said she never wanted to see him again. And Boyd had been happy. But that was then – and now everything was different. So different he could hardly face it.

As he watched Trina hurry away from him and he began his own slow walk home, it came to him that what he must keep in his heart was hope. Forget that Trina had defended Damon. Just hope that nothing would come of the fellow's return, and that Trina wouldn't see him again. And that all would be for her and Boyd as it had been before this evening happened.

Was it some poet who had said, 'Hope springs eternal'? Boyd knew for him it must be true. For without hope, he couldn't see how he could endure what his life would be like.

Forty-Eight

The November days went by, and suddenly it was December and Christmas was looming ahead. Not that all Scots celebrated the festival, some preparing to concentrate on Hogmanay, and some firms not even closing for Christmas Day. This was not the case with Meredith's Woollen Mill in Edgemuir which shut down completely for a two-day holiday, with the workers also being treated to a party organized by the management, something Nan particularly enjoyed and was constantly urging Isla and Boyd to attend.

'Now, do you think you'll manage it?' she asked, when Isla had looked in one afternoon and was sneaking a peep at her mother's Christmas cake, stored away in all its richness until it was time for it to be iced. 'It's not till the Wednesday before Christmas, so you've time to organize it.'

'Depends what I'm doing then, Ma.' Isla replaced the lid of the cake tin. 'I'll have to let you know nearer the time.'

'And see if you can get Boyd to come. He's been in such a mood lately, I hardly dare speak to him.' Nan sniffed in disapproval. 'It'll be something to do with that girl I've never been allowed to meet. I suppose you'll know all about it, eh?'

'Not really, Ma,' Isla answered uneasily. 'He doesn't confide in me.'

'Aye, she'll come between him and all of us, I reckon. But try to see Boyd, eh? Your dad and me'd like both of you to come to the do – it's always a grand night out.'

'I'm not promising anything, but I'll see what Boyd says. Now, I've got to go.'

'Like always,' sighed Nan.

If only she could get Boyd to say something with any meaning, Isla thought on her way back to the hydro, but talking to him lately, she'd hardly managed to get a word out of him. It had been a case of: 'How are you, Boyd?'

'Fine.'

'Seen anything of Damon?'

'Nothing at all.'

'What does Trina think about him coming back?'

'We don't talk about him.'

Every time Isla had sought her brother out, there had been a similar exchange, which had been of no help at all and had only made her anxious that he was keeping something from her. Something to do with Damon, which did not promise well for future peace, but what could she do about it? Trina would never allow her access to her private life, which meant that with Boyd's unwillingness to talk, Isla would just have to accept that their lives were their business and nothing to do with her.

Yet that was hard, when she and Boyd had always in the past been close enough to share their troubles, even if they'd had disagreements over them. Still, if she couldn't bring the old ways back, Isla felt she might at least find out if Boyd wanted to go to Meredith's Christmas party.

'Oh, God, is it that time again?' he groaned, when she asked him. 'The last thing I want to do is spend time playing games at Meredith's.'

He sighed and ran his hand over his brow, while Isla, studying

him, thought that he looked thinner, even careworn. Could that
be? Her handsome brother, always so fit, looking careworn? Or was
some secret worry eating away at his health?

'It'd please the folks,' she said quietly.

'Maybe.' Boyd was shaking his head. 'But I've got too much on
my mind to go to that sort of do. I'm sorry.'

It was the nearest he'd got to admitting that there were problems
for him, and Isla impulsively caught at his hand.

'Boyd, won't you tell me what's wrong? I know there's something.
Maybe I can help.'

For answer, he jerked his hand away. 'Isla, just leave it, eh? There's
nothing wrong – nothing that can't be sorted out.'

'If you say so,' she said slowly. 'But Ma says it's very difficult
to talk to you these days. That's why she asked me to see what I
could do.'

'Don't worry about it. I'll speak to her myself.'

'All right, then.'

Heavy of heart, Isla made her way back to the treatment rooms,
where she was surprised to find Noreen from Reception looking
for her.

'Letter for you, Isla – just come by second post.'

'A letter? I don't usually get letters sent here.'

'Probably a Christmas card.' Noreen, moving away, laughed. 'From
a grateful patient, eh?'

Her guess was correct. The large envelope she had handed Isla
did indeed contain a Christmas card, a very handsome one, showing
an artist's snow scene, and the sender was, yes, a grateful patient.
For so he had described himself in his Christmas message, in firm,
strong writing.

To Isla, my wonder nurse, with best wishes for Christmas and the
New Year, and heartfelt thanks from her most grateful patient, Mark
Kinnaird.

Feeling her colour deepen and a smile begin to play around her
mouth, Isla quickly put the card into her locker, glad that no one
had noticed Noreen's giving it to her. There was no reason why
people shouldn't know that Mark had sent her a card – patients
often did send cards, and presents, too, at that time of year – but
somehow she didn't want to discuss Mark's card with her colleagues.
One thing was sure, though; it had raised her spirits, except for the

sudden realization that she hadn't sent him one. Was it too late? She didn't even know his address.

'Are you with us, Nurse Scott?' she heard Staff Craddock calling, and, blushing harder, took her place with others to hear Staff's order that everyone – 'when they'd time' – should lend a hand in putting up Christmas decorations in the main rooms of the hydro. There were boxes of streamers set out ready at Reception, and bags of holly, and the tree – kindly donated as usual by Dr Lorne – was already in place in the entrance hall. Miss Guthrie knew where the decorations were for that and she'd be getting them out tomorrow.

'Do what you can, then, everybody,' Staff finished brightly. 'I know you'll say you haven't got time, but a lot of the patients will be going home for holiday soon, which means there won't be so much to do.'

'So why are we decorating?' asked Sheana. 'I mean, if there'll be no one but us to see what we do?'

'Not everyone will be leaving, Nurse, and we must do our best for those who stay. Now, let's get back to work, shall we?'

'I still think it's a waste of time,' Sheana said in a low voice. 'But roll on Christmas anyway, eh? I've got the two days off.'

'So've I,' said Ellie. Isla was about to say she only had Christmas Day when a tall, gangling young man wearing a waiter's suit came wandering uncertainly into the crowd of nurses who were about to find their patients. This was Ben Ferryman, the replacement for Damon Duthie, a shy fellow not yet used to coming out of places he knew, though some thought he'd be glad to get away from Mr Paul's hectoring even for five minutes.

'Yes, what is it Mr Ferryman?' Staff Miller asked briskly. 'Are you looking for somebody?'

'Er . . . yes,' he answered cautiously. 'Mr Paul's sent me to find her, because she didn't come to serve the lunches, but I don't know where to look.'

'Who didn't serve the lunches? What's her name?'

'Miss Morris. We call her Trina.'

Trina? Isla's heart missed a beat. She didn't know why she should feel so suddenly afraid. What was so worrying about Trina's not turning up to serve patients' lunches, then? She'd probably gone out in the morning and mistaken the time, or something, and would just come wandering in and flutter her eyelashes at Mr Paul and get away with the sort of thing he'd blow others sky high for. On the other hand . . .

But Isla didn't want to think of any other reason Trina shouldn't be at her post.

'Well, Miss Morris is certainly not here,' Staff Miller told Ben. 'In fact, I don't think she's ever even looked in on the treatment rooms. Not her sort of thing, I'm sure.'

There were nods from those around, Trina not being a favourite with the nurses. Far too full of herself. And not one who'd ever want to see sick people.

'I'd better try somewhere else, then,' Ben said disconsolately. 'But thanks very much.'

'Have you tried her room?' Isla asked, hurrying after him into the corridor as he went on his way.

'Went there first. No sign.'

'But I was thinking – could you check to see if her things are there?'

'Things?'

'Her clothes. In the wardrobe.'

Ben seemed mystified. 'Why shouldn't they be there?'

'I expect they are, but just supposing . . .' Isla hesitated. 'Supposing she's left? Gone away?

'Left the hydro? She'd never do that.' Ben was looking as nervous as though he'd attempted to do it himself. 'Not without telling Mr Paul!'

'Look, Ben, I've got to go, but Daisy shares a room with Trina. If you don't want to check it yourself, ask her to see if Trina's taken her clothes. Remember, people don't always give notice before they go.'

At least, Damon didn't, Isla thought. On her way to her patient, she was filled with apprehension that Trina might have done as he had done. To be with him. She had no reason to think that, didn't know if Trina had even been seeing him, but something was eating away at Boyd's peace of mind and almost certainly it was something to do with Trina.

How long before Isla could know definitely what Daisy had found? If the worst had happened and Isla's suspicions were correct, the news would be all over the hydro as soon as Daisy had made the discovery. In which case, Isla must try somehow to be with Boyd, for he would be feeling . . . But at that point, her mind closed. She couldn't even bring herself to think what he would be feeling.

'Isla, have you heard the news?' Sheana asked, running to catch her as she left the lift after escorting a rheumatic patient back to her room. 'You know Trina didn't turn up to do the lunches? Well, she's gone. Done a bunk. Daisy says there's not a thing of hers left in their room!'

Isla stood, still as a stone, as the news washed over her. So it was true: Trina had gone. Isla must go to Boyd, but she seemed unable to make herself move, even though Sheana's sympathetic eyes were on her.

'You're thinking of Boyd?' Sheana asked quietly.

'I don't know how he'll take it.'

'He might have already known she was going. She might have told him.'

Isla shook her head. 'He'd have told me.'

'I heard Damon Duthie was back in town. Trina surely wouldn't have gone with him, would she? After all the trouble he caused?'

'I must go to Boyd!' Isla cried, suddenly jerking into life, but Sheana was touching her arm.

'You needn't,' she whispered. 'He's here.'

And as Sheana tactfully left her, Isla saw her brother walking towards her. Or was it his ghost?

Forty-Nine

He could have been a ghost, he was so pale, so lacking in life-colour. Even his grey eyes, usually like Isla's, were so shadowed, so empty of expression, they might have been a spectre's.

'You've heard?' he asked. 'You've heard Trina's left me? Left the hydro?'

'I've heard,' Isla stammered. 'Oh, Boyd—'

'Didn't have the guts to tell me to my face – wrote me a note and asked Larry to give it to me after three o'clock. That would give them time to be well away.'

'*Them?*'

'Her and him. Don't ask me to say his name.'

Suddenly dragging his eyes from Isla, Boyd took a packet of cigarettes from his pocket and, with shaking hands, lit one and drew on it as though he couldn't do without it. He'd never smoked since his army days, and Isla, staring at him with wondering eyes, couldn't imagine where he'd even found the cigarettes.

'Don't look like that. I know it's forbidden,' he said shortly. 'But a patient left these behind and I say thank God he did. I couldn't have read that letter without them.'

'What – what did she say?'

'Look, I can't talk here – some damn fool will come past and want to stop. Where can we go?'

Isla was frantically looking at her watch – she had another patient to see in half an hour – but she must listen to Boyd, must do what she could to help him, though what that could be, she'd no idea.

'Outside,' he was saying roughly. 'We can go out of the side door – here, take my jacket, I don't need it. Shan't be long, anyway.'

Like a couple of fugitives, they made for the side door, luckily seeing no one until they were safely in the garden where, in the December chill, they were bound to be alone.

'What did the note say?' Isla pressed, shivering even with Boyd's heavy jacket around her shoulders, but he only shook his head.

'You know what it would say. She'd found him again and he was right for her; they were two of a kind – selfish, not willing to give a damn. She admitted it. I was much too good for her, things would never work out – God, I could have written it myself as soon as I heard he was back in Edgemuir! I knew she would see him again, and she did, but she never said a word, just left me waiting for the blow to fall.'

Even in the cold, Boyd was sweating and paused to wipe his brow. 'Isla, I was on the rack, but it's true – she didn't give a damn, didn't care what she put me through. And now . . . now she's gone and I despise her. But I can't do without her – I don't know what I'm going to do!'

'Oh, Boyd!' Isla whispered. She would have thrown her arms around him to comfort him, but he wasn't ready for comfort and simply stood still, breathing fast and again wiping his brow.

'The thing is, Isla, I've got to get away. I can't stay – where she was, where I had all those stupid dreams. Of her loving me, marrying me, settling down – what the hell was I thinking of?'

'Boyd, what do you mean, that you can't stay here?' Isla grasped his hands. 'You can't leave. It's what I nearly did, but Mark made me see it was better to stay, and you must stay. This awful pain, it'll pass – I know – so where would be the point in running away?'

'Plenty,' he said definitely. 'It's different for me. I'm not running away. I don't care what folk think about me. All I want is to leave the place where she was and begin a new life. Cut out the memories, start from scratch. It's the only thing for me, Isla, and the sooner I face up to it, the better.'

'You wouldn't go before Christmas, Boyd? Think of Ma and Dad; they're going to be so upset anyway, but at least you could let them have that, eh?'

He waited for some moments before replying, no sign of his thoughts changing the blankness of his face. Finally, he shrugged.

'OK, I'll stay. Just till after Christmas. I needn't be like her, not giving notice. Doctor Lorne doesn't deserve that of me.' He gave a great shuddering sigh. 'I'll tell him it's a personal matter, me leaving. He might even give me a reference.'

'It won't be the same here without you,' Isla said in a low voice, her eyes filling with tears. 'But you will keep in touch?'

'I will.' Boyd took her arm. 'Come on, you're getting frozen; let's go inside.'

Back in the warmth of the hydro, they looked at each other.

'I have a patient,' Isla whispered.

'And I should open up the gym again, but I can't. Not today. I've put up a notice' – Boyd laughed briefly – 'owing to illness, et cetera . . . But now I'm going to walk.'

'Where?'

'Anywhere.'

'Take care, then.'

'Oh, I'll take care! I'm not giving anybody the satisfaction of anything happening to me.'

'Boyd!'

'Look, don't worry. And, Isla . . .'

'What?

'Thanks.'

'I didn't do anything.'

'For being with me,' he said quietly.

And they went their separate ways.

Fifty

That Christmas Day, spent by Isla at home, was the strangest she'd ever known. It was as though they were all, except for Boyd, playing a part they'd learned – going through the motions of having a good time, opening presents, enjoying Ma's cooking, laughing over Dad's jokes as he opened the Christmas port. But none of it was real. Only Boyd was real in his silence, his failure to join in. Only the darkness that surrounded him was genuine.

He did agree to play rummy after they'd finished the Christmas meal and cleared away, but when, as usual, he'd won and the cards were gathered up, he relapsed into another silence which drove Nan to speak.

'Oh, Boyd, don't take it so hard, eh? She's not worth it.'

'Makes no difference.'

'I don't see why you have to leave your job, though. You're happy at the hydro – why give it up?'

'I *was* happy. Now I need to get away.'

'And do what?' asked Will, for the first time feeling able to question Boyd.

'I'll find something.'

'In the week before Hogmanay? Never!'

'I'll have to find somewhere to live first. I can stay at the YMCA to start with, till I find a bedsitter. Then I'll look for work.'

'Why not stay here with us?' cried Nan, 'Go into Edinburgh by train – a lot do that, eh? You've got your own bed, you'll have proper meals—'

'Ma, I need a new life. An independent life. Doctor Lorne's given me a good reference, I'll find something to suit, and I'll come back to see you from time to time – no need to worry about that. But I'm not staying in Edgemuir.'

With a sigh of defeat, Nan slowly rose and said she'd put the kettle on.

'Isla's to get back to the hydro, she'll want her tea. And Christmas cake.'

'Christmas cake? Ma, I don't think I can manage it.'

'Sure you can. And you can take a bit back with you and all.'

'I'll walk you back,' said Boyd. 'Could do with some air.'

'It'll seem funny, you not going back to the gym after the holiday,' Will remarked. 'What's going to happen to it?'

'Oh, there's no worry there. Larry's taking it on. He's got some experience, should do well.'

'And what about the saunas?' asked Isla. 'Larry can't do both.'

'They're going to advertise for somebody. So, Ma, what about that tea? Want me to give you a hand?'

She shook her head, sudden tears making her hurry away, and silence fell once more.

At least Boyd had been talking again, thought Isla, and some of the pall over him appeared to have lifted just a little. But, as it had been for her, so it would be for him; the only thing that would really help was time and its progression. One day, as she'd told him, the pain would go. You just had to wait until it did. Easy to say, eh?

After they'd had tea and managed a piece of Ma's delectable cake, Isla put on her coat and hat and hugged her parents in farewell, willing them both not to be too upset about Boyd, though there she had little hope of success.

'We'll see you again soon?' asked Nan, as Isla picked up her bag of presents and Boyd stood impassively by.

'Aye, we've got to see one o' you,' put in Will.

'You'll see me all right, but Boyd'll come back when he can. He's said so – isn't that right, Boyd?'

'It's what I said.' He took Isla's bag. 'Best be going.' He looked at his parents. 'I won't be long.'

Out in the cold air, he took deep breaths, slowing his stride to Isla's as they set out for the short walk to the hydro.

'Ever feel back there you're under a great soft blanket?' he asked after a few moments.

'With Ma and Dad? Not really. It's just that they care about us.'

'Best not to live at home, though, once you've grown up.'

Isla gave him a quick glance. 'You're looking forward to going now?'

'Suppose I am. As long as I find the right job.'

'At least you've got a good reference. Nice that Doctor Lorne was so understanding.'

'Yes, I appreciate that. His daughter wished me well and all.'

'What, Miss Lorne?' Isla was interested. 'I knew she was back for Christmas, but I didn't know she'd seen you. Did she come to the gym?'

'No, she just happened to be with her dad when he gave me the reference. Had some friend staying until Christmas Eve, I believe.'

'Fancy her being so polite! Wishing you well!'

'Oh, she's all right.' Boyd's voice had trailed away, as though he could make no more chat, and it wasn't until they reached the hydro that he spoke again.

'Isla, we'll keep in touch, eh? When I get an address, I'll send it.'

'I'm feeling like Ma,' she said shakily, 'wanting to cry.'

'Och, I'm only going to Edinburgh!'

She shook her head. 'No, Boyd, much further than that. Things will never be quite the same again.'

They hugged, exchanged long solemn looks, then Isla rang the bell of the main door. After Tam had admitted her, she looked back once at Boyd, who waved. Then the door was shut and locked, and he turned abruptly away.

Fifty-One

Although she still greatly missed Boyd, Isla found herself accepting, in the dreary weeks of January, that she would no longer see him around and that Larry Telford had his job at the gym and seemed to be doing well. The arrival of Bart Angus, the ginger-haired young man who now looked after the saunas, had caused hardly a ripple, he being so quiet, and with the return of Magda Lorne to Switzerland, and Dr Morgan keeping everything on an even keel, life at the hydro seemed to have become boringly quiet.

Not that Isla complained. These days, a quiet life suited her, for having had her fill of passionate exchanges and anguish, she was relishing being free again of any burden of unrequited love. Sometimes she thought of Mark Kinnaird and realized she still missed him, too, and was glad he'd sent her a card at Christmas. Her own card to him would have been late, but still she'd sent one, had kept in touch. She rather wished she might have heard from him again, but so far that hadn't happened. No doubt, back in his own busy life, he'd forgotten her. That was the way things went.

As for Boyd, she longed for the time when he would be like her – free of his burden of love – but there was no hope of that just yet, for whenever she saw him, on his hurried visits home, it was plain he was not yet himself. He seemed to be settling into his new life, though, having found not only a bedsitter but also a job, working as assistant to a sports master in an Edinburgh school. Not doing any teaching, but helping to look after equipment, standing in for supervision duties, generally making himself useful.

'Not the same as being in charge, like I was at the hydro,' he told Isla one February evening when they were both at home and alone in the parlour. 'But it's given me the idea of going into teaching myself. In fact, the chap I work for said I should look into that. Maybe apply for training.'

'Why, Boyd, that would be wonderful!' Isla's eyes were shining. 'And you do seem – you know . . .'

'Better?' He shook his head. 'Not yet.'

'Too soon, I know. But I'm sure you're managing better than you thought you would?'

'I'll tell you something that's helped,' he said after a pause. 'Though it's not easy to talk about.'

'Tell me anyway.'

'Well, you know I don't like to talk about the war? Never have, never want to. But there was one night, a couple of weeks ago, when I felt – oh, God, I don't know – I felt so bad, I was thinking – sounds crazy – I couldn't go on.'

Reluctantly, Boyd's eyes met Isla's and, seeing the fear in their depths, he looked away.

'Just couldn't go on. Can you imagine I'd feel like that, Isla?'

'No, no, Boyd, I can't imagine that. I won't.'

'No, well, suddenly – it was the oddest thing: all their faces came back to me. All the faces of the fellows I'd known, at the front. And I seemed to see what happened to them all over again, and when I'd seen it Isla, seen them, I was so ashamed. I thought of what they'd gone through, what they'd have given for life, and I thought, here I was, acting up like a spoiled wee bairn, when I'd got what they'd lost.' Boyd put his hand to his eyes and for some time was silent. Then he took his hand away.

'And I tell you, Isla, I decided I couldn't face wondering what they'd have thought of me, and I made up my mind I'd never let myself get so low again over Trina Morris, never.'

'That's good, Boyd, that's right,' Isla said earnestly. 'But those pals of yours, they wouldn't blame you for feeling bad over Trina. They'd have understood.'

'Maybe.' Boyd smiled grimly. 'But you know what sparked it off – that terrible feeling I had? She told me they were married.'

'Trina and Damon married? No, I don't believe it. When? When did she tell you?'

'Sent me another note. To let me see there was no hope, I suppose.' Boyd shrugged. 'Apparently, it was a registry office wedding, all very quick, and now they've gone to London. Got work in some posh hotel. End of story.'

'Oh, I hope so!' Isla cried. 'I do hope so!'

'Now, what are you two doing, sitting in here in the cold?' asked Nan, bouncing in, very flushed in the face from the heat of her stove, and waving a spoon. 'Come away and get warm in the kitchen. Your dad's home and the cottage pie's all ready, so look sharp now!'

'Grand to see you two home together again,' Will remarked, when they were tackling the cottage pie at the kitchen table. 'And looking so well, eh?'

'Glad you think so,' muttered Boyd, staring at his plate.

'Well, you do look better, Boyd,' Nan said firmly. 'I knew you would, soon as you got shot of that girl.'

'You never even met her.'

'Didn't want to see me, did she? But I saw that terrible Doctor Revie and I expect she was the same. Wrong for you, like he was wrong for Isla. Just remember, there's far better fish in the sea than ever came out of it, eh?'

'Yes, Ma,' sighed Isla.

'Who's looking for fish?' asked Will, and even Boyd managed to laugh.

Fifty-Two

As the year progressed into spring, worries began to grip the country that it would soon be heading for industrial unrest. A general strike, no less, if the unions had their way and workers came out in support of the miners. Whatever would ordinary folk do? The newspapers were saying that all railway workers would be called out, and the tram drivers, dockers, iron and steel workers – anybody who could cause a shutdown of services. How on earth would people manage?

And what was it all about, anyway? Seemed you could blame the Germans for the start of it, some said, seeing as they'd been able to sell their coal again after the war, which had brought down the price of British coal. The mine owners, of course, still wanted profits and, when government subsidies ran out, made the miners work longer hours and cut their wages. No wonder the men wanted to strike.

Backed by the Trades Union Congress, out they would come, together with all those workers who were in sympathy with them, and then, for the first time anyone could remember, the country would grind to a halt. When would this be? On a knife edge, everyone waited for a date. So far, it had not been announced.

While so many were apprehensive of what might come – and their number included the patients at the hydro – the nurses at Lorne's felt a certain odd excitement at the thought of such a change to the nation's life and their own. No trains to and from Edinburgh, for instance. No trams. No goods coming into shops as the docks would be closed. What would Mr Paul do if he had no food to prepare for the dining room? Heavens, he'd be raising the roof! At least, it seemed the staff wouldn't be asked to go on strike themselves, but if they'd have drawn the line there anyway, most felt sympathetic towards the miners' cause, with only Staff Miller declaring that to withdraw one's labour was disgraceful, whatever the reason.

'Trust her,' commented Sheana. 'All I can say is I feel sorry for folk having to do so such terrible work underground and getting paid so little. I wouldn't do it for a fortune.'

'Nor me,' said Ellie, 'but they haven't got much choice. Where are the jobs for them if they don't go down the pit?'

'If only there was something we could do to help,' said Isla, who was feeling very despondent over the plight of the strikers' families. How would they get on with only strike pay to keep body and soul together?

'I suppose I agree with Staff in a way,' she added slowly. 'It does seem wrong for people to withdraw their labour, but if they're desperate, what else can they do?'

'Thing is, will striking work?' asked Sheana. 'I bet it doesn't and everyone will end up worse than before.'

'Don't be so depressing,' Ellie retorted. 'Let's wait and see if they call this general strike anyway.'

They – the TUC – did indeed call the strike, to begin on the first of May, and by the fourth of May, nearly two million men were out, which seemed to the strikers a successful start. Of course, volunteers were doing what they could to man essential services, but these appeared no threat, and as all proposals to end the strike were turned down, it looked as though a long debilitating dispute lay ahead.

'So what can we do?' Isla asked her father, who, as a staunch Labour man, was himself fretting that he could do nothing to support the strikers, as the woollen mill workers were not considered essential to the cause and were not being called out.

'I was going to tell you about something you might like to do,' Will now told Isla. 'Not that it'd be any real help, except to show sympathy for the miners. Maybe you could join a wee march some of us are laying on in Edinburgh tomorrow? I can't get time off and neither can Boyd. How about you?

'I could go; I've some time due to me. But how will I get into Edinburgh when there's no transport?'

'Is anybody going in from the hydro with a car?'

Isla thought for a moment. 'I think Doctor Morgan might be driving in to stock up on supplies from the pharmacy. I could ask him for a lift.'

'Well, if you can get in, meet at Shandwick Place in the West End at two o'clock and march down Princes Street to the Mound – we've got some good speakers there. It's grand you're joining in this, Isla – I appreciate it.'

'I never thought I'd be involved in anything political, Dad, not being interested usually, but maybe this is different.'

'Of course it's different! This isn't political; it's humanitarian.'

To which, Isla agreed.

Dr Morgan having said he'd gladly give her a lift, Isla, wearing her navy suit, drove in with him to Edinburgh, telling him where she was going and hoping it was all right with Dr Lorne that she should go marching for the miners. Not that she would have given it up even if the director had not approved, but Dr Morgan said there'd be no problem, for Dr Lorne had some sympathy with the strikers.

'I have myself,' Dr Morgan added, 'until I think about essential driving, but now I'm wondering how long my petrol's going to last. My garage told me there'd be no more petrol coming in until the strike's settled, and when will that be?'

'If they'd give the miners what's right, it could be settled tomorrow,' Isla declared, but Dr Morgan smiled.

'If the mine owners had been willing to do that, there'd never have been a strike in the first place.'

'"Not a penny off the pay, not a minute on the day" is what the chaps are asking for – seems reasonable to me.'

'You're not a mine owner,' said Dr Morgan. 'Now, this looks like Shandwick Place ahead – where can I drop you? And how will you get home? I'll be going back in an hour or so but I expect you'll be much longer than that.'

'Don't worry, I'll get home somehow,' she answered, realizing that both she and her father had forgotten about the return trip. 'But thank you very much for the lift in, anyway. I'm really grateful.'

'Telephone Lorne's if you're stranded,' he told her, looking worried. 'Don't want that.'

'Honestly, Doctor Morgan, I'll be all right. And if you let me out here, this'll be fine. I can see people gathering ahead.'

Waving and smiling as he drove away, she tried not to think of just how she'd get home and walked forward to join the crowd of people of all description, who were holding banners of support for the miners and jostling together as they began to march away.

'Wanting to join us, hen?' a woman asked, smiling. 'Come away, then. We're just starting.'

'Oh, yes, I'm joining you,' Isla told her, forgetting any worries about getting home as she fell into step with those around her on a Princes Street emptied of traffic. *Am I really marching?* she asked herself. That was a first for her. If only it would do some good.

She knew that wasn't likely, but as she strode along, she still felt cheered that she was doing something to show sympathy, even if it was only a token. In fact, she was feeling so much involved with those around her that she didn't at first notice a tall, dark-haired man marching a little ahead of her, but when she did, she couldn't quite believe it. Was it him? Probably not. Why would he be marching for the miners? Most Edinburgh lawyers, she felt sure, would agree with Staff Miller and think they shouldn't be on strike. All the same . . .

Suddenly, she was sure. It was him. It was!
'Mark!' she called. 'Mark, wait! Wait for me!'
And ran to catch Mark Kinnaird, marching ahead.

Fifty-Three

At the sound of his name, he had swung round, and when she
reached him, he seemed unable at first to believe that it should be
Isla from the hydro facing him.

'Why, Isla, is it really you?' he asked, after recognition had swum
into his large brown eyes. 'I thought at first you were a mirage.'

'I felt the same about you,' she told him, laughing, and thinking,
as they moved aside to the pavement, how well he looked. She had
never seen him so casually dressed as he was then, in sports jacket
and checked shirt, nor with such colour in his face and brightness
in his eyes. But even as she thought that, he gave a harsh dry cough,
and his face changed, his colour fading, his eyes losing their lustre.

'Damn,' he murmured. 'Take no notice of that. It's just because
I've been hurrying—'

'I was thinking how well you're looking,' she told him quickly.
'Better than I've ever seen you.'

'Yes, well, it's true. I am better, on the whole. I do cough, I
suppose – but why are we talking about me?' He caught at her hand.
'It's so splendid to see you, Isla, I can't tell you. And to find you
on this march – never in the world did I expect that!'

'You think I'm permanently trapped in the hydro?' Her own eyes
were shining as she looked up into his face. 'I'm sure supporting
the miners is not so surprising for me, but you – you're the surprise.
Surely lawyers aren't in sympathy with the strikers?'

'Now, why would you say that? Lawyers have feelings, the same
as anyone else, and I certainly have sympathy with those poor fellows
on strike.'

Mark's gaze held Isla's.

'When I think of their work and how they've to bring up a family
for a week on what I might pay for a bottle or two of wine, I have
to admit I feel guilty as hell. I knew I had to come on this march
when I read about it in the paper; it was the least I could do.'

'Snap!' Isla dropped his hand but took his arm. 'I'm sorry I was wrong about you, Mark; it was thoughtless of me.' She glanced at the people surging past them. 'Shall we go back to the march?'

'Together,' said Mark.

As they slipped back into the crowd, both so obviously pleased at meeting up again, there was, for Isla, something else on her mind, which was a small feeling of worry. Yes, only a small one – she didn't think it need be more than that – but what was the truth behind that harsh cough Mark had given just after they'd met? Perhaps it was just a one-off, brought on by the exertion of marching?

Was he better or not? Would he mind if she asked him about it if she got the chance? She'd just have to wait and see how things worked out. First, they had to get to the Mound.

Purposely holding back a little so as not to have him moving too quickly, she glanced across at his profile as he strode beside her, his fine nose and strong chin, and was surprised to realize just how handsome he appeared and how she hadn't always realized that when he was her patient. Of course, when he'd first been admitted, his looks had been coloured by his illness and the fact that his spirits had been so low. Even when she had come to know him better, she still hadn't defined his looks as handsome, only thinking that his face was truly kind and sympathetic. A nice face, in fact; one that pleased, but not perhaps to be compared with Boyd's classical looks or Grant Revie's obvious appeal. Now, seeing Mark again after an absence, she decided she wasn't so sure. He was a good-looking man and should be admired as such, as indeed he was admired now – by her.

Sensing her study of him, he turned to smile, at which she blushed and looked away.

'Mound coming up,' he announced cheerfully. 'And what a scrum is here already!'

The famous Mound that rises from Princes Street to give access to George IV Bridge and the Old Town, was originally formed from the earth thrown up when the New Town was created, but in more recent years it had come to be known as a meeting place. People would gather in summer to lie on the grass and look up at the jagged silhouette of the Assembly Hall, a meeting place itself for churches, while for speakers the Mound was a favourite spot for their public oratory.

On that day in May, when the marchers arrived, there was already a speaker on the Mound waiting to begin, while crowds milled around, some standing, some finding places to sit.

Mark looked at Isla. 'Want to sit down? I can spread my coat.'

'Oh, no, the grass will be dry enough. All we have to do is find a space. There's a chap getting ready to speak.'

He spoke well, whoever he was, not really saying anything new but putting the miners' case in a concise, easy-to-understand manner, which drew passionate applause. The second speaker, echoing the first, also asked for funds to help the families, and after tins were passed round, and Mark and Isla contributed, it seemed to them that they might be on their way.

'You're going back now to the hydro?' Mark asked, as they made their way from the Mound back down to Princes Street.

'To Edgemuir, but not the hydro. I've a day or two off and I'm at home just now.'

'And you have transport?'

She hesitated. 'Good question. I got a lift in with Doctor Morgan, but – well, I haven't organized anything back yet.'

A look of concern sharpened Mark's brown eyes. 'You mean you've no one taking you back? What were you thinking of? There are no trains, no buses —'

'I know, I was stupid. Doctor Morgan was a bit upset but he couldn't wait for me. He did say I could ring the hydro for a lift if all else failed, but I don't want to put them to such trouble. And petrol's so short.'

A smile lit Mark's face. 'No need to worry. Look, we're standing right outside Logie's. We can go and have something to eat and then I'll run you home.'

'You have a car?' she asked breathlessly.

'Sure. Got my own now; I'm not sharing with my father. If you don't mind walking back to Gloucester Place later, we can collect the car then.'

'Mind? I should say I don't mind!' She gave a nervous laugh. 'Mark, are you wearing shining armour? I think you must be a knight at least.'

'And you're a damsel in distress? No, come on! I'm starving. Aren't you?'

She didn't know. In fact, as she followed him into Logie's, the largest and grandest of Edinburgh's department stores, she wasn't altogether sure she wasn't dreaming.

Fifty-Four

At first glance, Logie's well-appointed, top-floor café seemed so crowded that Mark and Isla thought they might not get a table, until, as they were about to turn away, a stout Edinburgh matron left her corner table and a smiling waitress fitted them in.

'What a bit of luck!' Mark exclaimed. 'I was just about to give up hope of recommending the mushroom omelette.'

'You often come here?' asked Isla, studying the menu.

'Sometimes for lunch. They do excellent light lunches and suppers, but I usually have dinner with my father – we share a house and have a housekeeper.'

Isla was interested, wondering what had happened to Mark's mother, for it occurred to her that only his father had visited him in Lorne's.

'You'll have gathered that my mother's dead,' Mark said quietly, perhaps recognizing a question in the grey eyes turned towards him. 'I hardly remember her – she died when I was very young. There was supposed to be a brother for me, but I'm afraid Dad lost them both, and so did I.'

'Oh, Mark, that's so sad!' Isla cried. 'I'd no idea.'

'No, well, it all happened a long time ago.' Mark laid down his menu. 'Thought what you'd like to eat?'

'The mushroom omelette sounds lovely.'

'Right, two mushroom omelettes it is, then. And afterwards, shall we make it a real high tea and have some of their beautiful cakes?'

'I can't say no,' said Isla, smiling.

When Mark had given their order to a waitress, he turned back to Isla and asked her to tell him about her family.

'I know your parents are nice, anyway,' he added.

'How can you say that without seeing them?' she asked, laughing.

'Because I know you and I know Boyd.'

'Oh, Boyd . . .'

As she said her brother's name, Isla's slight change of expression was not lost on Mark, who looked at her enquiringly.

'Everything all right with him?'

'Not really. Well, in a way, he's better than he was, but he's left the hydro and is working as an assistant to a school sports master here in Edinburgh.' Isla sighed heavily. 'I'm afraid Damon Duthie came back to Edgemuir, and Trina left Boyd to be with him. In fact, they are married.'

'Oh, Lord, no!' Mark's eyes were outraged. 'I thought everything was settled between her and Boyd. How could she do that to him?'

'I think now she never really cared for him. She's a bit of a wild one, you know, and he was always too quiet. When Damon reappeared, she said he was the one for her and they went off to London together.'

'Two mushroom omelettes,' announced their waitress, at which both Isla and Mark fell silent, Mark looking so stricken, thinking of Boyd, that Isla eventually changed the subject by talking of her easy-going father and her more excitable mother, and of how she believed her family was a happy one.

'We've always been pretty steady, you know,' she remarked, after the waitress had cleared their plates and brought tea and their choice of delicious almond cake iced with chocolate. 'Even if Ma does get worked up from time to time. There's never been much money, but Dad's a foreman now at the woollen mill, and life's a bit easier all round.'

'To be happy at home, you've been fortunate, Isla. I suppose I could say the same.' Mark finished his tea. 'I've always got on well with my father. So, no complaints' – his face darkened – 'except for my damned chest, I suppose.'

Isla hesitated. 'How has it been, Mark? Since you left us?'

'Oh, I'm much better,' he said readily, though his eyes didn't meet hers. 'Still got a cough, but it's not bad.'

'Really? You do feel better? Be honest, now. I'd like to know if we really succeeded with the treatments.'

'You did, you did. I am better, honestly.'

'Better, but not cured?'

'Well, I suppose I'd have to say no, not altogether, but look, let's not talk about me. I'm OK. I can manage. So, I'll get the bill and then we'll go for my car.' With obvious effort, Mark gave a smile and rose to find a waitress. 'You must be feeling pretty tired, eh?'

'No, I feel fine.' Isla managed a smile, hiding her disappointment over Mark's present state of health after all their efforts to help him at the hydro. Well, they had helped him, and he was better than he'd been; she must take comfort from that. 'I feel as though I've done something for the miners, though, to be honest, it's not going to help a lot – what I did.'

'They'll be helped by any kind of support, the way things stand. Ah, here comes our girl – next stop, Gloucester Place.'

Fifty-Five

Although still worried for Mark, Isla had to admit to herself that she was also feeling a new excitement being with him, almost as though she was seeing him in a totally different light. And also, she was, of course, curious to see where he lived. This turned out to be a large stone-built terraced house in a quiet New Town square, exactly the sort of place she'd imagined as his home. With three floors and a basement, it was surely too big for just Mark and his father? Perhaps they only had part of it?

'You have the whole house?' she asked.

'Yes, I'm afraid we do. Seems selfish to have so much space, I know, but Dad came here when he was married, and he doesn't want to convert it, and I . . . well, I've stayed with him. Really would like my own place, but haven't suggested that yet.'

'I can understand, Mark. You don't want to leave him on his own.'

'Yes, I suppose that's it. There's no garage and only a strip of garden at the back, but we each have our own studies and don't get too much in each other's way.'

She couldn't help thinking this new Mark she'd found was a rather lucky man, materially, at least.

'And is this your car?' she asked, seeing the small blue car at the kerbside.'

'Yes, it's a Hillman. Not a bad little motor. Good on petrol which is handy, seeing as it's in pretty short supply at the moment.'

'I feel bad about your using it for me, Mark.'

'Come on, that's what it's for, to help someone out, especially at a time like this,' he answered swiftly as he unlocked the doors and they took their seats. 'So, let's away. I'd like to have taken you in to have a word with Dad, but he's at a meeting tonight. I know he'd have wanted to meet you again.'

'Please remember me to him, Mark.'

'Sure, I will.'

Driving back to Edgemuir in the still bright sunshine of the May evening, Isla found her worries over Mark's health gradually receding and just took pleasure in being with him in a way that seemed particularly special. There'd always been a rapport between them, and when he'd gone, she'd certainly missed him keenly, but somehow she'd just never thought of him, even when she'd got over Grant, in a truly romantic way.

After all, he'd never shown he'd thought of her that way himself. He'd given her the lovely Chanel, but patients did like to give presents, and after he'd left, he'd made no effort to get in touch apart from one Christmas card. True, he seemed delighted to be with her now, and it might be that he did care for her, and she just didn't know. Just as she didn't know about her own feelings for him — except that there was that new excitement she felt in being with him.

When they reached Edgemuir, she instructed him in finding her home, and when they drew up at the door and looked at each other, it seemed quite natural to ask him to come in for a moment to meet her parents.

'Why, I'd like to very much, Isla, but I don't want to disturb them.'

'Heavens, they won't be doing anything special, and they'd like to meet you, Mark. Especially when you've brought me back — I know they'll have been worrying.'

'If you're sure, then.'

Isla, of course, knew that she was on dangerous ground when she brought Mark in and introduced him to her parents, for though her father was his usual friendly self as he heartily thanked Mark for bringing Isla back, her mother was instantly making all the wrong decisions. An ex-patient from the hydro? The one who was a lawyer? The one who was already a friend of Isla's?

Oh, my, this is exciting, eh? What about some tea? Shortbread? A piece of sandwich cake? Nan was all of a flutter, and Isla was inwardly groaning, but what else could she have done? She'd had to ask Mark in, hadn't she? But when he'd gone, she'd just have to be very firm in correcting her mother's idea — very firm indeed.

In fact, he didn't stay long, thanked Mrs Scott for her offer, but said he must be back for his father's return when their housekeeper would have prepared supper. Not that he'd need much – he gave Isla a sideways look – after all he'd eaten at Logie's.

'Oh, you've been to Logie's?' Nan cried. 'Was that after the march? You must tell us all about it.'

'Now, Nan, we must let the laddie get home,' Will remonstrated, shaking Mark's hand again. 'But I'll just thank you again, Mr Kinnaird, for giving Isla a lift back. I was that worried, wondering how she was going to get home. Should never have let her go, if I'd had my wits about me.'

'It was no trouble, Mr Scott – my pleasure, in fact, to bring her home, and also to meet you and Mrs Scott.'

With final smiles and thanks all round, Mark left for his car, accompanied by Isla, who said she'd just see him out. Ignoring her mother's smiles, she wanted a moment or two to thank Mark herself for all his kindness to her that day.

'Look, I meant what I said to your father: it was my pleasure to bring you back and to be with you earlier. In fact—'

He stopped, keeping his eyes on her face.

'In fact, I was wondering . . . if we might – you know – meet again?'

Meet again? All she had been expecting was a fond goodnight! Now – well – her eyes returning his gaze were alight with true pleasure.

'Mark, I'd like that very much. If we can manage it.'

'Manage it? Why shouldn't we manage it?'

'I was thinking of transport – I mean, between here and Edinburgh.'

'Of course. I'd come over to you by car – there'll be no problem. I'll get petrol somehow or other.' Mark was smiling, as though relieved. 'All we need to arrange is when you're free. I know you're limited by the hours you have to work, but you do get evenings off sometime, don't you?'

'Oh, yes, of course. My next one's today week. A Friday. Would that be any good?'

'Perfect.' Mark's smile had broadened. 'Shall we say I'll come over about six to the hydro?'

Come over about six to the hydro and wait for her, probably at the gate? Even if she asked him to wait away down the road, it was all too much like the arrangements made by Grant Revie and she didn't want anything to remind her of those.

'Come into the grounds,' she said firmly. 'I'll be looking out for you.'

There would be no secrecy this time. They had nothing to hide, she and Mark, for Mark was no longer her patient and they were both free to do as they liked.

'And I'll be there. Till Friday, then.'

'Friday,' she repeated, and after a hesitant silence they drew closer together and, yes, exchanged a goodnight kiss, sweet in itself, but full of promise.

She watched, as he gave a last wave before driving away, leaving her to go into the house to face her mother's interest. Better damp down the speculation, she decided firmly, for in spite of all her pleasure at the idea of seeing Mark again, Isla had really no idea how things would go. Better just to let things happen as they would. That would be best.

Fifty-Six

'What excitement,' was Boyd's comment when he came to see his parents for Sunday dinner, having cycled over from Edinburgh. 'Isla's going out next week with Mr Kinnaird? Wonderful.'

'You're not being sarcastic?' asked his mother, serving Yorkshire puddings as his father carved the joint. 'You should be pleased for her.'

'I'm not being sarcastic and I am pleased for her. Mark Kinnaird's a nice chap.'

'A perfect gentleman!' cried Nan. 'And as different from that Doctor Revie as chalk is from cheese. Did you no' think so, Will?'

'Aye, I liked him.' Will passed the plates of beef he'd carved. 'Mind you, I wouldn't think there'd be anything in it.'

'Whatever do you mean? He's taken with Isla, that's for sure, and they've always been friendly – she said so.'

'Maybe, but he's a lawyer, eh? Might make a difference.'

'I don't agree. Isla's a nurse; she's educated and very bright, though I say it as shouldn't. Girls like her marry professional people all the time.'

'Oh, Ma, they've not even been out yet, and you're talking about marriage,' Boyd protested. 'And what might make a difference, I'd say, is not Mr Kinnaird's job, but his health.'

'Why do you say that?' asked Nan sharply. 'He got better, didn't he?'

'Who's to say he'll stay better?' Boyd poured the last of the gravy over his plate of beef. 'Just don't go getting your hopes up, Ma. Doesn't do, does it?'

She was silent, watching him eat, before finally turning to her own meal. He had seemed so much more himself lately; she hoped his thoughts had not gone back to 'that girl', as she called Trina. How well she'd got her hooks into him, eh? And all for nothing. What he needed was to meet someone else. Someone who'd care for him as he deserved. Maybe there would be a nice girl at this school where he was working? Something made her think, if there was, it would be a long time before she got to know about it.

'How's things at the school, then?' Will asked Boyd, as though Nan's thought had somehow conveyed itself into his head. 'Any news on that course you were wanting to do?'

'Oh, yes, I was going to tell you!' Boyd brightened as he spoke. 'I've been accepted – start in September! Couldn't be more pleased. I won't end up teaching arithmetic or anything like that, but I'll be able to be a sports master and that's what I want.'

'Why, what a funny lad you are, Boyd, not to tell us all this before!' cried Nan, but he only gave a crooked smile.

'When you were so full of news about Isla? I couldn't get a word in edgeways.'

'Now, that's just unfair, Boyd! As though I don't care about your news just as much!'

'Now, Nan, don't take on,' Will said mildly. 'Boyd doesn't think that, and you know it. Don't spoil a nice dinner, eh?'

'Och, I'll clear the plates,' she said, tossing her head. 'Who wants apple pie?'

'As though you need to ask!' cried Boyd, rising and giving his mother a kiss. 'Bring it on, eh?'

After the meal was finished and cleared away, they had some tea and studied the Sunday paper with news of the strike, which did not look hopeful.

'Says here the TUC met that Samuel fellow who did a report some time back, and worked out some proposals for ending the strike,' Will remarked. 'But the miners turned 'em down.'

'Which means they're no further forward,' said Boyd. 'Everybody says it'll be a long dispute.'

'I'm wondering now if the TUC might just give in, get the other workers back, and if the miners want to stay out, leave 'em to it.'

'Oh, no!' sighed Nan. 'That'll be too hard. They'll be no better off!'

'It's what I thought would happen all along,' said Will, folding the paper. 'The owners of the mines hold all the cards. When the strike pay runs out, the miners'll have to go back and it'll be on the owners' terms – mark my word.'

After that, there seemed nothing more to say, and Boyd said he'd better be getting ready for his ride back. Luckily, the weather was fine and he was extremely fit, though Nan still worried that he'd be doing too much, cycling all that way. At least, he could take some sandwiches with him and a slice of cake, which, to please her, he said he would.

'Can't promise when I'll come again,' he told his parents when they stood at the door, ready to wave him off. 'Depends on when we get the trains back. I don't mind doing the ride this once, but I don't fancy making a regular thing of it.'

'That's all right, son, we understand,' said Will, and with final hugs, Boyd left them, riding easily away through the spring sunshine.

'Grand to see him, anyway,' his father added, as he and Nan went into the house. 'I think he's a good bit better, eh?'

'He is, and this new idea of doing teacher training will make all the difference.' Nan, beginning to tidy her kitchen, was looking quite cheerful. 'Wouldn't it be nice if we could get our children settled, Will? It's all I want.'

'Shouldn't expect it just yet,' said Will. 'There's a lot o' water to flow under the bridge yet.'

Boyd had not ridden far – was, in fact, only passing the empty railway station – when he was astonished to see a young woman waving him down. And at her side was Dr Lorne. Dr Lorne? Well, of course. The young woman smiling at Boyd was, he now realized, Dr Lorne's daughter, who was supposed to be in Switzerland. So, what was she doing back in Edgemuir?

Both Magda and her father were dressed casually, she in a white summer dress and emerald cardigan, the doctor in a light jacket and twill trousers, and both were studying him in the sympathetic way he'd come to accept from those who knew his story.

'How nice to see you, Boyd,' Dr Lorne said jovially, unusually using his first name, perhaps because Boyd was no longer a member of the hydro's staff. 'Have you been visiting your parents?'

'Just for the day. It's nice to see you, too, sir, and Miss Lorne.'

Turning to meet her green gaze, Boyd saw that she was looking, as usual, very striking, her dark hair, now rather longer, framing the perfect shape of her face, her charming mouth still smiling.

'Like the bike,' she said lightly. 'Don't say you're cycling all the way to Edinburgh?'

'Well, there are no trains, as you know.'

'I certainly do know.' Slipping her arm into Dr Lorne's, Magda was suddenly rather serious. 'I came over from Switzerland to see my father – he's not been well, poor Daddy – and now I can't get back again. Not that I mind – I'm finishing soon anyway, and then I'm hoping to go to art school – if I can get in.'

'Of course you'll get in,' her father said fondly. 'You draw very well, I've always said so.'

Although he had seemed at first to be his usual self, Boyd could see now, as the doctor smiled down at Magda, that his face was thinner and there were lines at his eyes and by his mouth that hadn't been noticeable before.

'I'm very sorry to hear you've been ill, sir,' Boyd said, a little awkwardly. 'I hope you're feeling better?'

'Oh, I'm fine, thank you, quite all right.' The doctor laughed a little. 'There was no need at all for Magda to come over – just Miss Elrick being a bit over-anxious writing to her.'

'Daddy, that's not fair!' Magda cried. 'You were ill and needed me – I'm glad she wrote to me!'

'It was just a bit of trouble with the old ticker. I had to take it easy for a while, but I still covered for Doctor Morgan; we didn't need a locum. Now Magda's ready to go back, except that she can't at the moment. But tell us how you are doing, Boyd – are you enjoying being in Edinburgh?'

'I am, sir, thank you, it's working out well, and I'll be starting a teacher training course in September – I'm aiming to be a sports master.'

'Why, that's excellent, Boyd, really excellent! Let us know how it goes – keep in touch.'

'Yes, keep in touch,' chimed Magda.

There was a short pause before Boyd said he'd better be getting back – he wanted to avoid the dark – and the doctor and his daughter, agreeing that he should, watched him mount his bike and self-consciously ride away, waving once and not trying to look back.

'We'd better get back, too,' Magda said, turning away. 'Don't want you to be over-tired, Daddy, after our walk.'

'I'm not too tired and it's good to walk, but I'll have to admit, I'm glad I'm not having to cycle back to Edinburgh!'

'Oh, Boyd Scott is very fit – anyone can see that.'

'And a very nice young fellow. I'm so glad he's doing well, getting over his problems.'

'Handsome, too.'

'Oh, yes, he's considered so,' the doctor agreed. 'Though it seems his girlfriend didn't think he was handsome enough.'

To this, Magda made no reply.

Fifty-Seven

As the time drew near for Isla's outing with Mark, she found herself remembering her meetings with Grant Revie, and was relieved that this time all would be different. There would be no secrets over her seeing Mark; he was to drive directly in to collect her, not hide in the street outside, and to make everything perfectly open, she told all her colleagues one tea break what was happening.

'You're going out with that sweet Mr Kinnaird?' asked Kitty Brown, her eyes widening. 'Oh, I always thought he was such a dear man. Aren't you the lucky one, then?'

'Aye, how did you get so lucky?' asked Sheana. 'I mean, how d'you meet up with him again?'

'Don't laugh, but we met on a march for the miners,' Isla told them, and watched them all laugh anyway. A march for the miners? Talk about a romantic setting!

'Not that Sheana and me can talk about romantic meetings, anyway,' said Ellie. 'I mean, where'd we meet our guys? Right here in the hydro and it took 'em all their time to get round to asking us out even then!'

Everyone laughed again, for it had been a great source of amusement that Larry Telford, now looking after the gym, had taken months to find the courage to approach Sheana, and Bart Angus, in charge of the saunas, would never have got round to asking Ellie out if she hadn't done a little prompting.

'No, but seriously, it shows Mark is a caring sort of person,' Isla pressed on. 'I mean, to be thinking about the miners, when some folk like him don't think of them at all.'

'To be fair, some do,' Ellie remarked. 'At least, until the strike stops 'em getting the trains they want, and such like.'

'Might have done better not to have had a general strike,' Kitty said brightly. 'Maybe there'd have been more sympathy if the miners had just come out on their own.'

'They need more than sympathy,' said Sheana. 'They need the owners to pay 'em their proper wages. I bet that never happens, strike or no strike.'

Though not forgetting the miners and their woes, on the evening she was to meet Mark, Isla was preoccupied with what she should wear. It was a perennial problem for women, of course, but hers was special for she was determined not to wear anything when seeing Mark that she'd worn when seeing Grant. Which meant, of course, that she didn't have much choice, for after she'd cleared out all the clothes that reminded her of Grant, there wasn't much left. Oh, Lord, what should she do?

'Och, just wear a summer dress and a cardigan,' Sheana advised. 'It's a lovely evening – where's the problem?'

'You think this one will do?' asked Isla, holding up a dark blue dress she'd worn several times. 'Just with my white cardigan?'

'Perfect. Now get yourself away, or you'll be late. Don't want the poor chap sitting in his car in the drive and everyone wondering what he's up to, eh?'

'Oh, don't!' cried Isla, Dressing in haste, she dabbed on some lipstick, combed her hair and ran through the hydro to the front door, just in time to see Mark pulling in on the dot of half past six.

How had it happened, she wondered, that when she'd wanted to look her best, she'd ended up in such a scramble that she must look as though she'd been pulled through a hedge backwards? But as Mark ran round to open the passenger door for her and she took her seat, she quite suddenly relaxed, for she'd seen the welcoming look in those brown eyes of his and knew that he hadn't even noticed what she was wearing. He just wanted to be with her − that was plain − and as she wanted to be with him, on this first date they were together, she was truly content.

'I thought we'd take the Galashiels road,' he told her as they drove away. 'There's a nice little restaurant I know where we can have a meal, and then maybe walk a bit. That all right?'

'Sounds wonderful. And we're so lucky − it's such a lovely evening.'

Driving through the countryside, decked out in fine May colours, with all the trees and hedges freshly green and spilling blossom, Isla felt buoyed up with a serenity that was almost joy. Until she sensed that Mark was not with her, not feeling quite as much as she was feeling, and was instantly brought down to earth.

'Everything all right?' she asked cautiously.

'Fine. It's just that − well, have you not heard the news?'

'What news?'

'The TUC have called off the strike.'

A shadow seemed to fall over the radiant colours around them, and for a moment Isla closed her eyes. When she opened them, the shadow was still there.

'Oh, no,' she said quietly. 'No, Mark, it's too soon. They haven't given it time.'

'They've done it, anyway.'

'When? When was it called off? We haven't heard anything.'

'Only happened today. A client came into the office; someone had telephoned him from London.' Mark shrugged. 'It'll be all over the papers tomorrow.'

'What about the miners? Are they going back to work?'

'No, they're staying out. They're not giving up.'

'"Not a penny off the pay, not a minute off the day",' Isla said sadly. 'Who will listen to them now?'

For some time, Mark drove in silence, then he gave Isla a quick glance and shook his head.

'Look, I'm sorry, Isla, I shouldn't have told you − not yet. I knew you'd be upset.'

'Of course you should have told me, Mark! I am upset, thinking about the families, the poor wives and bairns, wondering how they'll manage, but I don't want to pretend nothing's happened. Where would be the point in that?'

'I know, I suppose I was just thinking – I didn't want to spoil our evening. Being selfish, you see.'

'It needn't spoil our evening.' She waited a moment, then said quietly, 'I like being with you, anyway.'

'Do you, Isla?'

'I always have. Even when you were a patient, I always looked forward to seeing you.' She laughed gently. 'Seem to remember crying on your shoulder once or twice.'

'And you told me I wasn't supposed to hold you, didn't you?' Mark was laughing a little, too. 'Well, maybe now's the time to tell you that I always liked being with you. If anyone came instead of you, I always felt badly done to, nice though they were. Just weren't Isla, you see.'

But Isla was thinking, trying to come to terms with the news, searching for a way to do something . . .

'You know, Mark, I can't help feeling guilty about it – I mean, having a nice evening with you, while the miners must be feeling terrible – but maybe we needn't have a special dinner? Maybe we could just go into Galashiels and have a light meal, or something?'

At that, Mark shook his head. 'You think that would help? We never have a restaurant meal again? I told you once I always felt bad, thinking of what I spend compared with what the miners can afford, but I don't know what the answer is. Except give to their funds.'

'But tonight, couldn't we find somewhere cheaper?'

'Would it make you happier?'

'I think it would.'

'Right, we'll make for Galashiels. Let's hope we can find somewhere.'

'If we don't, we can always go back to Ma's and I could make us omelettes. Without mushrooms, I'm afraid.'

'Ah, Isla, I don't give a damn about food!' Mark exclaimed, beginning to speed up his driving. 'We've said we like being with each other – that's what matters.'

Yes, that was the truth of it, Isla thought, for though this was the first time they'd gone out together, they already knew each other quite well. Already knew they liked being in each other's company, sharing that affinity she'd noticed from the very early days, and however they spent this evening, those were, as Mark had said, the things that mattered.

Fifty-Eight

As it happened, when they reached Galashiels, a busy Borders town, specially known for its textiles, they soon found a small café which was exactly what they were looking for. There were things on toast, sausages, fish pie or macaroni cheese, with jam tart or apple crumble to follow, tea or coffee, but no alcohol.

'Sorry, folks, we don't have a licence,' the waitress told them cheerfully. 'We reckon we're cheerful enough without.'

'Too right,' Mark commented when they'd ordered fish pie and apple crumble. 'This menu makes me think I'm a schoolboy again – all my favourites are here! How about you, Isla?'

'Well, we're not giving up much, are we?' she asked ruefully. 'I mean, these things are my favourites, too.'

'It is cheaper, though. As I said, we could put all we've saved on wine and such into the funds for the families.'

As she still looked dubious, Mark caught her hand.

'It was a good idea, Isla, and shows you're a caring person – which I knew, anyway. Maybe it wasn't practical, but it's worth something, to know we wanted to make a difference.'

'I suppose so.' Her brow cleared. 'Yes, you're right.'

Their meal came, and for some time they ate in silence, until Mark said, 'Penny for them, Isla. You seem far away.'

'No, I'm not.' She blushed a little. 'I was just thinking about something you said once. About having had your share of disappointments?'

'Oh, yes?' He smiled at that. 'Fancy your remembering.'

'It's not so strange. I was wondering – seems awful, asking you – who'd been disappointing you.'

She put her knife and fork together and sat back, her face still pink as her eyes slid away from his. 'You needn't say if you don't want to.'

'Isla, I don't in the least mind talking about them − that's if I can remember who they were! But here comes the waitress with our puddings. Hang on till she's gone.'

When they were alone, eating their crumbles, Mark said he'd have to take a trip down Memory Lane if Isla really wanted to know about his old loves.

'I do, Mark, just out of interest.'

'Can't see the interest now; it's all so long ago. But there were three heartbreakers, if I remember rightly. One worked in the admin department of the university where I was a student. She emigrated to Australia with a rugby player. Another was Dad's receptionist, about five years older than me − said she was too old and got engaged to a wealthy patient who used to come to the surgery. Last one − now, who was she? Ah, yes, Joanna, I think she was called − she seemed ideal. Met her at a dance a friend dragged me to − only in the end, she preferred the friend.'

Mark laughed as he finished his crumble.

'Isla, I was a broken man − for about a week. We're not talking about real relationships here − just the sort of casual thing a young fellow could get involved in. Probably it was the same for you in the early days?'

His tone was light and Isla knew he wasn't talking about Grant Revie; there'd been nothing casual about her feelings for him.

'Oh, yes, I did go out with one or two people,' she admitted. 'It was before I started nursing and there was never anything serious.' She lowered her eyes. 'That came later. We needn't say any more.'

'You won't mind if I ask . . . that is well and truly over?'

'Oh, well and truly!' she cried, looking up. 'And I couldn't be more relieved!'

'Let's have some coffee,' Mark said, smiling.

The light was finally fading when they came out of the little café and took their seats in Mark's car.

'Time's getting on,' he observed. 'I suppose you shouldn't be too late back at the hydro? Eleven o'clock, is it?'

'They prefer eleven,' she agreed, unwillingly recalling that she had once given the same information to Grant Revie. Why did such memories haunt her? There was no doubt that she felt truly happy, truly relaxed with Mark, and if there were to be comparisons, he came off better than Grant every time. Which meant that if memories of Grant came into her mind, they meant nothing. It was only natural that she should remember being with him, even though she was with Mark, because . . . well, you couldn't just cut out the past, could you? What you did was concentrate on the happier present, as she was doing now, as they drove through the darkening countryside on their way back to Edgemuir.

So far, Mark had not stopped in some secluded lane. Isla had been wondering if he would, but she somehow wasn't really expecting that he would. This was their first real date, and although she was over her feelings for someone else, he might be thinking he should be cautious, should not rush her. Yet they'd already had their first kiss and it had seemed to promise . . . well, more.

But as her mind was crowding with these thoughts, Mark did in fact turn suddenly off the main road. They had been driving by the river, a chain of hills not clearly visible in deepening darkness rising on their right, and very soon, Isla knew, they would be on the outskirts of Edgemuir. Where there would be people and lights.

'Shall we stop for a bit?' asked Mark. 'Just to say goodnight?'

Promise. If there had been promise in that first kiss outside her home, it was now certainly fulfilled, as they stepped out of the car and slid into each other's arms, kissing gently, kissing strongly, until slowly, reluctantly, after an age they quietly drew apart and returned to the car.

'Oh, Isla, you don't know how long I've wanted to kiss you like that,' Mark murmured, his breath coming fast and for a moment worrying Isla that he was going to cough. But he didn't, only continued to smile at her in the darkness, while she ran her hand down his face, then smoothed back his dark hair.

'And I've wondered if you would.'

'I never thought the time would come. But then we met again.'

'You knew where I would be.'

'Yes, but I didn't think . . . I didn't know if you were really – you know – free.'

'I'm glad you know now.'

'So am I!'

They were silent for a while, then Mark took a torch and looked at his watch.

'Help! It's getting on for eleven! I've got to get you back to the hydro, Isla.'

'It won't matter if I'm a bit late.'

'It will be easier if you're not.'

After his smooth, fast driving on the quiet roads, she wasn't late at all, which she was in fact relieved about as there need then be no teasing from her room-mates. First, though, there was the real goodnight which they said at the gates, without kisses, of course, but with quick pressing of the hands and exchanges of long looks.

'When can we meet again?' Mark asked, and after she'd given him the date of her next free evening, it was arranged that now the trains would be back, she'd travel into Edinburgh and they'd meet at Haymarket station.

'Should be in at six,' she told him, preparing to leave him.

'I'll be there.'

'Where shall we go?'

'Don't worry, I'll have something booked. Goodnight, Isla.'

'Goodnight, Mark. Thanks for the lovely evening.'

'My pleasure.'

And mine, thought Isla. More than she'd anticipated, perhaps. For so long, Mark had been her patient – now, he seemed to have become her lover. Was she his? This man who had been her special friend? Friends need not be lovers. But as she returned to her room, preparing to be quite noncommittal about her evening if anyone asked, she felt she was walking on air. A sign of being in love, if ever there was one.

Fifty-Nine

After that first evening together, Isla and Mark began to see each other as often as Isla's free time would allow, which wasn't as often as they would have liked. Sometimes, although she still loved her work, Isla found herself wishing she had a nine-to-five job like Mark, with every evening off, but really she knew she shouldn't complain; they still managed to meet regularly, and when they did – on long light evenings, or the occasional Sunday – she was totally happy, confident that Mark felt the same.

Sometimes, they'd meet in Edinburgh and go to a theatre or a cinema, sometimes stopping off at Mark's home, where they might meet his father and be given tea by Mrs Fernie, the housekeeper. More often, though, Mark would collect Isla from the hydro and they'd drive into the country, where they'd walk, spend time passionately kissing, and eventually stop somewhere for a meal before returning to Edgemuir, for a prolonged goodnight.

Only two things marred this new relationship for Isla. One was concern for Mark's health. She guessed that he kept from her any bad bouts he'd had, but there were times when he could not conceal his coughing, which he preferred her not to mention, and she could only feel frustration.

'It's difficult for me,' she told him once, 'I want to help.'

'I'm fine,' he answered. 'This passes. I can cope – no need to worry.'

At least, the symptoms were intermittent, and their being together brought such joy that Isla learned not to make too much of Mark's problems and tried to put them to the back of her mind.

But then there was the other thing that bothered her: why, when they were so obviously in love, had Mark never put his feelings into words? Well, of course, neither had she, but she was chary of being the first to speak, being well trained as a woman to believe that the man should make the first move.

It was simple enough, wasn't it? All he had to say were the three little words – I love you. They would mean so much; for women they always did. Many men, everyone knew, were happy enough to make love and never give a thought to what women might want, but Isla was sure Mark was not like that. He was one who cared for others; he would know, surely, that Isla, who had once been so hurt, would appreciate commitment, would need to hear those words lovers down the ages had always been ready to say: I love you. But Mark never said them.

There was nothing she could do and sometimes, she had to admit, she felt a bit down, even wondering whether there was a divide between her and Mark. He was, after all, a professional and from a professional family, and she was not, but she quickly dismissed the thought from her mind. Not just because she truly believed she and her family were as good as anyone, but because she knew Mark wasn't the sort to mind about such distinctions – and even to consider he might be was to do him an injustice.

But, then, there was his father. Maybe he did not approve of her? Parents' views could matter. Whenever she'd met Mr Kinnaird, though, he'd been most friendly and courteous, no hint of disapproval in his welcome, and the more she reflected on him, the less she thought he could be the reason Mark seemed not to want their relationship to progress.

On one occasion, when they were having tea with Mr Kinnaird in his handsome drawing room, furnished with heavy mahogany furniture, loose-covered chairs and a chesterfield, her eyes fell again on a photograph of Mark's mother, a sweet-faced woman with dark hair like Mark's and large expressive eyes.

How would she have seen me? Isla wondered, deciding that if she'd thought Isla could make Mark happy, Mrs Kinnaird would have welcomed her. Just as her own mother had welcomed Mark. At the thought of Nan, Isla groaned inwardly. It was getting more and more difficult facing her mother's bright questioning eyes when she had nothing to tell her, especially as the weeks were going by – soon it would be September – and Isla couldn't really say she and Mark didn't know each other well enough to be serious.

It didn't help that both Sheana and Ellie had become engaged. Yes, there they were, sporting their rings and talking of wedding plans, with everyone congratulating them, and Larry and Barty, and sending sideways glances at Isla, who was truly as happy for her friends as everyone else. It was not that she wanted a ring herself, anyway; only that she envied the plans for the future that the others had.

I should concentrate more on my job, she resolved; after all, that had always been so important to her. If her future were not to change, she must make the best of what she had.

But then, walking with Mark in Princes Street on one of her afternoons off, news came that made her wonder if even work was going to give its old satisfaction. And it came partly from Boyd, now busy on his teacher training course, and partly from someone whose appearance in Edinburgh could only be described as a surprise.

Sixty

Isla and Mark had been on their way to the National Gallery of Scotland on the Mound, where Mark had said he would like to introduce Isla to Scottish art. She had always freely admitted that she didn't know anything about art, never having had much opportunity to go to galleries, but she was very willing to learn, especially as it was an interest of Mark's.

'There are so many wonderful Scottish artists,' he had been saying as they made their way down a crowded pavement. 'Raeburn, McTaggart, Peploe – you'll soon get to know them – and we're so lucky here to have so many galleries to visit.'

'I'm looking forward to seeing them—' Isla was beginning when she stopped mid-sentence and, staring ahead, gave a little gasp. 'I don't believe it, Mark, but there's Boyd!'

'Boyd? What's so surprising? He works in Edinburgh.'

'Yes, but he's with Magda! Miss Lorne, Mark! Look at them – they seem to be together!'

Following her gaze, Mark picked out the tall figure of Boyd, though he was wearing a hat over his blond hair and wasn't easy to spot. The girl with him, however, was easy to recognize. She, too, was wearing a hat over her mass of dark hair, but her face, turned to Boyd's, was in profile and so distinctive that Mark had no difficulty whispering, 'Oh, yes, that's Boyd, and with Miss Lorne. Does look as if they know each other, doesn't it?'

'Quick, let's catch them up!' cried Isla, hurrying along the pavement and calling her brother's name.

He stopped and, as Magda stopped with him, turned to look back at Isla and Mark coming towards them.

'Why, it's you!' he called. 'Isla and Mark!'

'Hello, Boyd. Miss Lorne,' said Isla, thinking how well her brother looked, and how relaxed – surely, better than he'd looked for a long time?

'Er, you know Miss Lorne?' he asked Mark, who smiled and said he did, but she might not remember him.

'I was a patient at the hydro for a time – Mark Kinnaird.'

'Oh, yes, I'm sure we've met,' she answered, her green eyes studying his face as they shook hands. 'How nice to see you in Edinburgh – and Nurse Scott – or may I call you Isla? And you must call me Magda.'

'Thank you,' said Isla, marvelling at Magda's smooth politeness – Switzerland must have rubbed off some corners. 'I'm just over for the day, but Mark lives in Edinburgh. Are you at college now? We heard you'd left Switzerland.'

'Oh, yes, I'm at the art college here in Edinburgh.' Magda smiled.

'That's how I came to meet Boyd – just bumped into each other one day, didn't we, Boyd?'

'We did.' He too was smiling. 'I'm on half-term from my course at the moment.'

'And I'm playing truant.' Magda slipped her arm into his. 'But we're going to the National, so I think you can say that's arty enough.'

'I can see you're looking mystified,' Boyd said to Isla, 'me knowing nothing about art, but Magda's going to instruct me.'

'Snap!' cried Isla. 'Mark's going to instruct me. We're going to the National, too.'

'I'm not planning on doing any instructing,' said Mark. 'I just want Isla to decide what she likes. But why don't we all go to the National together?'

'That would be lovely,' Magda answered, glancing at Boyd, who nodded, and they made their way to the gallery as a foursome, deciding, on reaching its impressive entrance hall, that they should have tea first.

'I always say you should have sustenance before you start looking at things,' Magda declared. 'Otherwise you get too tired. Well, I do.'

'Excellent idea,' Mark agreed. 'Seem to remember they have rather good sticky buns here.'

'There you are, Boyd!' Magda laughed. 'It won't be so bad looking at pictures if you've had a couple of sticky buns first!'

'Hey, I have to keep fit, remember?' he asked, in a teasing tone Isla couldn't remember him using for quite some time. 'If I get to teach pupils, I'll have to set a good example.'

Watching her brother and Magda during tea, Isla was fascinated by the changes in both of them, for Boyd was as relaxed and easy in his manner as if Trina had never existed, and Magda seemed to have completely cast aside her frostiness to show herself in as pleasant a light as possible. What had come over them? Was it possible that they – Boyd and Magda – were . . . well, attached? Or, at least, very good friends? Isla felt she didn't know what to make of it and wondered if Boyd would ever explain, but then she saw him so rarely it would be difficult to pin him down.

As for Magda, it seemed incredible that she and Isla might one day have a special relationship. No, Isla couldn't see that happening. Couldn't see Magda and Boyd really having a permanent relationship. Supposing . . . oh, no. Supposing he got hurt again?

Sixty-One

Glancing quickly at Magda, Isla was surprised to see her sitting in sudden silence, staring at her plate, far away in thought from where she was. What could be wrong? A few minutes ago, she'd appeared happy enough not to have a care in the world. Now, clearly, something had come to her mind to upset her. But what?

Isla would have liked to help, ask if there was anything she could do, but knew that wasn't possible, and even as she was thinking it, she saw Boyd's hand reach out to cover Magda's.

'Please don't worry, Magda. He's all right, I'm sure of it,' Boyd whispered.

'No, Boyd, he's not all right,' Magda answered, her voice very low. 'He wouldn't be resigning if that were true – you know it's the last thing he'd ever want to do.'

Resigning? Who was Magda talking about? Something cold seemed to be running down Isla's spine, and she turned hastily to Mark to see if he had heard what she had heard and was thinking the same impossible thing. He had been looking at Magda, who was still holding Boyd's hand, but as he felt Isla's gaze on him, his eyes moved to meet hers with the same sort of questioning. Who was Magda talking about?

It could only be her father, Isla knew, though the thought made her catch her breath and instantly try to deny it. Resigning? Dr Lorne? No, it wasn't possible. He *was* Lorne's, he'd created it; you couldn't think of it without him.

Yet here was Magda, releasing her hand from Boyd's and looking straight at Isla, whose face must be showing what she was feeling, who certainly couldn't hide it, and saying she was sorry.

'I'm sorry, Isla, you must have heard what I said – I didn't mean to talk about it – just came over me . . .'

'It's Doctor Lorne,' Boyd said quietly. 'He's got a heart problem – angina – and high blood pressure. Seemingly never wanted to tell anybody.'

'I never knew until Miss Elrick told me he was ill and that I should come back and see him,' Magda said brokenly. 'Even then, he pretended he was all right.'

'Magda, he'll be fine,' Boyd declared firmly. 'As long as he takes care.'

'But he's been told he should give up work!' she cried. 'Give up work! And he's agreed. He's agreed to give up the hydro.' Her voice trembled. 'Can you imagine it? My father giving up the hydro? It's been his life – it's all he cares about!'

'Except you,' murmured Boyd.

'Oh, never mind about me.' Magda put her hand to her eyes. 'I just know he's very ill, or he'd never be letting it go.'

'He knows he has to.' Boyd turned his gaze towards Isla and Mark. 'Magda hasn't mentioned yet that things aren't going so well at the hydro – Doctor Lorne told her himself.'

'Not going so well?' Isla repeated. 'Why, I've never heard that; none of us has. What did he mean? We've plenty of patients.'

'Now, but not for the coming months, it seems. Bookings are down and there's talk that folk are going off the idea of the water cure. They fancy just going to hotels for "rest cures", apparently, and you can imagine what Doctor Lorne thinks of that!'

'It's ridiculous!' Magda said sharply. 'I just don't believe things are as bad as they say – Daddy must have been misled.'

'He's admitted he should retire,' Boyd reminded her, at which Magda's lower lip trembled and her eyes filled with tears.

'He's a doctor himself,' Mark put in gently. 'He knows he's doing the sensible thing, cutting down on stress and worry, but that doesn't mean he's dangerously ill now. I'm sure, if he takes care, as Boyd says, all will be fine.' Mark leaned forward. 'He'll be retiring for you, Magda; he'll know you want him to stay well – that's all it is.'

'You think so?' she whispered. 'I wish I could believe it.'

'You can believe it,' Boyd told her. 'Mark's right, your dad's doing the right thing and it's for you.'

'So try not to worry,' Isla added quietly. 'I know something of angina – the paroxysms can be very painful but they can be controlled with amyl nitrate, and if the patient doesn't exhaust himself, he's every chance of keeping going. Without the strain of running the hydro and all this talk of bookings falling off, I think Doctor Lorne will feel much better, honestly I do.'

'Thank you for that, Isla,' Magda answered earnestly. 'I feel better now, listening to you all. As long as Daddy's all right, that's all that matters – though I know no one will be happy seeing someone else in charge at the hydro.'

'Oh, that's true!' cried Isla, with feeling. 'We'll none of us be happy!'

'Would you mind if I asked you not to say anything about this for the time being, though? My father doesn't want to announce it until a new director's been appointed.'

'Of course, I understand, and I promise I won't say anything.' Isla's face was bleak. 'In fact, I don't want to talk about it.'

After a short silence, they all rose from the table and when Mark, allowing no arguments, had called for the bill, Magda apologetically said she didn't think she wanted to look round the gallery, after all.

'I'm sorry, Boyd, but I can't really put my mind on anything today. I'm just – you know – so low.'

'I feel the same,' said Isla. 'This news – it's just blocking out everything else for me.' She turned to Mark. 'Maybe we'll try another time?'

'Of course,' Mark agreed, while Boyd told Magda she didn't need to apologize: no one, least of all him, would expect her to go round the gallery when she felt so anxious.

'As long as you don't mind,' she said, sighing. 'It's too late for me to go back to college – let's just go to my flat.'

They were going back to her flat? Isla's eyes slightly widened and she knew that at one time she would have been intrigued and excited by this new relationship her brother appeared to be sharing with Magda. But now, all she could think of was the news she'd heard over the tea table and wonder desperately what the future would hold.

'Tell the folks I'll be over to see them soon,' Boyd whispered in her ear, and when she turned to look at him, the message in his eyes and the slight shake of his head told her that she was not to mention Magda. As though she would! The repercussions would be endless. Let Boyd tell their mother himself when the time was right, if that ever came.

When she and Mark had waved Boyd and Magda away outside the gallery, Mark said he'd drive Isla back to the hydro, where she was to be on evening duty, and they walked slowly back to his house to collect the car.

'I know this news from Magda has been a terrible blow for you,' Mark told Isla when they were driving away through the darkened streets, lit now by the mellow light of gas lamps. 'You've always thought so much of Doctor Lorne.'

'He was the reason I'm at the hydro at all, Mark. He made me believe in what we do, and I just can't take it in that people are turning against it.'

'Some maybe, but not all. We don't know too much about the situation yet.'

'I just feel too depressed to think about it.'

'Well, on to something different, I thought Boyd was looking very much his old self. Magda seems to have worked a certain magic.'

'Yes, I suppose so.' Isla heaved a sigh. 'As long as she doesn't let him down.'

'I thought she was much easier to talk to than everybody said.'

'That's true.' Isla, glancing at Mark in the dusk of the car, suddenly tried to smile. 'Oh, I'm sorry, Mark, I'm not being much fun to be with at the moment. I wish I'd been able to have had a quiet afternoon with you, looking at the pictures.'

'Good heavens, you've no need to apologize! You know I like being with you, anyway!'

Do you? she wondered to herself, returning for a moment to her earlier nagging worry. *Do you love me, Mark?*

As she could not ask the question, there could be no answer, and as she kissed him goodbye at the hydro and hurried into the workplace that might any day be changing, she felt problems crowding in on her like falling snow.

Sixty-Two

Act the part, she had to keep telling herself when she was with her colleagues. Pretend everything was just as usual. That she had no need to dread the future, wasn't sick with worry over Dr Lorne's health and the state of the hydro's bookings, and wasn't waiting anxiously for Mark to say the words she wanted to hear.

Certainly, everything seemed just as usual at the hydro itself, with Dr Lorne, when he appeared to relieve Dr Morgan, appearing cheerful, though Isla wasn't so sure that Joan Elrick wasn't also acting a part in looking cheerful, too. But then she'd already proved she could do a good cover-up when necessary, for she was the one who'd asked Magda to come to see Dr Lorne, yet she'd said nothing of his illness to anyone else. And he, of course, had kept it quiet.

As for the fall in bookings, nothing had been said, as far as Isla could tell, which made her wonder about the situation – until, very suddenly, Matron announced her retirement. And the news spread round the hydro like wildfire that she was not to be replaced.

'Not to be replaced?' cried Sheana at tea break. 'What do they think they're playing at?'

'Who's they?' someone asked.

'Why, those folk who run the company – the ones we never see but who make the rules, eh? Why should they say we can suddenly do without a matron?'

'Doctor Lorne must have agreed to it,' Ellie remarked. 'He has a big say in what goes on.'

'I'm wondering what Sister Francis is thinking,' Isla said, keeping her voice down in case the Sister or Staff Miller were around. Too late. Staff Miller, appearing suddenly from nowhere – a favourite trick of hers – had heard her and at once rattled out a reply on the Sister's behalf.

'I can tell you all that Sister Francis was fully informed of the decision not to replace Matron, and has accepted that she will be taking on some of Matron's duties. There's no need to add that she is quite capable of doing anything that is required of her, and I hope that the same can be said of all of us here.'

'But Staff, why don't they want to replace Matron?' Sheana asked. 'I mean, we are a sort of hospital, eh?'

Staff Miller pursed her lips.

'Obviously, it's been decided that someone of that rank is not absolutely necessary now. It's not for us to question decisions when we don't have the full facts. Now, if tea's over, can we get back to work?'

'Seems to me, Sister Francis is being exploited,' Sheana muttered as the nurses returned to their duties. 'Just hope they give her a couple of bob extra, eh?'

'If she's like the poor miners, she won't get a thing,' said Ellie gloomily. 'They've gone back to work and didn't even get their old wages back. "Not a penny off the pay, not a minute on the day" was what they wanted, but they couldn't last out any longer. Had to go back and just do what the owners said.'

Isla, remembering that the miners had not been in her thoughts recently, bit her lip and turned away. Seemed the strike and the hardship had all been for nothing, and she'd been so wrapped up in other things, she hadn't give the men and their families a thought. Oh, she couldn't say that Dr Lorne's health or the state of the bookings were of no importance – they were, they had to be – but she should have remembered the miners, whose struggle was for their very existence, who had been living on the edge for so long they had almost gone over.

Surely there must be a better way of organizing people's lives?

When she saw Boyd again, she put the question to him, but he only shook his head and sighed.

'The way of the world, they call it,' he told her. 'Money talks, always has – if you haven't got it, you've an uphill job if you want to change anything.'

They drank the tea they'd brought to a table in the hydro canteen, scene of many a chat they'd enjoyed when Boyd was one of the workforce. Now, of course, he had to be Isla's guest, when he'd taken time from his visit to their parents to look in to see her, and knew, after she'd spoken of the miners, what she'd want to talk about.

It was true, for though she'd plenty of other things to occupy her mind, she'd come round to wondering about her brother and Magda Lorne, and what sort of relationship was theirs, if indeed there was one.

'Come on, then,' he said, smiling. 'Ask me about Magda. I can see the questions already trembling on your lips.'

'Well, I must admit, seeing you together the other day was a bit of a surprise. How did it happen?'

'Like Magda said, we met in town one day – sheer accident – and got to talking. Then she said how about a coffee – I'd never thought to ask – and we went to one of the cafés, carried on talking and, in the end, went to the pictures. When we came out, we agreed to meet again – and it just went from there.'

Boyd, beginning to eat a buttered teacake, raised his grey eyes to Isla's.

'Hard to believe, I suppose? Doctor Lorne's daughter and me? but the truth is – I don't know how to put it, without sounding big-headed – she likes me.'

'I think I understand,' Isla said softly. 'She makes the running?'

'If you like to put it that way.'

'I've been worrying in case you got hurt. She could be such a heartbreaker.'

'She's beautiful enough, but you know what she told me? She's always liked me, ever since she first saw me here when she was still a schoolgirl. She said she'd made up her mind that one day we'd be together. Can you believe it?'

'I'm beginning to wonder now if she'll be the one to get hurt,' Isla said with a laugh.

'Oh, no,' Boyd said firmly. 'I'd never hurt Magda. Because I do care for her, you know? Maybe not quite as much as she cares for me, but she can rely on me. I won't let her down.'

'I'm glad, then.' Isla finished her tea and said she must get back to work. 'Just want to say, Boyd, that Magda does seem quite different, as though all the hard corners have gone. Don't you think so?'

'It's since her father's illness. She says it's changed her. She admits she was difficult before and says it all happened when her mother died. Her mother was everything to her and then was taken away, and somehow she felt the whole world was against her. Her dad, it seems, was nowhere.'

'Yet she seems so upset now over his illness.'

'She is, because she's realized how much he means to her and she's terrified he'll go, too.' Boyd heaved a sigh. 'You've no idea how insecure she feels, Isla. She does need someone.'

Isla shrugged. 'Such a privileged girl, Boyd? How many in the tenements would want to swap places, do you think?'

'Can't buy happiness, however you live,' he said quietly.

Outside the canteen, Boyd gave Isla a quick hug and said he'd better be getting back to see Nan and also Will, who would be home soon. Then they'd be having the slap-up meal Nan would no doubt be cooking at that very moment.

'Of course, you haven't said a word about Magda?' Isla asked.

'You bet I haven't! I'd never have got out of the house if I'd let on I had a young lady – and Doctor Lorne's daughter at that!'

'You might have to tell Ma some time.'

'I'll cross that bridge when I come to it. In the meantime, you'll not say anything?'

'Of course I won't.' Isla hesitated. 'How about Doctor Lorne? Does he know about you and Magda?'

It was Boyd's turn to pause, but after a few moments, he said lightly, 'Not yet. I expect he will, though. I'm leaving it to Magda. But listen, you'll let me know what happens here? I mean when Doctor Lorne announces what's going to happen?'

'I'll keep in touch. Remember me to Magda.'

'And me to Mark.'

'Oh, yes, Mark . . .'

As Boyd left her and Isla returned to the treatment rooms, she thought of meeting Mark at the weekend as they had arranged and how she was looking forward to it. And yet – and yet . . .

If only she knew what was in his mind! Sometimes, she doubted if she ever would know.

Sixty-Three

The blow that Isla had been expecting fell at last on a moist, dark afternoon in November following a farewell ceremony to Matron. As usual, this was held after lunch when the patients were resting, which meant that all staff were free to make their presentation and say their goodbyes – in this case, to Mrs Walker, or Matron as she was better known, who shed a few tears over Dr Lorne's kind words about her. And quite a few more after he'd put into her hands the handsome leather bag that was her leaving present, as well as a large bouquet of flowers.

'Oh dear, oh dear, I don't know what to say!' she exclaimed. 'You've all been too kind – and I'm going to miss you all so much! But, thank you – thank you, everyone. Every time I use this lovely bag, I'll think of Lorne's!'

'And now for tea!' cried Sister Francis, 'And, of course, one of Mr Paul's cakes!'

She seemed cheerful enough, but as she glanced back at Dr Lorne, her look seemed watchful, even apprehensive, and Isla thought, *She knows, he's told her.* And Joan Elrick, from her tearful face, obviously knew as well – but when would he tell the others?

Sooner than Isla thought, for when tea was over and Matron had left, and before the rest of the staff were moving away, Sister Francis raised her hand.

'Could everyone wait for a moment? Doctor Lorne has an announcement.'

People paused, their eyes turning on the doctor who had been standing with Dr Morgan – surely they could see, thought Isla, that he wasn't well? He had that look of an invalid that men always took on when their collars seemed too big for their necks, and though he'd been putting on a very good act, there was no doubt that he was not the man he'd been. His act continuing, he smiled as he moved to the centre of the room to address his staff, and held up a hand for their murmurs to quieten.

'I'm sorry to use this occasion of Matron's farewell to make my little speech, but it's difficult to get everyone together and it seemed a good opportunity. I won't keep you long – you have your duties – but I have to give you some important news. First, something sad, for me – as I have decided to retire.'

Retire? A wave of shock ran through his listeners, so strong no one could speak, or even gasp.

'I know this will come as a bit of a shock to most of you,' Dr Lorne continued, 'but these things happen. Sometimes the time is right for a certain course of action, and for me that time has come. I couldn't tell you before because I thought it important we should know who is to succeed me as director. I'm glad to say I can tell you that now. It may come as a surprise to you, but you will have no difficulty recognizing his name.'

Dr Lorne paused, cleared his throat, and looking nowhere in particular, declared, 'The name of the new director is Doctor Grant Revie.'

As a second shock wave hit the doctor's listeners, their eyes widened, their mouths opened, though sheer shock held them silent. And Isla, too, was silent; she too was shocked, yet, standing with her colleagues, felt only quite alone.

Grant Revie? The new director? It didn't seem possible. How could Dr Lorne have chosen him? Surely, surely, he hadn't?

Apparently, he hadn't chosen him, exactly, for, as he told his staff, the decision to appoint Grant Revie as the new director had been taken by the shareholders' board and had been unanimous. Almost certainly – though he didn't mention it – Dr Lorne had been asked to give his advice, which must have been favourable, for he said now that he was happy about the appointment. In fact, he had every confidence in the new director, who was young, had ideas and might well be just what was needed for the future.

Unfortunately, he had recently lost his father – here looks were exchanged between Isla and Sheana – but it was to be hoped that his new post would provide him with the kind of challenge he needed to help him recover from his sad loss. With Dr Morgan still at the hydro to be of assistance, Dr Lorne seemed certain all would go well for Lorne's in the future, and ended his announcement by stressing that he knew he would be leaving the hydro in very capable hands.

From such a ringing endorsement, it seemed he had nothing against the new director and had perhaps never known of his attempt to court Magda. Who could say? All that was certain was that very soon Dr Lorne would be gone and in his place would be Dr Revie – the last person Isla and others would want to see.

'All right, I was wrong,' Sheana murmured to Isla when Dr Lorne had returned to his office, accompanied by a depressed-looking Joan Elrick. 'Grant Revie didn't make it up about his dad, but that's about the only good thing I can say about him.' She studied Isla's withdrawn face. 'How about you?'

'I don't want to talk about it now,' Isla said in a low voice. 'I'm due to give Mrs Noble a herbal bath.'

'And I'm due upstairs, but I've got time to say I think I'll just leave. I don't want to work for Doctor Revie and neither does Ellie – we'll both be on our way.'

'Both of you?' Isla stared. 'I'm thinking of it myself – never thought of you two going too.'

'Well, Ellie wants a change, and Larry wants me and him to get wed. Why not? Maybe I've had enough of going to work.'

'Sheana, you'd be bored stiff in no time, staying at home!'

'Well, what will you do? Find a new job?' Sheana's eyes were bright. 'Or follow my example?'

'I think you know what I'll be doing,' Isla replied evenly. 'At the moment I don't have a ring on my finger. Now, I'll have to dash.'

'Isla, I'm sorry—' Sheana called after her, but Isla was hurrying away, already putting out of her mind Sheana's reminder of her usual preoccupation, thinking only of the Lorne's she'd lost, now that Grant Revie was to be in charge. As was only to be expected, nothing had been said by Dr Lorne of possible trouble ahead from reduced bookings, but if it was true that things were going to be difficult, there might well be a great shake-up at the hydro, whoever was in charge, and Isla would be well out of it.

Oh, how quickly things could change! If it hadn't been that she mustn't show any feelings before her patient, Isla would have been bursting into tears. As it was, old Mrs Noble still asked, as she had once asked before, if she was all right, to which Isla replied in the same words.

'I'm quite all right, Mrs Noble, thanks.'

Sixty-Four

Mark's reaction to the news of Grant Revie's return was, as Isla had expected, one of incredulity followed by anger.

'I just don't understand how that can have happened,' he declared when they were having a meal in a Princes Street restaurant. 'I mean, why has Doctor Lorne not vetoed the choice? Surely, as the founder of the hydro, his opinions had to be considered?'

'The point is that he seems to have nothing against Grant,' Isla replied. 'He never knew what Grant was like, and Magda seems not to have told him how Grant made a play for her.'

Mark drank some wine and shook his head. 'Such a shrewd man, Doctor Lorne – and never to have known what was going on in his own hydro? It was his job to know, wasn't it?'

'Who was going to tell him about Grant and me? That was just between us and nothing to do with work. Doctor Lorne always knew exactly what was happening where work was concerned.'

Mark smiled. 'You're very loyal to the doctor, Isla. I can see how much you're going to miss him.'

'Yes, except that I probably won't be at the hydro when he's gone.'

'Oh?' Mark's eyes widened. 'What's this, then? You're leaving the hydro? When? I'd no idea.'

'You think I want to stay and watch Grant Revie running the place?' Isla laid down her knife and fork. 'That's not for me, Mark. I stuck it out before, working with him, but to see him in Doctor Lorne's job – oh, no, I couldn't put up with that. I'll look for another job.'

'In Edinburgh? Why, Isla, that would be wonderful! It'd be so much easier for us to meet!'

Studying his smiling face, Isla returned no smile of her own.

'You're pleased?'

'Well, of course I am. I want you to be happy and there's no way you can be happy with Revie back and in Doctor Lorne's job. You're definitely doing the right thing. Do you think you'll find it easy to get a job here?'

She shrugged. 'We'll have to see, won't we? I've discussed it with

Ma and Dad. They'll be sorry if I leave Edgemuir, but they understand the situation. They're furious, of course, that Grant Revie's coming back to the hydro – Ma's face was like a thundercloud!'

'Guess mine is, too. What would you like now, Isla? Cheese or a pudding?'

'Just coffee, please. I'm feeling a bit tired, tonight; I don't want to be late back.'

Mark's brown eyes were wonderfully sympathetic, even loving, Isla thought as they rested on her, but she felt too low in spirits to think about love. Anyway, how could she rely on Mark's love when it was still leading nowhere? He seemed delighted that she was planning to work in Edinburgh again, but what would it mean if she did? Just that they would see each other more easily, then go on as before? And because she loved him, was that what she must accept? Best not try to face that one now, she decided.

'Of course you're tired,' Mark was saying. 'It's the emotional stress that takes its toll. I'll see you get back early to the hydro, don't worry about that.'

'I'm afraid I'm not very good company at the moment.'

'You'll feel better when you're more rested – and when you're settled in a different job, away from Grant Revie.'

Which was true, thought Isla.

'Put your notice in yet?' asked Ellie, when Isla was preparing to go to her bed. 'We're wondering when would be best.'

'I say before Grant Revie arrives,' said Sheana, rubbing cold cream into her face. 'Anybody heard the date?'

'Beginning of December,' Isla replied. 'I'll put my notice in then. Before that, we'll have Doctor Lorne's farewell.' She sighed. 'He's planning to be out of his flat next week, Joan says, so it can be made ready for you-know-who. Then he's going to stay at some hotel until he can move into his house.'

'He's bought a house?' asked Ellie with interest. 'Where?'

'In Edinburgh. Seemingly, he bought it some time ago. Must have thought he'd be moving on and would need one.'

'Well, whatever happens, this place isn't going to be the same without him,' said Sheana. 'What's Joan going to do? Did she say?'

'She thinks she might go, too.' Pulling on pyjamas, Isla climbed into bed and sat back against her pillow, combing her hair. 'She's not keen on being Grant's secretary.'

'Looks like the rats are leaving the sinking ship!' Sheana laughed. 'Only needs the patients to back out and there'll be nothing left for our new director to direct!'

Isla, turning on her side to try for sleep, made no reply. Obviously, Sheana didn't know that her joke might have more truth in it than she realized, not having heard yet of the concern over future bookings. Was there real cause for worry? Isla wondered. Probably, the hydro would keep going and Grant Revie would make a huge success of running it, but by then she would be elsewhere.

'Lights out!' cried Sheana, which was the signal, thank heaven, for sleep and some relief from all the girls' problems.

Sixty-Five

In spite of all his efforts to make it cheerful, Dr Lorne's farewell was a sad affair. Organized by Dr Morgan and the two nursing sisters, it was held in the larger of the two lounges and attended not only by hydro staff, including Boyd and Bob Woodville from the past, but also patients, who had gladly given up their afternoon rest to say goodbye to dear Dr Lorne. Such a terrible loss to the hydro he would be, wouldn't he? However would they manage without him?

No one, at that stage, mentioned the name of the new director, this being Dr Lorne's day when the spotlight should be only on him, even if at her entrance, all eyes went to his daughter who always looked so striking. But after she'd taken her place near her father, attention, of course, went back to him, as he stood listening to what was almost a eulogy from Dr Morgan, afterwards exclaiming over his leaving presents of a portable gramophone and large framed picture of the hydro. It was at this point that a number in his audience dissolved into tears, only controlling themselves when Dr Morgan announced that Dr Lorne himself would now say a few words.

Practised speaker as he was, he did not keep his listeners long, first thanking them for the wonderful gifts which he would always treasure, and then describing what an immensely privileged time he'd been lucky enough to have at Lorne's, how proud he'd been of the achievements of his staff, everyone one of whom, whether medical or maintenance or in whatever field, had been wonderful. He couldn't have had a better way to spend his working life than at the hydro, and though it was with a heavy heart that he was now to depart, they wouldn't have seen the last of him; he hoped to look in from time to time and would always be thinking of them.

'It will be au revoir, not goodbye,' he finished, his voice now slightly husky. 'Once again, my thanks to you all.'

There was applause and there was emotion, with Joan Elrick valiantly not looking at Dr Woodville but failing to conceal her tears for Dr Lorne, and tears also from Magda, Isla, Ellie and Kitty, and a few sniffs from unsentimental Sheana, as Larry and Barty looked gloomily on. Even the arrival of Mr Paul and his staff with trolley-loads of refreshments – tea, coffee, scones and chocolate cake – did little to lighten the atmosphere, but when Isla suggested they should try to say goodbye to Dr Lorne personally, the young men said they'd wait, maybe start on the scones. At which the girls said they'd go anyway, and lined up with the others who'd had the same idea, one of whom was Boyd.

'Nice of you to come over,' Isla whispered to him. 'You'll be support for Magda.'

'Ssh,' he whispered back, 'we're not exactly supposed to be together at the moment.'

'Oh, Boyd, when are you going to tell folk what you're up to?'

'All in good time. I think it's nearly my turn – or do you want to go ahead?'

'No, you go. I'll wait with Ellie and Sheana.'

Isla was glad she'd waited, for when it came to their turn to shake Dr Lorne's hand and wish him well, he rather mysteriously asked them to step aside with him for a moment; he had something he'd like to ask them.

Exchanging looks, the three nurses moved with him to a corner of the room, where he smiled at them and thanked them for their good wishes, then for a moment or two hesitated.

'I do hope you'll forgive me for putting an oar in, so to speak,' he said at last, 'and if I've got this all wrong, I'll apologize in advance.'

As they gazed at him expectantly, he coughed and went on: 'The thing is, it's been reported to me that you three, who have done so much for Lorne's, are actually thinking of handing in your notice. Now, please, I know you have a right to do whatever you wish, but if this is true, I want to ask you, for the sake of Lorne's, to reconsider. It's been a shock, perhaps, that there's been such a shake-up here, but I know Doctor Revie is capable of doing a very good job only if he has the cooperation of his staff – really good nurses, as you three are.'

As his kindly eyes went from face to face, they stood in silence, amazed that he'd known what they were planning to do, very much shaken that he had requested them not to do it. Clearly, though he hadn't put it into words, what he was asking was that they should think of his beloved hydro, of all that he'd loved and built up, rather than Dr Revie. So, what were they to say?

The first to speak was Sheana. 'I am thinking of getting married,' she said quietly. 'I suppose then I'd have to leave.'

'Not necessarily,' he said eagerly. 'There are no rules banning married women here, and it would be a great loss if you were to go, Sheana.'

Sheana? He'd used her first name? Nothing seemed to show more clearly that Dr Lorne was on his way out from his hydro, and a further cloud of sadness wrapped around the nurses as he still fixed them with his gaze.

'If you really think we matter,' Ellie said diffidently, 'I could stay on.'

The doctor's face lit up. 'Excellent! If you really feel you could, I'd be most grateful.' His eyes moving to Sheana, then to Isla, he waited, and after a quick glance at Isla, Sheana said if it were true she could stay on if she married, well, yes, she would. Which left Isla.

What could she say? She raised her eyes to Dr Lorne's. Cleared her throat: 'I'm like Ellie – if we're needed, I'll stay.'

'Thank you,' he said simply. 'I give my thanks to all of you. And to Joan, who's also agreed to stay. Now, what about some of Mr Paul's excellent chocolate cake?'

While he moved back to shake hands with those waiting to say goodbye, the girls stood, looking at one another.

'How did he know?' asked Ellie. 'That we were planning to go?'

'I expect Staff Miller overheard us,' Sheana replied. 'She always gets to know things – or it might have been Staff Craddock. She's as bad.'

'It doesn't matter how he knew,' Isla murmured. 'Once he'd asked, I knew we wouldn't say no.'

'Hope you'll be all right,' Sheana said sympathetically. 'I mean, with Grant Revie in charge.'

'Why, Isla's got Mark Kinnaird!' Ellie cried. 'She'll be all right.'

'Of course I will,' Isla agreed, wondering how she would tell Mark she was not leaving the hydro after all.

In fact, she still had not told him, even when Grant Revie arrived.

Sixty-Six

On a day in December, cold and grey, Grant Revie arrived back at the hydro to take up his new position as director. No one from the treatment rooms saw him in the morning, when, after being shown round his flat by Joan Elrick, he was given a hand-over talk by Dr Lorne who'd come in specially, and then had lunch in the flat he'd just been shown.

Kind words were exchanged by the outgoing director and the man who was to succeed him, after which Dr Lorne quietly departed, being escorted to his car by tearful Joan, while Grant, accompanied by Sister Francis, prepared himself for his first meeting under new circumstances with the hydro staff.

They had been earlier called together in the large lounge, as usual during the patients' rest period, and no one could deny that there was a certain feeling of excitement at the thought of meeting the man who had once been such a favourite but had left under something of a cloud. Who would have thought he'd come back in such style? What sort of director would he be? Very different from Dr Lorne, was all anyone could be sure of, though no doubt he would be pulling out all the stops to charm folk as he'd done before. Which was not to say he would succeed.

It was kindly Dr Morgan who presented him to his staff that afternoon, the one, everybody thought, would only be a foil for the charismatic Dr Revie, but that was where they were wrong. For where was the famous charm that had been expected from the new director? Where was the smile, the ease of manner, the far-reaching rays of the brilliant blue eyes?

Well, the eyes were still there, obviously, and their blueness was just as vivid, but there was only the briefest of smiles. As for the ease of manner, Dr Revie seemed almost subdued. Handsome still, it was as though in the time he'd been away, he'd lost part of himself, which was so unexpected that people didn't know quite how to react.

It was only when he'd been talking a few minutes, saying how glad and proud he was to be back at Lorne's, that the eyes of his audience found a probable reason for the change in him. Unlike Dr Morgan, he was not wearing a white coat over his dark suit, and it was on one of his sleeves that the black armband was finally spotted, and all became clear. Of course, Dr Revie had just lost his father, and from the look of him, had taken it pretty hard. Couldn't be all bad, then, could he, if he'd cared about his father? Even Isla, nervously watching from a distance, felt a sudden sympathy, although Sheana, standing close to her, was sighing and shaking her head, as though she were unconvinced.

What was he saying, anyway, in this new serious style of his? Something more, it seemed, about how it was wonderful to be back, and Lorne's was as splendid as ever, the best thing for him being to find the excellent staff he remembered still in place, which meant that together they could face the future with confidence.

'And yet,' he said slowly, 'I think, even at this early stage, it's important for me to tell you that there may be difficulties ahead. Difficulties we've not had to face before, as good bookings have never been a problem for us. Now, after Christmas, I'm afraid they are undoubtedly down.'

Here Dr Revie gave a rueful shrug.

'It appears there's been something of a falling off in people's interest in hydrotherapy, though the reason isn't clear. But it's general and certainly Lorne's isn't alone in feeling the effects of it. What we have to do is counteract this new trend, which means a number of changes will have to be made. I can't tell you more at present, but you will be informed of all plans as soon as they are made. In the meantime, remember that I have the welfare of this hydro and all of you who work for it very much at heart. Please feel free to come to me at any time if you need me. I'm here, I'm back, and happy to be so. Thank you all for your attention.'

As he withdrew to stand near Dr Morgan and Sister Francis, there was a small amount of applause, after which people looked at one another, deciding what to say about what had been a decidedly gloomy opening speech from their director. At least, though, there was tea being served by Mr Paul, though no cake, and as they drank their tea, tongues were loosened and the staff began to question just what Dr Revie had meant by 'changes'.

'I don't like changes,' Sheana stated, as Larry and Barty joined the
nurses. 'I fear the worst, eh? As for that black armband, I'm not impressed.
I bet that's just a ploy for sympathy. What do you think, Isla?'

'I think he could be missing his dad,' she answered slowly. 'I
believe he was very fond of his parents. But about the changes – I'm
like you, Sheana. I'm worried.'

'We'll just have to wait and see what happens,' said Ellie, setting
down her cup. 'Now it's action stations – Staff's looming up, wants
us to get back to work.'

'At least we have work,' Kitty Brown declared cheerfully, 'for now.'

There was a silence, the sort that can follow an odd and unexpected remark. Sheana was the one to speak first.

'What do you mean, *for now*, Kitty? Who's said we might lose
our jobs?'

'No one yet,' Kitty replied, unconcerned at Sheana's tone. 'But
when a new boss starts talking about changes, you can guess what
sort of changes he means.'

'Redundancies?' asked Larry. 'Can't see Revie sacking me. Who'd
run the gym?'

'Might close the gym,' Kitty retorted. 'If there aren't enough folk
wanting to use it, it'd make sense, eh?'

'Oh, come on!' cried Ellie. 'You're just teasing, Kitty. Doctor
Lorne specially asked us to stay on, said we were needed. I don't
think we have any need to worry.'

'That's right,' Sheana agreed. 'Let's try to be as cheerful as we can
and look on the bright side. There might be a load of bookings in
the New Year – folk wanting to undo Christmas overeating!'

Everyone laughed as they made their way to their various duties,
Isla among them, though when she was hurrying to keep her
appointment with a patient at the pool, she became aware of
someone calling her name and, recognizing the voice, stopped and
turned with a sinking heart.

'Isla, I've been trying to catch you,' Grant Revie said, with only
the slightest of smiles. 'I just wanted to have a quick word.'

'I can't stop. I have a patient to see.'

'I won't keep you. Just wanted to say I'm glad you're still here at
Lorne's. I thought . . . well, that you might want a break.'

'Doctor Lorne asked me to stay on, Sheana and Ellie as well. We
were all planning to leave.'

'Doctor Lorne?' Grant appeared disconcerted.

'For the sake of the hydro,' Isla told him coolly. 'Seemed to think it couldn't manage without us.'

'So you didn't want to work for me?'

'Didn't fancy the changes. You're the new broom, aren't you?'

'I hope to do well; I want Lorne's to prosper under me. That's why I'm glad you're here to help me.'

He was very serious, very sincere, but Isla, moving away, made no comment. Only when she was some distance away, did she turn and say she was sorry he had lost his father.

'It must be hard for you; I know you were close.'

'Thank you. Yes, we were close and it is hard. Work helps, though. Work always helps.'

'Yes.' She gave him one last cold look before moving fast down the corridor towards the entrance to the pool. After some moments, he turned away.

I must tell Mark what I've done. That was all Isla could think as she found her patient and began to help him into the water. Why had she not told him before? There would have been no reason for him then to mind too much that she would be working for Grant Revie, because she could have honestly said she would probably see very little of him, now that he was director. And she'd been sure, anyway, that he would avoid her as he had done before. Instead, though, he'd sought her out, had wanted to talk. What was he playing at?

'All right, Mr Drew?' she asked, reminding herself she should be concentrating on her work. 'This is just a partial immersion, not a full one; there's nothing to worry about. And you'll find it really helps the arthritis, when the water supports you.'

'Oh, I'm not worried,' he answered cheerfully. 'Not when you're looking after me, Nurse Scott!'

And Isla smiled, putting Mark to the back of her mind, aware of what she had to do.

Sixty-Seven

Well, she told him. Eventually. Still hoping that he would not take it as badly as she feared he would. Often, when you were worrying about something, it turned out not to be so terrible; after all, she'd only stayed on to please Dr Lorne, which should count in her favour. Mark liked and admired Dr Lorne; why shouldn't he want her to do what the doctor asked of her?

Because, as she knew in her heart, doing what the doctor wanted would mean she would be working again with Grant Revie, and in spite of the break between her and Grant, Mark wasn't happy about her seeing him in the workplace. He would have wanted Isla to tell him as soon as she'd changed her mind about staying on, which was exactly what she hadn't done. And now, when she was really faced with telling him, she was anxious.

They'd been having a meal at the little restaurant Mark knew on the Galashiels road, and were having coffee away from their table alone in a quiet lounge. The noise from the other diners, though filtering through to them, was not troubling, and as they drank their coffee and looked at one another, Isla knew that this was the time.

And Mark himself gave her her cue.

'Have you thought any more about which hospital you're going to try for?' he asked, as he refilled their cups from the pot the waiter had left.

She drank some coffee. 'Hospital?'

'Well, you must have been thinking about it, haven't you?' Mark's warm brown eyes were gently questioning. 'Is it to be Edinburgh Southern?'

'Mark, I'm not actually applying anywhere.' Isla set down her cup. 'The thing is – I should have told you before, don't know why I didn't – but I'm staying on at Lorne's.'

'Staying on? I don't understand. That wasn't your plan, was it?'

'No.' Her voice was low. 'It wasn't.'

'So, why the change? The last time we discussed this, you were only thinking of getting away from the hydro. There was no way, you said, you could ever work with Grant Revie as director. Suddenly, that's all changed. He's director, all right, but you find you can work with him after all? So, what's going on?'

'You make it all sound so suspicious,' she protested. 'It's just that Doctor Lorne asked me, and Sheana and Ellie as well, not to resign. He said we'd be needed and shouldn't go. So, we agreed to stay.'

'Doctor Lorne wanted you to stay?'

'Yes, it was all done for Doctor Lorne.'

'That being the case, why haven't you told me before? Why keep it a secret?'

Why had she? Isla looked down at her empty coffee cup. 'I'm not sure, Mark. I suppose I thought that you wouldn't be happy about me staying on at Lorne's.'

'With Grant Revie as director? You're damn right I'm not happy. I persuaded you to stay on at Lorne's after his shameful behaviour towards you because I knew it was better for you to stick it out, regain your self-respect, which you did. But it's all different now. I don't trust him.'

'What do you mean, you don't trust him?

'I mean, where you're concerned.'

'Where I'm concerned? Mark, that's ridiculous!' Her cheeks flushing, her eyes stormy, Isla was quick to speak what was only the truth – or what was probably the truth. And she would have had no hesitation in believing what she was saying, had Grant not followed her down the corridor as he had on his first day, had he not sought her out when he need not have done. It might have meant nothing, it might have meant something – she just wished he hadn't done it – but in any case she'd been right to say what she'd said to Mark. It was ridiculous to think that there could ever again be anything between herself and Grant Revie.

'Why ever do you say such a thing?' she asked, her colour still high. 'You have nothing to fear from Grant Revie.'

'Think not? I'm not so sure. Look what's happened – he appeared to have a genuine love for you, but when Magda came in his sights, he tried for her, thinking she could be of help to him. When she rejected him, that made him look a fool and he took himself off. But since then he's had time to think, time to remember you, Isla, and has maybe learned his lesson.' Leaning forward, Mark fixed Isla with a troubled gaze. 'Can't you see why I don't want you working with him again? Why I want you to leave the hydro? Just as you said you would?'

'Mark, I can't leave the hydro. I promised Doctor Lorne I'd stay. I couldn't go back on my word.'

'You just want to please him?'

'It's not a question of pleasing. As I say, it's about keeping my word.'

'And you won't consider doing what I ask? What you said you'd do, anyway?'

For some time, she did not speak, her thoughts too confused over her situation. At one time, no question, she'd have done what Mark wanted. It would have been the right thing to do; they were in love, they would have a future together – of course she'd have been ready to do what he would like her to do.

But now, since her own love had grown, his had seemed to remain static. Never once had he put into words that he loved her. There had been no talk of their future, no ring on her finger, which wasn't in itself important – only what it signified. For some reason still unknown, Mark did not consider her as a future partner. Why, then, should he ask her to leave the hydro just because Grant Revie had returned there? What right had he to ask her to do that?

No more right than she had to put her cards on the table and tell him of her feelings for him, to ask him why she wasn't suitable for him, even to hint at marriage? The fact was that, as a woman in 1926, she had no right to propose to a man, because he was the breadwinner and she wasn't, which meant she would be asking him to keep her for the rest of her life. Why, even if she'd had a job of her own, she'd be expected to give it up. Such was the situation and there was nothing she could do about it – except now, at least, to tell Mark plainly that she was not prepared to do as he asked.

'Aren't you going to answer me?' he asked suddenly. 'For God's sake, Isla, what's in your mind?'

She raised her eyes to his.

'I'm sorry, Mark, but I can't do what you ask. And I don't think you've any right to ask me.'

'No right?' He appeared shocked, his eyes searching her face as though trying to make sense of what she'd said, but then he let go, sank back in his chair and looked away. 'Well . . .' He ran his hand over his face. 'Maybe that's true.'

'Are you all right?' she asked, noticing worriedly that his breathing was becoming fast. Clearly his chest was tightening; soon he would begin to cough.

'I'm fine. It's just the usual thing. But I think we ought to go. I'll get the bill.'

*   *   *

There was no question of stopping anywhere for kisses of farewell. Apart from Mark's coughing fit, which did come, everything was different anyway, for they had had their first quarrel. Maybe even their last, for who knew if they would meet again?

'Mark, I'm worried about you,' Isla said as they drew up outside the hydro. 'When you get home, see if the steam kettle will help, then try to rest.'

'It's all right, Isla, I know what to do. This will ease off; always does.'

In the dusk of the car, they could barely see each other's faces, but they needed no vision to recognize the sorrowing of parting. How had they come to this? But Isla knew relationships could only develop or end, and it seemed clear that this one was ending.

'Perhaps we shouldn't see each other for a while,' Mark said, with a struggle, and Isla, though inwardly wincing, was quick to agree.

'Yes, that would be best. I'll go now, Mark, so that you can get home quickly. And do get the doctor if you have real trouble.'

'I will. But let me open the door—'

'No need. You stay where you are.'

There was no farewell kiss, no pressing of hands, just Isla leaving the car and Mark gazing out at her, and then he was gone, his car's rear lights the last thing she saw as he drove through the gates and away.

For a long, long moment, she stood by the side door, letting the pain wash over her, breathing hard herself as though she were ill like Mark, until she felt able to face the world in there, in the hydro, and opened the door.

Sixty-Eight

She had decided not to tell anyone – not even her mother – of her parting with Mark. After all, it was her business and Mark's alone; no one else need know of it – at least, for now. Of course, as time went on, it would become known anyway, and then she might have to say something; in the meantime, she would say nothing.

As the days went by, she was relieved not to see much of Grant Revie, who was caught up in all the work of being the new director, only appearing in the treatment rooms to take over from

Dr Morgan, when he had made no effort to speak again to Isla. So, she'd been right all along, and there had been no need for Mark to worry about Grant's wanting to rake up their old attachment. Yet she didn't try to deceive herself: what had gone wrong between herself and Mark had had a much deeper cause than Mark's fear of Grant's pursuing her again. With no real hope of a solution there, she knew for the time being she couldn't escape heartache.

Now that there was no fear of seeing Damon Duthie at the little café where he'd worked in the High Street – he and Trina still being in the south, as far as anyone knew – Isla felt safe to go to the café for a snack lunch. Sometimes, she would go with Ellie or Sheana, but sometimes, depending on her shifts, she would just go alone, order eggs on toast and read a book. It was pleasant, she found, not to have to talk with others and pretend to be happy.

On a chill December day, when the café was decorated with paper chains and balloons, she was almost contentedly eating her eggs and reading the paper, when someone slid into the chair opposite hers.

'Mind if I sit here?' came a well-known voice, and looking up, her heart plummeting, she saw Grant Revie.

'Don't look so startled,' he said quietly, as he rose to hang up his coat and hat before returning to his seat. 'I'm only going to have something on toast, like you.'

'Don't you have lunch in your flat?' she asked bluntly. 'There's no need for you to come here.'

'Well, you're not in my flat, are you? And I want to talk to you.'

'Grant, this is all a waste of time. We've nothing to say to each other.'

'Hang on – I'll just put my order in.'

Smiling at the waitress, almost in the old way, he asked for eggs on toast with bacon and tomato, and coffee to follow. 'Coffee for you, Isla? Make that two coffees, please.'

'What on earth can you have to say?' she cried desperately. 'I don't even want to listen.'

'Please, Isla, please listen.' There were no smiles now on Grant's face, and the brilliant blue eyes were serious. 'You've no idea how bad I feel when I look at you and think what I did – how I hurt you, how I threw away my chance of real happiness. I know it's a lot to ask, but would you let me explain just what happened. Please?'

'I know what happened, Grant. You saw Magda and you realized she was what you wanted, so I had to be dropped. There's no need for you to explain that.'

He was silent, resting his cheek on his hand and shaking his head.

'I know it sounds bad, put like that,' he said at last, 'but it wasn't quite the way you think. When I saw Magda, I wasn't being cool and calculating, as you seem to believe. I was just . . . bowled over. It was like a thunderbolt – the sort of thing you read about. Love at first sight, no rhyme or reason about it. I couldn't eat or sleep, or think of anything but her. But the truth is, Isla, the person I fell in love with wasn't a real woman. Not someone like you, a person who belonged to the world. She was someone I'd sort of created, made for myself – sounds crazy – but nothing to do with Magda.'

'Eggs, bacon and tomato on toast,' the waitress intoned, dashing down a large platter in front of Grant. 'Want your coffee now, or later?'

'Now, please,' ordered Isla. 'I can't stay long.'

'Oh, God, how stern you look!' Grant cried. 'Don't you believe what I've told you? Doesn't it explain how I went wrong?'

'Better eat that before it gets cold, Grant.'

'I suppose I can't blame you, for not believing me,' he muttered, beginning to eat. 'I lie awake at nights thinking how badly I treated you, but I wasn't myself – I didn't know what I was doing.'

'As a matter of fact, I do sort of believe you,' Isla told him. 'I know this sort of thing can happen because it happened to my brother, when he first saw Trina Morris. But if he'd wanted to give some other girl up, he'd have done it more gently than you did, Grant.'

Grant looked down at his plate and pushed it away.

'You don't need to tell me how it was,' he said in a low voice. 'As I've said, I lie awake at nights, remembering it. But if you know how badly I feel, couldn't you forgive me?'

'Two coffees,' said the waitress, looking at Grant's plate. 'No' want that?'

'Not hungry, after all, I'm afraid.'

When she had removed his plate and left them, Grant reached across to take Isla's hand.

'Couldn't we at least be friends? You liked being with me once, didn't you?'

'Things were different then.' Isla drank her coffee. 'I don't really see us being friends after what happened. The thing is I stopped caring for you a long time ago, Grant, and now I care for someone else.'

'Not Mark Kinnaird?'

Isla's colour rose. She made no reply.

'It's him, isn't it?' Grant pressed. 'I always knew he was keen on you. Most people knew.'

'I don't want to talk about him.'

Stirring his coffee, Grant studied her averted face.

'It's not going well, though, is it?' he asked softly. 'I know how people look when they're happy, and since I came back, you haven't looked happy.'

Isla stood up. 'I have to go. I'm due back on duty.'

'Wait, I'll pay the bill.'

'Not for me; I'll pay my own.'

'Oh, come on, what's a couple of bob?'

She shrugged and went for her coat. 'Thanks, then.'

Outside, as they faced the bleakness of the afternoon, he made no move to leave her, though she'd been waiting for him to say they shouldn't walk back together. Of course, he is the boss now, she remembered, half smiling. He can do what he likes.

Turning to him, she continued to smile.

'Know what's happened to Magda now, Grant? And my brother, Boyd?'

'I've no idea.'

'They're in love.'

He almost stopped in his tracks, but recovered himself, trying not to show his chagrin.

'Handsome Boyd and Magda? How did that happen?'

'He's on a teacher training course in Edinburgh, she's at the art college, they met in the street one day and it went on from there.'

Grant laughed. 'Good luck to them, then. As you know, my feelings for her are quite dead, but she's very beautiful – they'll make a handsome pair.'

'And they really are happy,' Isla said quietly, to which Grant made no reply.

Only when they reached the hydro did he halt and put his hand on Isla's arm.

'I haven't given up,' he told her. 'I still believe we might be friends again, and perhaps more than that. Who knows?'

'You don't really care about being friends with me, Grant,' Isla replied, her grey eyes wintry. 'You just want to feel good about yourself, and if I don't come running back to you, that's not so easy, is it? It would be best if we just stay out of each other's way.'

He shook his head. 'You still don't understand me, Isla. I've changed, and just for once I'm not thinking of myself. But we'll talk again, eh?'

Not if I can help it, she thought, as they entered the hydro and parted.

Sixty-Nine

'They really are happy,' Isla had said of Boyd and Magda, and this was true.

So true that when they were sitting out in a secluded corridor after an eightsome reel at the art college Christmas dance, Magda suddenly said, 'Boyd, why don't we get married?'

'Married?' He stared, then laughed. 'Now, how many glasses of punch have you been drinking?'

'Boyd, I'm serious. Look, I know women aren't supposed to do the asking, but as you haven't come up with the question, I thought I'd ask it myself. So, think about it.'

As she leaned forward towards him, her face so deeply flushed and her green eyes so strangely bright, she did give the impression of being a little the worse for drink, though Boyd knew it wasn't so. If she was drunk, it was on excitement and – yes – love, which was not surprising to him, considering the fact that he felt that way himself. But such feelings were dangerous, not to be taken seriously. To do so could lead to 'morning after' regrets, which could be long-term if you actually went about tying legal knots.

'Why should you be serious about getting married?' he asked lightly. 'You're far too young.'

'I'll soon be nineteen. Loads of girls get married at nineteen – and younger!'

'And spend how long regretting it?'

'Why should they regret it?'

'Because they're so young – they're still changing, becoming different. Maybe falling out of love with the one they've married.' Boyd's look was now grave. 'Too late then to do anything about it.'

'Are you saying that could be me?' Magda demanded. 'That I could fall out of love with you?'

'You could realize you'd made a mistake. I was years older than you and I made a mistake, didn't I? I fell out of love with Trina.'

'Only after she'd let you down, Boyd. We wouldn't do that to each other.' Magda took Boyd's hand. 'I know I've found the one I want. With you, I'm at ease, I'm happy. Not difficult, like I used to be.'

'You've never been difficult with me,' he agreed softly. 'And if I make you happy, that's grand. But I can't let you take the risk of marrying me – at least, not yet.'

'Not yet?' Her face brightened. 'What does that mean, then?'

'It means we wait. See how things go. And give me time to save up after I finish the course and get a job. I'd need to do that, Magda.'

'I've got money—'

'No.' He released his hand from hers. 'I know I'm old-fashioned, but I want to provide the home. Would you mind about that?'

'Not if I could contribute – I mean, add things I'd like. That would be fair, wouldn't it?'

'Sure, it would.' Looking round to see if anyone was watching, Boyd quickly held Magda close and kissed her. 'Shall we leave it like that, then? We wait. And see.'

'I won't change, Boyd.'

'Nor will I. But we'll just take our time.'

For some moments, they gazed into each other's eyes, thinking of the step they had newly taken together.

Then Magda asked quietly, 'Boyd, would you like to see my father some time?'

'Your father?' Boyd's face had taken on a hunted expression. 'Oh, God, Magda, I'd be terrified. I've never dared to suggest it. Supposing he throws me out?'

'He won't. I'll just say you've been a good friend to me since I moved to Edinburgh. Oh, Boyd, will you see him?'

'Of course. It's just that – well, you know how it is. But I will see him. I want to. It's been worrying me for some time, that we've never told him about us.'

'There's your parents to see, too, Boyd. I'd like so much to meet them.'

'And you'll also be a friend?' he asked wryly. 'All right, we'll see all the parents without putting too much into words, eh? And then we'll feel better.'

He ran his hands through his hair and shook his head.

'But I just wish we could be on our own now, instead of being surrounded by other people. Why don't we leave early?'

'Too late!' cried Magda as a group of people she knew came up to seize her and Boyd by the hands and pull them from their seats.

'Come on, you lovebirds!' they cried. 'Stop skulking round here and get back to the dancing. There's a sixteensome starting up and we want feet on the floor!'

'I'll need a drink before a sixteensome,' said Boyd, joining in the laughter, but he was borne away with Magda to the ballroom, where he forgot about leaving early.

Seventy

On her free Sunday afternoon, two weeks before Christmas, Isla arrived for tea with her parents to be met by Nan at the front door in a state of quivering excitement.

'You'll never guess who's here!' she said in a stage whisper, drawing Isla into the hall. 'Never in a thousand years!'

'Tell me, then,' Isla said, laughing, as she took off her coat and hat. 'Though I'll see in a minute anyway.'

'Yes, but I'll tell you first.' Still whispering, Nan put her face close to Isla's. 'It's Boyd and Miss Lorne! Doctor Lorne's daughter — can you believe it! With our Boyd? She's asked me to call her Magda. Boyd says she's just a friend, but honestly, you've just got to look at them—'

'Ma, calm down a bit, eh? And let's go in. Where are they?'

'In the parlour, of course. Your dad's lit the fire and we've plenty for tea, but they should have let me know they were coming—'

'Come on, Ma,' Isla said firmly and, taking Nan's arm, moved with her into the parlour, where Will was looking dazed on the sofa and Boyd and Magda were sitting either side of the fireplace, looking very happy and rather pleased with themselves.

'Isla!' cried Boyd, leaping up, as his father rose too and came to hug her. 'Never expected to see you today!'

'What a bit of luck,' said Magda, who was eye-catching as usual in a dark blue woollen dress with a matching scarf. 'We really only came on the spur of the moment. Should have given some notice.'

'That's quite all right,' said Nan breathlessly. 'We're just so happy to meet you, Miss Lorne.'

'Magda, please.'

'Yes, so happy,' said Isla, smiling and shaking Magda's hand, then clapping her brother on the back. 'It's grand to see you both. You've not been over to the hydro lately, Boyd.'

'Not since Grant Revie took over from Doctor Lorne,' he agreed, glancing at Magda, whose face had lost its smile. 'We're not too happy about that, are we, Magda?'

'Not happy at all,' she replied coldly.

'I'll make the tea,' said Nan. 'Everything else is ready. Will, come and give me a hand, eh?'

'I can do that,' Isla offered, but Nan shook her head.

'No, you stay and talk to Boyd and . . . Magda. We won't be but a few minutes. Come on, Will.'

There was a little silence when the young people were alone, until Isla smiled and asked, 'Well, what did you tell them?'

'Just what we told my father,' Magda answered. 'That we'd become good friends since we met in Edinburgh.' She laughed a little. 'Only he didn't altogether believe it.'

'I was in a state, having to see him,' said Boyd, shaking his head. 'Isla, I was like a wee laddie starting school or something, but he was so nice, so friendly, I couldn't believe it. Like Magda says, he saw through us straight away, but he said we were right to take our time, make sure of what we were doing, and if it all worked out for us − well, he'd be happy.'

'The thing is, Isla, he thinks we're right for each other,' Magda told her seriously. 'He thinks I need someone like Boyd − very steady, very conscientious, but ambitious, too − and he thinks Boyd needs me.' She looked across to Boyd. 'Why did he think you needed me, Boyd?'

'Ah, he didn't exactly say, but he was sure you'd be right for me.' Boyd came over to take her hand. 'As though you wouldn't be!'

'So now you want the folks to accept your story?' Isla asked. 'I mean of being very helpful friends? I think they'll be just like your dad, Magda, and see through you, but they won't say anything. At least, not until you're ready tell them the truth. But it's really nice you've come to see them − they're thrilled.'

'I think they're lovely people,' Magda said earnestly. 'I hope they'll like me.'

'No problem there. Just to make sure, though, eat as many of Ma's scones and cakes as you can!'

After they'd laughed, Boyd went back to his seat and looked at Isla.

'So, how are things under the new regime? Grant Revie treating you all well?'

Isla hesitated. 'He's OK. Hasn't started bossing us about or anything, but it's not the same as when your father was there, Magda. I can't put my finger on it exactly, but the atmosphere's different. We don't feel as relaxed as we used to do.'

'Bet you don't,' Magda commented. 'Grant has different ideas from my father. In fact, he more or less said so, when he came to tell Daddy about the changes.'

'Changes?' Isla was alert. 'What sort of changes? He told us there'd be some, but we don't know what they are yet. We're afraid there'll be sackings.'

'Probably. I know Daddy was pretty upset anyway, by what's being planned.'

'Grant gave him details?'

'Yes, he was decent enough to do that. Apparently, he's got permission from the board to make the hydro more of a hotel. That's the trend, he says. People are going off full water cures, but they still fancy coming to a hotel with a sort of spa or water treatment attached.'

'A spa?' cried Isla. 'A hotel? That's what he's planning for the hydro? I don't believe it. It would make it all quite different.'

Magda shrugged. 'He said it was what people wanted. All the facilities of a hotel, plus entertainment, a golf course . . . and spa and water treatments thrown in. I suppose it could work.'

'I can imagine what your dad thought,' said Boyd. 'He was always the serious doctor, eh? Grant's out to make money. There's the difference.'

'And some staff will have to go,' Isla said slowly. 'Obviously, they won't need as many nurses if the treatments are just a sideline. I wish now I hadn't promised Doctor Lorne I'd stay.'

'He'd no idea then what was going to happen,' Magda said sympathetically. 'But you needn't stay now.'

'You mean I should go before I'm sacked?'

'I bet Grant won't sack you, Isla,' Boyd put in. 'Though what you should do, if you ask me, is marry Mark Kinnaird – that'd solve all your problems!'

A rich red colour rose to Isla's brow and she lowered her eyes.

'Oh, there's still a problem, Boyd,' she said lightly. 'Mark hasn't asked me.'

'Oh? I thought . . .' As Magda shook her head at him, Boyd looked embarrassed. 'I thought you were both – you know—'

'No. As a matter of fact, I'm not seeing him at the moment. We're . . . having a break.'

'Here comes the tea!' cried Nan, entering with a loaded tray, while Will followed with another. 'Now I'll just set this on the table. Oh, isn't it grand we're all together and so happy?'

It was some time later, when the family party had broken up, with Boyd and Magda on their way to the station, and Nan and Will talking over Magda's amazing visit, that Isla arrived back at the hydro for evening duty. Still trying to come to terms with the awful news Magda had passed on, she was hoping she wouldn't see Grant Revie, or she would be bound to tell him what she thought of his future changes and that she for one would not be staying around to see them.

And then, of course, she did see him, strolling through Reception, where a telephone was ringing and Noreen's Sunday replacement, Ruthie Atkinson, was running to answer it.

'Isla, how nice to see you!' Grant cried. 'We haven't talked for a while, have we? You must admit I've been very good staying out of your way.'

She was about to open her mouth to speak when she heard her name called and looked across to Ruthie beckoning her.

'Isla! Telephone!'

'For me?' She didn't know anyone who would ring her, especially not on a Sunday night.

'Who is it?' she asked Ruthie as she came to pick up the receiver. 'Are you sure they want me?'

'It's some man from Edinburgh. He rang earlier, said he'd try again. Definitely wanted you.'

'Hello? This is Isla Scott speaking,' Isla said, wondering, with a beating heart, if it could be Mark trying to get through to her.

But it wasn't Mark; it was his father.

As she listened, Grant, watching closely, saw the colour drain from her face, and when she laid the receiver down and turned to him, he went to her.

'Isla, what is it? Tell me!'

'It's Mark. He's ill, very ill.' Her lips were trembling, her eyes enormous, full of fear. 'He has pneumonia.'

'Oh, God – with his medical history!' Grant took Isla's cold hands, as Ruthie, at a distance, looked on with awe. 'That's bad, Isla, that's bad.'

'He's asked for me, Grant. I must go.' Isla looked round wildly. 'I'm on duty, but I must go. There's a late train I can catch—'

'No train, Isla; I'll drive you.' Grant released Isla's hands. 'Quick, run up and pack a bag – you'll be staying on, I take it? Yes, get what you need and I'll try to catch Sister Francis – she won't have left yet – and tell her you won't be here. Don't worry, she'll cope. You just meet me on the steps in ten minutes. All right?'

'Grant, I don't know what to say—'

'Just pack your things, Isla. Then we'll away.'

Seventy-One

Isla knew that she would never forget that drive through quiet roads, with Grant driving as fast as he dared, his handsome face grim, their only talk of Mark's illness and what they might expect to find when they reached him in Edinburgh.

'He's being nursed at home with his own doctor and a private nurse,' Isla said, her voice low. 'The doctor thinks he'll be better there than in hospital; he has everything he needs, including oxygen.'

'That's fine. Sometimes patients are better off at home.' Grant gave her a quick glance. 'But you know as well as I do that there isn't a great deal we can do for pneumonia. It's an inflammation of the lungs with no magic formula to clear the symptoms – might happen one day, but for now we're dependent on the patient's own will to survive.'

'I know,' sighed Isla, thinking of all the pneumonia cases she'd nursed, of how the patients had suffered, with high temperature, pain and racking cough . . . the difficulty in breathing, the struggle to clear the lungs of secretions, the nightmare of facing the crisis, the turning point, which some survived, but many did not.

And now this dreaded disease was being faced by Mark – her own dear Mark, who she'd been stupid enough to quarrel with, who meant so much, but who might now be taken from her before they could be reconciled. All right, it was true, he hadn't declared his love, but deep down she knew it was there – it was hers – and

maybe all she'd had to do was speak to him about it. But he'd been
upset with her over Grant, and she'd been upset anyway, so they'd
quarrelled and – oh, God – parted. Please, please, she prayed to the
unknown, may we not be parted now.

'How long has Mark been ill?' Grant was asking. 'Did his father
say?'

'No, I wish I'd asked him.' She was trying to control her fears.
'You're thinking of the crisis?'

'Between the sixth and eighth days, yes. All will depend on that.'
Grant was having to slow down as they reached the outskirts of the
city. 'What's the address again?'

'Gloucester Place. I think I can guide you, if you like.'

'No, I know it. We'll be there very soon.' Again, Grant glanced
at Isla. 'What's your plan, then? To work with the nurse who's
already there?'

'Oh, Grant, I have no plan.' Isla was shivering, longing to reach
Mark's home, dreading what she might find there. 'I just want to
see him, know how he is.'

Parking the car in Gloucester Place, Grant said quietly, 'Isla, I
won't come in with you. Don't want to get in the way.'

'No, no, you won't be in the way. I'm sure Mark's doctor and
his father would want to talk to you.' Isla put her hand on Grant's
arm. 'Come in with me, but first I want to thank you for driving
me here. I'm so grateful – I can't tell you how grateful.'

'I was glad to do it, Isla. Made me feel I'd been of some use.'

'Come, then.' Taking a deep breath, Isla left the car, Grant
following. With trembling finger, she rang the bell of Mark's home.

The front door was opened by Mrs Fernie, looking worn and
red-eyed. She instantly drew them in, taking Isla's small case and
her coat, though Grant kept his, saying he wouldn't be staying
long.

'I'll just call Mr Kinnaird, sir – Miss Scott. He won't be a minute—'

In fact, he was already with them, his hand outstretched,
exclaiming how wonderful it was to see Isla, and how quick she'd
been – was it thanks to Dr Revie, then? How very kind, very
kind.

He, too, looked worn and rather older as he held her hand and
said he would take her at once to see Mark. Oh, things would be
better now, he was sure of it, now that Isla was here; Mark had
been so anxious to see her.

'I'll wait,' Grant said quickly, at which Mr Kinnaird called Mrs Fernie who took him into her care, while Mr Kinnaird asked Isla to follow him up the stairs.

'Just to the door on the right, my dear. Then you'll see Mark.'

Even before she saw him in his bed in his large airy room at the top of the stairs, she could hear the deep wrenching sounds of his breathing, sounds she knew so well but were so particularly painful to her now that she could hardly bear to listen.

Oh, Mark, Mark!

She ran to him where he lay, his eyes closed, his face darkly flushed, and sank down beside his bed to take his hand.

He stirred, his eyelids slowly moving, and then his shadowed eyes recognized her and his whole face seemed to change, to come alive for a moment or two, as he brought out her name.

'Isla? You're here?'

'Yes, Mark, I'm here,' she whispered, tears stinging her eyes but held back so that he should not see. 'I'm here and I won't leave you. You're going to get well again, I promise.'

'Promise . . .' he tried to say, but even as she watched, he began to cough, and two people she had only vaguely sensed in the room moved to be with him, one a young woman in nurse's uniform, the other a middle-aged man in a dark suit. The nurse and the doctor. Oh, yes, Isla knew she must now step aside, let them do their job, and, rising, she moved back, still keeping her eyes on Mark. But the doctor came to her.

'I'm Doctor Wynn,' he whispered. 'I believe you're Miss Scott from the hydro? Mr Kinnaird has just asked me to speak to Doctor Revie before he leaves. Perhaps we can talk later?'

'Yes, of course.'

Suddenly feeling strangely weary, she sank into a chair as the doctor withdrew, and watched as the nurse helped Mark to bring up sputum, then settled him against his pillows before turning to glance and then faintly smile at Isla.

The face, the smile − were they familiar?

Isla, failing to manage a smile back, thought they might be. But from where? The short bobbed hair didn't ring any bells, but surely she had seen the friendly, pretty face somewhere before?

'Remember me?' whispered the nurse, coming close. 'I'm Margie MacCallum. We met at the interview at the hydro.'

'Margie MacCallum . . . Yes, I do remember! I'm Isla Scott. But you look different somehow—'

'Only my hair. I had it bobbed. It was always coming down.' Margie's smile had faded. 'But you're Mr Kinnaird's friend, aren't you? Oh, you must be feeling so bad, but you mustn't despair. The doctor is very hopeful, and, see, the breathing is a little better, isn't it?'

Looking back at Mark, his breathing did seem rather easier, though his eyes were closed again and he appeared to be sleeping.

'You look all in,' Margie said softly. 'How about a cup of tea?'

'I just want to be with him.'

'Tea first. Quick now, I'll watch over him.'

'I won't be long, then.'

With a last look at Mark, Isla, knowing she must have something to keep her going, left the sick room to make her way to the dining room, where she found Grant with the doctor and Mr Kinnaird. She would have gone directly to Grant, if Mrs Fernie hadn't insisted that she have some of her chicken soup – perfect for energy.

'I was thinking of tea . . .' Isla began, but it was easier just to take the soup, until Grant came up and whispered that he must be on his way.

'Finish that soup, though, it'll do you good, and then come and see me off, will you? I've made my goodbyes to Mr Kinnaird and Doctor Wynn.'

Obediently, she followed him into the hall where he turned to her, his blue eyes serious.

'Tell me how you found Mark. He was my patient once. I feel so bad for him.'

'I'd say he's holding his own, but' – Isla's voice shook – 'there's no doubt he's very ill.'

'As you know, pneumonia is always a danger to chronic bronchitis, but his doctor here is confident he'll fight it. Don't give up hope.' Grant gave a final press to her hand. 'If you can, will you let me know how things go?'

'I will. And thank you, Grant, thank you again for all your help. You know what it meant to me.'

'Meant a lot to me to do something for you and Mark.' He paused a moment. 'Goodbye, then, Isla.'

'Goodbye, Grant.'

'Come back when you can.'

She nodded but made no reply, and after he'd kissed her briefly on the cheek, he was gone. She waited a moment, then turned away, thinking only of Mark, but first she had to have a quick word of encouragement with Mr Kinnaird, and be encouraged herself by Dr Wynn who said he was grateful to her for being there. Next, there was tea to drink and her room to see – and all the time she was on pins, waiting to be with Mark again, even if he didn't know she was there.

But when she was finally by his bed again, he did know she was there, for his eyes were open and on her face, and he even lifted his moist, hot hand to put into hers.

'Isla,' he whispered. 'You're back again. All . . . I wanted.'

'All I want, too, Mark, to be near you.'

There she stayed, until he fell asleep, when she lay on the sofa in his room, even though Margie tried to make her go to her bed.

'Tomorrow night, maybe,' Isla told her. 'Tonight, I'll stay here.'

Seventy-Two

When would the crisis come? That was the question on everyone's mind, as Mark's illness appeared to have reached a plateau of suffering, with continual coughing, pain and fever, the only change in sight being that terrible turning point when he would either come through to recovery – or not.

Six to eight days after the onset of the illness was when the crisis could be expected, which meant that it could come as early as two days after Isla's arrival.

'You will be staying on?' Mr Kinnaird had asked her anxiously after her first night spent by Mark's side, and she had assured him that she would. It was what she had come for, and she and Nurse MacCallum would manage all the nursing between them.

'That's wonderful,' he said fervently. 'We'd been about to engage a second nurse, but if you're willing to stay—'

'It's all I want,' she told him simply. 'To look after Mark and see him through.'

'Isla, you have all my thanks.' Mark's father's voice thickened and he briefly wiped his eyes. 'He's all I have, as you know. But if there's anything I can do for you – anything you need – you have only to say.'

'Well, there is something – if you wouldn't mind . . .'

'Anything, my dear.'

'May I use your telephone, then? I'm sending a postcard to my parents to tell them what's been happening, but I'd like to ring my brother at college and just speak to him.'

'Of course, of course, Isla! Please, ring him now.'

It was a relief to tell Boyd of Mark's illness and feel his sympathy even over the telephone. Of course, he wanted to come to see Mark, but Isla said it would be better to wait; Mark wasn't up to seeing visitors and they were waiting now for the crisis.

'He'll come through, Isla, I'm sure of it. He's young and he's got the will to live – that's what counts, they say. But keep in touch, eh? Let us know how things go. And don't worry about the folks. I'll see them at Christmas, while Magda goes to her father's. They'll understand that you have to stay with Mark.'

Deeply grateful, Isla hurried back to Mark, to do all that was required for him, while Margie cheerfully sorted and bore away a great quantity of laundry.

Cheerful – yes, that was the word for Margie, and Isla, who was finding it a real bonus to be working with so pleasant and caring a nurse, thought she'd been lucky.

There was never much time to talk, of course, but later that day, when Mark was sleeping, having been given medication by Dr Wynn to ease his pain, the girls did manage to have a cup of tea together, and Margie said how glad she was to be working with Isla.

'To tell you the truth, I was really scared of working with one of those battleaxes from the agency, you know. It's so much nicer with you – I remember thinking how friendly you were at the interview. Of course, we all knew you'd get the job!'

'Now, how could you have known that?' Isla asked with a smile. 'But I liked you, too. Did you never get into a hospital post, then?'

'Och, no, I think it was my hair! Always coming down. Folk probably thought I was too scatty. So I decided to go for agency work, got my hair trimmed, got a job, and everything's worked out well.'

Margie's eyes on Isla were suddenly full of sympathy. 'But I'm so sorry your young man's so ill, Isla. Try not to worry. We've both seen cases just like his, eh, and they've pulled through? He will, too.'

'There's the crisis ahead,' Isla said in a low voice. 'I never stop thinking about it. I almost wish it was here now.'

'Could come in a couple of days' time, or maybe four.'

'Then I hope it'll be sooner rather than later. All the time, Mark's strength is slipping away and he needs all he can to come through.'

'He's young, Isla – that's a plus – and there's something else that counts—'

'What?'

'He wants to. He wants to come through. For you.'

'Oh, Margie!'

'Yes, you can tell – the way his eyes follow you, the way he's looking around for you till you come.' Margie smiled a little. 'I know about patients, Isla, I can read their signs, and I know Mark will fight this to be with you.'

'I'd better go back to him,' Isla said softly. 'He may have woken up.'

He hadn't. Though breathing harshly, he was still asleep, and Isla was able to lean close and whisper, 'If it's true you want to come through for me, please, Mark, let it happen. Fight for us both. Never give in.'

And then his eyes opened and he said her name, and for some time she stayed by his side, holding his hand, until his eyes closed and he slipped back into sleep.

Two days later, when Dr Wynn paid his early morning visit, he took Mark's temperature as usual, but then glanced sharply across at Isla who was on her own, as Margie was preparing to go to bed after night duty.

'It's rising,' he said shortly. 'The temperature. I think this may be it, Nurse Scott.'

'The crisis?' Her heart was thumping in her chest.

'I believe so. We must be prepared; it will reach great heights. You've had experience of it, of course?'

'Oh, yes, often, Doctor.'

But never with one she loved, she thought, beginning to summon up all her reserves of strength. If Mark must be strong, so must she, and she reached out and pressed his hand, already burning like a brand.

Seventy-Three

The hours that followed were like a bad dream. Dr Wynn was there, and Margie, who had left her bed. Mark's father, too, who kept in the background, while Mrs Fernie went in and out, unable to do more than stand by as others supported Mark in his struggle, all working through the dream.

As his temperature rose, it was terrible to see him, the sweat pouring from him in rivers, his eyes wide with the knowledge that this was happening to him, yet uncomplaining, as they flung open the windows for the fresh air on which they set such store, and sponged him down and moistened his lips. It seemed impossible that he could withstand the forces that came from within, turning him into a furnace, yet sometimes his eyes would meet Isla's and he would try to speak, but then he'd lie back and they would try to soothe him, as they waited – had to wait – for a miracle.

'Oh, God, I can't stand this,' whispered Mr Kinnaird suddenly. 'I've seen it before – my little brother long ago – but this is my son. It's too much – too much—'

'Wait,' ordered Dr Wynn. 'There's a change.'

A change? Yes, a change, but pointing which way? For here was the turning point, here was the time when things could go either way. Isla had begun to shake, reaching for Margie's protective arm, as Dr Wynn once more took Mark's temperature and turned his eyes on the watchers. Oh, God, when would he speak?

'It's down,' he said in a hushed voice. 'Too early to say if this is really a sign, but it's down, thank God, it's down!'

'Oh, Isla, it's good news,' Margie cried. 'I know it, you know it! This is what happens when the patient wins!'

'Quiet, Nurse,' Dr Wynn said sternly, as Margie and Isla clung together, but Mr Kinnaird was already leaning at the foot of Mark's bed, offering up thanks, and Mrs Fernie was openly sobbing with relief.

'Is it true, Doctor?' Isla whispered, her eyes on Mark. 'Oh, please, has it gone his way?'

'Yes, he's easier,' Dr Wynn told her, putting his hand on her shoulder. 'He is coming through, as the lucky ones do. And when his fever has passed, I think we'll find that he makes a good recovery. Such has been my experience.'

With trembling hands, Isla and Margie sponged Mark down again, changed his pyjamas, and gave him a little water, while the heat gradually left him. His eyes rested on their faces, moving at last to his father who was now too overcome to speak.

No one knew what time it was, for they felt time had stood still during the battle, but Mrs Fernie said she would now make everyone tea or coffee or anything they wanted and bustled away, leaving the others to collapse into chairs, with even Dr Wynn admitting his legs didn't feel his own.

'Doctor, I can't thank you enough,' Mr Kinnaird eventually managed to say. 'Or you girls – I can't tell you – I'm so grateful—'

'No need for thanks,' said Dr Wynn. 'Just doing our job. It's Mark you should be thanking – he's the one who saved himself.'

Everyone looked at Mark, but he was too exhausted to speak, and only his expressive eyes told them all how he felt at being returned to the promise of life, finally resting on Isla who went to him.

It's true,' she told him, kneeling by his bed, the bad dream fading around her, relief and unbelievable joy taking hold. 'It's true what Doctor Wynn says, Mark. You saved yourself. Only you could have done it – oh, I'm so grateful . . .'

As her voice cracked and trailed away, all he wanted now was to look at her, but even as he improved, with his temperature falling all the time, weakness overcame him, his eyelids fell, and he lay still.

'Come away, my dear,' Dr Wynn said gently, helping Isla to her feet. 'You know that rest now is the best thing for him. I suggest we all have a cup of Mrs Fernie's tea. It's been a tough day.'

'And I've remembered what day it is,' Margie said, yawning, for she'd had no sleep. 'Tomorrow will be Christmas Eve.'

Christmas Eve? It seemed quite remote, nothing at all to do with them, yet Isla's thoughts went to her parents, who would be without her. Thank heaven, Boyd was going to be with them!

'If Mark recovers, I want no other Christmas present,' Mr Kinnaird suddenly declared, gazing round at everyone, his face very pale but his eyes bright. 'In fact, I doubt if I will ever want a present again.'

Nor me, thought Isla, her eyes returning to Mark's sleeping face, knowing she would go further. If Mark were really spared to those who loved him, she was inwardly promising that she would never ask for anything more. For what else could she want?

In the past, she had always said she wanted things to be clear between herself and Mark, and she was sure now in her heart that he wanted that, too. Only something was obviously holding him back. If he were really well again, were really spared to her, she'd try to sort things out, for he would want it as much as she. But for now, all that mattered was his recovery. And that the miracle should continue to work.

Seventy-Four

Two weeks later, on a January afternoon heavy with lowering cloud, Mark and Isla were sitting together in the Gloucester Place drawing room. They'd just had tea and were holding hands as they gazed at the cheerful fire in the grate of the handsome chimneypiece. All seemed pleasant, very tranquil, except that the memory of Mark's illness was still raw for both of them, and Isla couldn't help glancing at him from time to time, just to make sure he was still there.

'I'm all right, you know,' he said, smiling as he caught one of her quick looks. 'Doctor Wynn said I'd make a good recovery after the crisis, and I have.'

'You're a miracle,' she said softly, and they quietly kissed.

The last two weeks had been so hectic. Isla was still reeling, first with the euphoria of Mark's recovery, and then with the stream of visitors who wanted to see him. Boyd and Magda, Dr Lorne, Bob Woodville, legal colleagues Isla didn't know, neighbours and – to her own special delight – Will and Nan. They'd been overcome at seeing Mark, and afterwards had been so welcomed by Mr Kinnaird and Mrs Fernie that they'd said they didn't know what to say, they really didn't.

'Oh, Isla, that poor young man!' Nan had cried, hugging Isla later. 'To think you nearly lost him, eh?'

'He's not actually mine, Ma,' Isla had told her, but Nan had only smiled and said wasn't it lovely about Boyd and Magda? Seemingly, they'd finally admitted that they weren't just friends, and in fact were bringing forward the date of their wedding, which was to be as soon as Boyd finished college. After what had almost happened to Mark, Boyd had asked, who could be sure of how much time they had? He and Magda had decided to be happy while they had the chance.

'Very wise,' said Isla.

A few days after New Year, before Margie moved on to another client, Isla had taken the opportunity to go back to the hydro, to give news of Mark and also to find out what was happening.

Nothing yet, Sheana and Ellie had told her, but changes were in the pipeline and they had decided to leave anyway to be married. They'd be two folk Dr Revie wouldn't have to sack.

'You're really getting wed?' Isla cried. 'Congratulations, then, and don't forget to invite me to the wedding, will you? Oh, this place won't be the same without you two!'

'Won't be the same, full stop,' said Ellie. 'But how about you, Isla? Are you really coming back here?'

'That's the plan,' she said lightly.

'For the moment,' they laughed, and said no more.

Later, Isla had slipped in to see Grant, still glad to thank him for his help that terrible night when she'd had to go to Mark.

'Of course, I know you think I'm a monster for changing Lorne's, Isla, but the truth is I've no choice,' he'd told her. 'Bookings truly are down, and if we don't get clients, we'll have to close. At least, my way, we can keep the place open, and there'll still be some hydropathy, you know. I'll still want to be a doctor.'

'Oh, I understand, Grant. It's just a bit sad for me, that's all.'

'But surely, you won't be here? You'll be Mrs Mark Kinnaird and living in Gloucester Place, won't you?'

She'd hesitated, flushing. 'I'm coming back here next week.'

'For how long, I wonder?'

'I'm not sure.'

He shrugged and smiled, and as she moved to the door, he went with her. 'Thought not. But, Isla, may I just ask before you go – you don't think so badly of me after all, do you? I'm a reformed character now, you know.'

'Maybe you are,' she said quietly. 'You'll always have my thanks, anyway.'

He'd held the door for her, and she passed through, smiling. Putting him from her mind, she hurried from the hydro to snatch a cup of tea with her mother before returning to Gloucester Place and Mark.

Seventy-Five

Dear Mark, who was beside her now on the chesterfield that had been his mother's. Mark, whose look was so tender and whose hand was still in hers. Mark, who would listen to anything she had to say.

Is now the time? she asked herself, her heart beating fast. Did she dare take the risk of maybe spoiling what they had? Well, nothing ventured, nothing gained, and there couldn't be a better time than this, she decided, to try to make things clear between them. There were just the two of them before the crackling fire, Mark was so much more himself, and she herself felt that the time had come to put aside the past and reach forward to the future. Slowly, she loosed her hand from his.

'Mark, would you mind if I said something to you?' she asked, her voice still under control. 'Something you've never said to me?'

His eyes widened a little, but he said at once that Isla could say anything she liked to him, anything at all.

'Well, it's not the done thing for a woman to say, you see, and you may not approve.'

'Isla, I've said, you can say anything to me.' He laughed. 'I'm not going to disapprove of anything you want to say.'

'It's this then.' She swallowed, sat up straight, looked away towards the fire. 'This is what I want to say. Mark, I love you.'

There was a long silence, during which she gradually turned back to him and, raising her eyes, saw that he was just as astonished as she'd feared he would be, but that his smile on her was radiant.

'Isla,' he whispered, but she held up her hand.

'No, wait, Mark, there's more. I have to say it quickly before I lose my nerve. I'm acting like a man here, you see; I'm pretending I have the right.'

'I don't understand – what right? My darling, what are you trying to say to me?'

'I'm asking you to marry me,' she said quietly. 'Because I love you and I know you love me, but something always holds you back. If there's anything wrong with me, tell me, please, but don't let's go on as we have been up till now, loving each other and getting nowhere. Life's so short. It's like Boyd says: we must be happy when we can – if we're spared.'

There was a short silence, as Mark bent his head and held his brow. Finally, in a low, hesitant voice, he spoke.

'Oh, Isla, dearest, this is all my fault. There is nothing wrong with you. You're perfect, and I've loved you ever since I first saw you at the hydro. I know you didn't realize that and I didn't want you to, for what good was I ever going to be to you? A patient, an invalid? I had no right to expect anyone to love me.'

'Mark, that's not true! That's crazy! Where did you get such an idea?'

He raised his head and looked at her sorrowfully.

'It was what I thought – still think now, in fact. The worst thing was when I had to stand back and see you falling in love with Grant Revie, so handsome, so fit – nothing of the invalid about him! And when it all went wrong, and you were so broken-hearted, all I could do was sympathize.'

Sighing, Mark paused, once again putting his hand to his brow.

'When I had to leave the hydro,' he went on at last, 'I pretended I was glad, knew I had to cut myself away. I did send you a Christmas card—'

'It was so beautiful!' Isla cried. 'I was so touched.'

'Were you?' Mark smiled slightly. 'Well, I thought any patient might do that, but all the time I was promising myself I wouldn't get in touch with you. And that was a promise I might have kept – if we hadn't met, at the time of the miners' strike. That's when all my promises went out of the window.'

'Yes, and it was wonderful,' Isla said softly. 'Wonderful. That was the true beginning for me, you see. We'd always had an affinity, but it was when we met again in Edinburgh that I began to fall really in love with you.'

'I didn't know if you were, or not,' he murmured. 'I hoped – oh, God, I hoped – but I didn't know.'

'It was something that grew stronger, Mark, grew stronger all the time. The sort of love that's real, not built on romantic ideas.' She paused. 'That lasts.'

'But I shouldn't have let it happen, Isla. You were worth something better than me. I always felt that, but I was selfish, I didn't want to give you up, so I monopolized you and didn't offer you the love you knew was there.'

His long sorrowful gaze never left her face.

'You were right, weren't you, when you said I'd never told you in so many words that I loved you. You knew I did, but I never said it, so, poor girl, you began to think something was wrong with you – when, all the time, I was the one who was wrong for you.'

'No!' Isla cried, and drew him into her arms. 'You're not wrong for me, Mark. You're right because we're right for each other. I understand now how it was for you – you've explained it all – but you must see that I don't mind if you have problems from time to time. Plenty of people have problems, but it doesn't stop them from being loved. And I'm a nurse, so I can help.'

'That's just what I never wanted, my darling – that you should think I'd marry you to have you look after me. Oh, God, I'd never ask that of you!'

'You're not asking, Mark. I'm offering. And who says you'll need me, anyway. You're stronger than you think – look how you came through the crisis! I'm going to get you better!'

'And you won't go back to the hydro?'

'Only to give my notice.'

'You won't miss it? You were happy there once.'

'I was, and I learned a lot. But it's all going to be different now.'

'And you really won't mind leaving?'

'When I can be with you? What do you think?'

For a trembling, joyful moment, they stared at each other, wondering if it were true that, after all the trials and the heartbreak, they had come through to harbour. As though they'd been struggling on choppy seas, giving up hope, and then saw the lights ahead and knew they were finally home.

For some time, they clung together, kissing and caressing, and revelling in their love that could at last be put into words, until Isla finally drew away and laughed because they were almost in the dark and had switched on no lights.

'Who needs lights?' asked Mark, rising to make up the fire, but Isla, after smoothing her hair, only laughed again and went about switching on lamps. At the window, she paused to look out.

'Oh, look, Mark, it's snowing!'

'Snowing?'

He came to stand with her at the window, looking out at the snow quietly drifting down, so white, so perfect, as it always was at first. Then they kissed again, long and passionately.

Only when they parted, did Isla say, 'By the way, Mark, what was your answer to my question, then?'

'Question?'

'You haven't forgotten already, have you? Didn't I ask you to marry me a little while ago?'

'So you did. But I think it's my turn now. Isla, will you marry me?'

Once again, she moved into his arms, but neither of them felt this time that words were needed.